SILENT FALL

NICKY DOWNES

Storm
PUBLISHING

Ebook ISBN: 978-1-80508-240-8
Paperback ISBN: 978-1-80508-242-2

Cover design: Lisa Brewster
Cover images: Depositphotos, Shutterstock, Midjourney

Published by Storm Publishing.
For further information, visit:
www.stormpublishing.co

To Eliza and Molly Aston.
Be strong and bold.

PROLOGUE

'Fly away, bird. I've come to set you free.'

Those were the last words Ana Marlova heard.

He stood in silence, dressed in black from head to toe, reminding her of the necrotic tissue that had confronted her that afternoon. So dark, grim and unexpected. He just stared. His eyes were a striking blue against the pale white of his skin. She wiped her face with the back of her hand, concerned she still had a blood smear across it. She scanned his body, searching for any sign of a weapon. Had he been sent by her husband? A response to her failure? She held her breath for what felt like several minutes and still he stood before her without moving.

He was young and strong; she was weak – physically from the exertions of surgery, and mentally from the trauma of the child's death. No time to run. And what was the point of screaming for help? No one ever came. She'd learnt that the day she married.

I deserve it. Her final thought.

Every beating, every harsh word, every condescending look. She deserved them all, and maybe she deserved death too, for her failure to save poor Katie on the operating table.

Her skull shattered as it hit the corner of the fireplace. A thousand sparks flashed in front of her eyes as blood sprayed in a crimson arc across the white marble. No time for a movie of her life or even highlights of the best scenes. No time for regret.

Freedom at last from her caged life.

ONE

You can't consent to sex with a knife at your throat, despite the suspect's protestations to the contrary. In interview, he'd waved his family name around like a badge of honour, but he wasn't above the law and Detective Inspector Jack Kent was going to enjoy proving that. They were almost finished wrapping up this case and she was already thinking ahead to what she would work on next. Anything to keep her mind off what day it was. Get through today, and maybe she could sleep.

Just then, an email pinged into her inbox from the forensic lab. Jack mentally crossed her fingers before opening it. They needed one more solid piece of evidence to show that the sex wasn't consensual. A few days ago, a small pocketknife had been found on wasteland near Sara Millings' student flat, a knife that matched the description of the one that Steven Jacobs had used to threaten her. They just needed prints.

Jack opened the email. 'Bingo.'

Detective Sergeant Nadia Begum looked up from her laptop, tucking an errant hair back under her hijab. 'Boss?'

'We've got the little bastard.' There it was in black and white. 'Try buying your way out of this.'

Nadia gave a fist pump in response. She reached for her phone. Holding it up, she asked, 'Do you want me to ring her?'

Jack rubbed the back of her neck, grazing her hand against the shaved hairline. 'Leave it for now. I'd prefer to wait for a response from CPS before getting her hopes up.'

Frowning, Nadia placed her mobile back on the desk. 'If you say so, boss.'

A few hours later, Jack placed the last of the freshly printed sheets of evidence into Sara Millings' manila case folder. Detective Superintendent Anthony Campbell's office was on the same floor as the open-plan space provided for Jack and the rest of their team. It even occupied precisely the same square footage, like the architect's idea of irony. Jack knew that the other officers considered Jack's small team to be the station misfits, which often meant they were allocated the weird or difficult cases that were hard to convict. But they weren't relegated to a tiny basement office out of sight. The 'powers that be' liked them on show.

Jack adjusted her tailored navy jacket and rapped hard on her boss's door. He could see her through the tempered glass but still took a while to respond with a firm, 'Come.'

Striding in, she placed the folder on the desk in front of him. 'The Millings case. All complete and ready to be mauled by the CPS.'

He took his time opening it while Jack mused how tidy his office was. No piles of paperwork cluttered his desk. After opening a spectacle case and putting on his reading glasses, DSI Campbell turned to the first page in the file.

He tapped it with a finger. 'You know this is going to raise a stink.'

Jack sighed. 'And if his dad wasn't the newly elected mayor, would we even be having this conversation?'

'If this goes pear-shaped, we'll have the press at our door again.' He took off his glasses and waved them at her. 'It'll be your neck on the line, Jack. And don't go hiding out of the way up a bloody mountain.'

So he hadn't noticed, nobody had.

'Sara Millings deserves better, sir. Please tell me you'll push for a prosecution?' She slammed her hand down on the desk, not caring this time if she left a mark. 'I mean, really push. If he doesn't go down, what message does that give to any other survivor of rape? If the rapist's rich and white, then don't bother even reporting it?'

He stared at her, new worry lines forming at the corner of his red-rimmed eyes. 'Of course I will. You don't have to explain those things to me.' The frown remained. 'Now, you'd better sit down. I've got a fresh case for you and your mini-me out there.'

She perched, without comment, on one of the plush chairs usually reserved for visitors.

He rose from his office chair and sat opposite her, sinking into the fabric of an equally plush couch. Jack noticed he was piling on the pounds and his grey roots were turning white. Perhaps the golf course wasn't the best form of exercise for a cop approaching retirement? She wondered if things changed when you reached the rank of superintendent. It couldn't be that many years since, as a Black officer, he wouldn't even get through the front door of the golf course where he was now a leading member.

DSI Campbell cleared his throat. 'It's a B and E case.'

'A *burglary*? That's well below my pay grade.' Jack leant her head in her hand. 'You're kidding, right?'

'They didn't break in through the front door and the flats are all higher than the fourth floor. So, I guess they thought with your expertise...'

'Expertise? I investigate violent crimes, sir.' Never a murder though, despite it always being her turn for the next one.

'The climbing stuff... you know.' Her superintendent smiled, no doubt thinking he'd get her onside with that one remark.

The climbing stuff. She was a world-class mountaineer, not an occasional hill walker. Not that the force was that interested. They let her disappear for three months of the year so long as they could show her off at functions and send her into schools to talk about aspirations and life in the police. No one had even noticed that she hadn't put in a request to climb another 8000-metre this year. Nor did she intend to.

'I'm sure there are constables better qualified for this case than me. Why don't you ask one of the probationers to look into it?' She stood up, gaining a short-term advantage.

He stood too and immediately towered over her. 'Think about it. Discuss it with Nadia and get back to me by tomorrow.' Looking at the floor, he continued, 'The victims, well, they're all... wealthy... you know.'

'Tell me about it. If these were flats in Druids Heath, they'd get a crime number and not even a visit. But since these are upmarket flats in the centre of Birmingham—'

'I know, it's bollocks.'

'Yeah, it is.'

'So, I'll mark you down to take a look.'

Jack strode towards the door and turned. 'No, sir. With respect, you can forget it.'

She didn't wait for his response. She was right and he knew it. And insubordination was her middle name. He wouldn't complain because it meant filling in paperwork which, she knew, he couldn't be bothered with.

Despite the run-in with her boss, the rest of the day passed without incident, and she caught up on a pile of monotonous paperwork quickly enough to leave before the sun went down.

Many people asked why she worked in a city, not slap-bang next to a mountain range. There were two reasons: first, she could work as part of a large organisation in Birmingham and spend months away on expeditions without it affecting her cases too disastrously; the second was Danny Cavendish's climbing school, one of the best in the world, just on her doorstep.

Jack had known Danny for over twenty years. His father was a climber too, and they'd often found themselves on the same mountain as kids. Every Tuesday evening that she could, Jack went to the climbing centre to be trained and supported by Danny.

She parked her Range Rover – which had earned her the station-wide nickname of Vera – and grabbed her bag and climbing harness from the back. The climbing centre occupied space below and behind one of the tallest railway arches in the country. Above, high-speed trains took commuters to London; below, stood a range of the most difficult climbing walls in the country. It wasn't advertised anywhere as a climbing centre, and it didn't need to be. Danny didn't cater for the beginner; all his clients were established climbers who needed to test themselves or who wanted to practise routes for an upcoming ascent.

The one thing that cried out for improvement, though, was the cramped changing rooms, which had the aroma of clothes left too long hung out on a line. Jack quickly changed from her formal work suit into leggings and a long-sleeved T-shirt. She replaced her black Doc Martens with brightly coloured climbing shoes. Carrying her harness, she left the changing room and entered the gym. She needed to stretch her aching muscles and warm up before attempting a climb.

Danny came in as she completed her last set of stretches. 'I've set up a tricky boulder for you.'

Jack paused and smiled at him. He looked tired. His three kids must wear him out. At only thirty-two years old, he had crow's feet and was already greying at the temples, adding a touch of frost to his blond, curly hair. It reminded Jack of why she stayed single and had never even contemplated having any children. 'Thanks, Danny. I'll go take a look. You sticking around?'

'Yeah, I told Gem I'd be late...' He broke off and blushed.

A moment's silence passed between them, a mere punctuation mark.

Danny was right. The route across the boulder was tricky. Jack sat in front of it, knees bent, arms crossed as she pondered her plan of attack. In her head, she measured the distance between each possible handhold and foot placement. For each hold, she assessed the shape and angles. Would her fingertips be strong enough to take her weight in certain sections? Would she be able to make a leap?

After ten minutes of thinking time, Jack powdered up her hands. She knew the first few steps were pretty simple, luring the unsuspecting climber into a false sense of security before the boulder threw them off. Her first go was over quickly: failing to reach the fourth handhold, she slipped to the mat below. Jack shot Danny a look; he was trying to cover his grin with a hand.

She powdered up again, paying special attention to her fingertips. Her second attempt saw an improvement. She managed to get to handhold six before the familiar slip of a miss-angled hold. Even her slight body weight couldn't be balanced on the tip of a finger. She sat down again. She needed to be more fluid and flexible during the middle section or identify a different route. Her thoughts drifted to her last icy climb. She rubbed her hands on her leggings, reminding herself that she was safe, streaking them in white dust. The boulder mocked her. *One last try.*

Ideas whirred in her mind until, like the unpicking of a lock, the cylinders lined up and a solution formed. She passed hand-hold six, swiftly pushing off with her left foot. She managed to find the sweet spot on the next hold. Dangling for a moment, her weight threatening to dislodge her, she swung again to handhold seven, then used a heel hook before reaching out to the last hold and topping out.

Danny clapped. 'A bit slow, but well done.'

Jack grabbed a towel and wiped the sweat off her face before it could sting her eyes. Then she threw the towel at Danny. 'I'd like to see you do it.'

Of course, indoor bouldering was his thing, not hers. She preferred the thumping heart of a mountain.

Danny must have noticed that she wasn't on her best form. 'Sure. Fancy a race?'

Speed climbing always brought out the competitor in Jack. Mountaineering wasn't a sport, it was a chess game with each move eliciting a reaction from your opponent, one that could lead to you gaining the advantage or falling back. Speed climbing was just unadulterated fun. All you had to do was race up the same course over and over, shaving off the seconds until you reached perfection.

Both Danny and Jack belted up and clipped onto the wall using a fixed belay line, then placed a secure hand on their first hold and a foot on a lower rest. Danny counted down. 3... 2... 1.

Jack flew up the wall, Danny barely a breath away until they reached the midpoint. His foot slipped off a hold, faltering his progress. Jack, unaware, continued her ascent, topping seconds later. Hauling herself across the overhang, she watched Danny complete the run. 'Keep up, old-timer.'

He gasped. 'Lucky run for you.'

The speed climb at Danny's had a flat top that could also be reached by ladder. Danny had left a couple of cold bottles of water up there knowing that Jack liked to sit and chat at the end of a session. They both sat down and sipped water, neither speaking as they got their breath back.

'You okay?' Danny asked after a few minutes.

'Sure.' She patted him on the back. 'Are you, Grandad?'

Danny stared at her. She felt herself blush under his gaze and looked away. He gently said, 'Jack... I know what day it is. Are you okay?'

Jack leant into him, placing her head in the crook of his neck and shoulder. There was no hiding from her childhood friend. She muttered, 'No, not really.'

Neither spoke for a while. The air appeared heavier up here. It covered them with a comforting blanket. Putting his arm around Jack, Danny whispered, 'I know you loved her.'

There was no hiding. Still, she bit her lip and swallowed her emotions while a few errant tears escaped. *How did he know? I thought nobody knew.*

By the time Jack returned to the changing room, she'd recovered enough to brush it off. Danny had just meant that Hannah was her climbing partner, her best friend and confidante. He couldn't have known anything else. Even Hannah didn't know anything else.

Before changing, she sat on the bench and retrieved her phone from her bag. She'd missed a call from Shauna, who had followed up with a text. It simply said,

Fox?

Jack glanced at her watch. It was coming up to nine, but Lower Essex Street was only a few minutes' drive away. She replied:

Yeah, see you in 10.

In the bathroom at Danny's, she spiked her dark brown hair.

She now vaguely resembled Ruby Rose rather than Chucky. A dash of sheer lipstick and a touch of eyeliner completed the look. She'd just ditch the jacket; her tight-fitting trousers and work shirt would do.

Shauna Scott was one of Birmingham's forensic pathologists and as 'queer as hell'. Or at least that's what she said she wanted to have etched on her tombstone. Jack had a couple of well-hidden climbing-themed tattoos, but Shauna had a double sleeve and, except for her face, many other inks. Jack had multiple piercings in her ears; Shauna had multiple piercings full stop. Her shock of red hair completed the look.

Jack reached The Fox five minutes later and parked her car. She loved the vibrant colours and tone of the club, particularly when it wasn't too crowded. Since this was a Tuesday and the last week of the month, she hoped it wouldn't be too full of jostling women – or men, for that matter – as there were few she could tolerate, let alone be bothered to flirt with these days. Shauna had already got the drinks in, a bottle each of an IPA. They sat beneath huge prints of Marilyn Monroe and Audrey Hepburn and admired the view.

There was only one other group, chatting and laughing at the bar. Jack and Shauna sipped their drinks, neither speaking for a few minutes. Shauna ran her hand through her short, wavy hair and grinned. 'That's better. How are you, mate?'

Honest answer or expected response?

'Surviving... sent that case off to the CPS this afternoon.'

Shauna slammed her bottle on the table. 'If they don't accept it, I'll go round there, sort 'em out!'

Jack had no doubt she would. 'What about you? What's hot at the morgue?'

'We had a right one yesterday – dead pensioner. The body wasn't discovered for a week. Keep finding various insects.'

Jack nearly spat out her beer. 'Urgh. I swear you make this up.'

'At one point, the heart started to pulse, and we heard this odd buzzing. Opened it up and a blowfly flew out.'

'Gross.'

The pair studied their pints, each lost in their own thoughts for a moment. Then Shauna waved her arms and said, 'You'll never guess what happened at the centre yesterday.'

The centre meant the Centre for Forensic and Criminal Pathology where Shauna worked.

'Not another dark story,' Jack insisted. 'You'll put me off my pint.'

'No, sorry... I mean the Pride Centre. You know, I volunteer on Monday evenings?'

Jack didn't, or at least didn't remember. 'Oh! I'm sure you've never said.' She must have looked puzzled.

'Haven't I? It's nothing special. I help at the Sexual Health Clinic. They need medical staff, and it makes a change from dealing with stiff, cold bodies. Anyway, they had a massive donation left on the doorstep on Sunday night. Must have been at least £12,000 in cash. How bizarre is that?'

'Wow. At least it'll do some good... for the community, I mean. Don't suppose they left a note?'

'Nope, nothing.'

Jack glanced over at the other women in the pub.

Shauna nodded their way. 'I see Klaudie's back in town. You gonna say hello?'

Klaudie Robinson, the kayaker, was Jack's occasional lover and the centre of the group's attention tonight. As usual, the blonde, dreadlocked woman had an entourage of adoring young female fans with her. There were many reasons why: Klaudie was intelligent, naturally bronzed by being outdoors all the time, and softly muscular. She was also brutally honest and could appear and disappear in a heartbeat.

Shauna waited for an answer, grinning, obviously enjoying the sideshow.

Jack moved her chair slightly, so Klaudie was less in her line of sight. 'She's busy.'

'And you wish she wasn't.'

Shauna wasn't wrong – there were flutterings – but Jack could do without the drama. She hadn't come here to score a date, just for the good company that Shauna provided.

A short while later, Fran entered the bar with all the grace of some of the female legends whose images adorned the walls. She made a beeline for Jack and Shauna's table, sitting herself down on a stool opposite them. Jack wouldn't have minded, but she obstructed her view to the point that she now couldn't see Klaudie at all. No chance now of their eyes meeting by accident.

Taking out a compact from her bag, Fran carefully powdered her face. Jack watched her. Her features had softened over the last couple of years, but there was still a tinge of sadness and fear behind the foundation.

'What a day.' Fran folded her arms. 'But you don't want to hear about that. How are my favourite two law enforcers?'

Fran was one of the few people with whom the two friends talked about the stresses of their jobs, particularly after having come out at work.

Jack muttered, 'Fine.'

Shauna launched into another tale from the crypt. Jack tuned out and sipped her beer until, minutes later, she excused herself and headed to the ladies'.

She took her time, grateful for the enclosed space away from prying eyes. Her head thumped; she took deep breaths to steady herself. A scream was incubating in her stomach, tightening every muscle. She swallowed hard in the faint hope that this would quell it and stop it rising to her mouth.

Her hands pushed against the sides of the cubicle. Her head

dropped. She was back there, watching each frame like a film as Hannah was hit by the full force of snow and ice. The roughness of the rope scoured Jack's skin, like being dragged along a grater, as she clung on with little hope. Blinded by the deluge of falling snow, she held herself as close to the wall as she could. Silence.

Jack heard the running of a tap. Forcing herself back to the present, she flushed the toilet and left the claustrophobic cubicle.

'Hey, missed you!' Klaudie pulled her into a hug. Her citrus-scented locks scratched the side of Jack's face as she let her chin fall to Klaudie's shoulder as she hugged her back. She could stay here forever. They fit like two pieces of a jigsaw puzzle, both being the same height. She felt Klaudie's hand rub the back of her neck and up to the shaved part of her hairline. Jack held on tight. Maybe this was what she needed to erase the memories? Then Klaudie pulled away.

'It's been bloody ages. Sorry, found a new training centre, up north. How's it going?' Klaudie pulled herself up to sit on the shelf next to the two sinks, knocking over a basket of free sanitary towels.

Jack washed her hands at the nearest sink, not sure what to say. Why did everyone have to ask her if she was okay? Today, of all days!

Klaudie grabbed her arm as she moved past her to get to the hand dryer. 'You look dreadful.'

Jack felt like she'd been slapped in the face.

Klaudie must have seen her startled look. 'Sorry. That sounded brutal. It must be a year, right? I meant—'

'Yeah, it's a year and I do look like shit.' Jack made for the door, part of her hoping that Klaudie would stop her.

Jack stomped back to her friends and caught Fran in the middle of a raucous laugh. Klaudie rejoined her entourage and was swallowed up by them like a sugar lump in a welcome cup of tea.

After the laughter had subsided, Jack interjected, 'I've got to go, sorry. Work tomorrow.'

Shauna looked surprised. 'Another pint? You can stay at mine.'

That's what often happened. They'd have another pint and go searching for Shauna's narrowboat, which could be anywhere within a three-mile radius. Jack sometimes wished that her friend would invest in a permanent mooring, but she seemed to like having a new view every couple of weeks.

Lines of concern etched Fran's face. 'It will get better, I promise,' she said. 'You just need to talk more. Let it out.'

But it doesn't get better. And talking! Talking, just brings it closer to the surface. With that comes pain. All consuming, never-ending pain.

Jack leant over and kissed Shauna on the cheek and then blew Fran her own missive. 'See you both soon.'

Outside, she hugged herself, the May evening chill apparent. On the journey home, she couldn't help glancing up at the high-rise apartments. How would anyone climb their vertical sides? There were some adornments added by enthusiastic architects, but mountains had structure — natural cracks and ridges that a climber could cling to. She shook her head. It was someone else's problem.

TWO

All night, whilst she tossed and turned, sleep eluding her, Jack considered how she'd climb an apartment building – the ropes and equipment she'd need, if any, and what she could attach them to. At three in the morning, she gave up on sleep and sought out YouTube clips of Alain Robert, the French Spider-Man. Whoever was climbing apartment buildings in Birmingham would need ropes, surely? But who would belay if they were working alone? If there was anyone as skilled and experienced as Alain in the UK, then surely Jack would know of them.

She considered that they might, instead, be experienced in parkour or free running. She knew some coaches who specialised in all three, including urban climbing – they might have an insight into who the climber was. She noted that in her planner, then paused. If she took this case, she'd forever be the detective who would take on anything that nobody else wanted.

At some point, she dropped off to sleep on the sofa. For a change, she dreamt about the best moments with Hannah. Preparing for the Annapurna climb, they'd become close friends, sharing stories of their past over bowls of steaming Dal

Bhat in Nepalese guest houses. They'd talk into the night and then realise how late it was. Hannah always made the first move to kiss her on the lips – a soft, brief goodnight. Jack often wondered if Hannah realised how much those moments meant to her.

After napping for an hour, Jack jerked awake and concluded that she could just take one look at the flats to satisfy her gnawing curiosity, and that would be it. No investigating, just a sneaky peak at a crime scene. What harm would that do?

Jack arrived at Sheriff Tower, parked on the street and looked up, shielding her eyes from the sun. *Soulless and grubby.* Those were her first thoughts.

This block had twenty floors. The other blocks where the break-ins occurred were newer and not as tall. This one had been the first. It was at least thirty years old and not part of the growing developments that lined the canals, adding to the congestion of the city centre. She had arranged for the caretaker to meet her in the lobby.

A short, stocky man in a green hoodie and black combats stood by the elevators making notes in a spiral notebook with a gambler's stubby pencil. He wrote with his left hand. His right, Jack noticed, was in a plaster cast. He looked up as Jack exited the revolving door. Striding over to her, he put the pen and notebook in his back pocket and greeted her with a smile.

'Hi, I'm Pete. I'm the caretaker for this block and a few others nearby.'

'Great. I'd like to go to the roof first if that's okay.' Jack started to walk towards the elevator, expecting the caretaker to follow her.

When they reached it, Pete pressed the button to bring it down from the floors above. 'The roof's always locked.' He reached for his belt and held up a crocodile clip and ring with at least thirty keys in an array of sizes and shapes attached to it. 'But I should be able to open it.'

They entered the elevator and looked either at their feet or the glowing red numbers that displayed their progress. When this became uncomfortable, Jack turned to Pete. 'Can we get into the apartment too?'

Pete blushed. 'I've tried to get hold of Mr Hunani. He's not in the country at the minute.'

'So we don't have permission?' Jack didn't intend to break in.

'I'm allowed to enter if there's an issue, mind. Maybe a leak or summat... but, well... no, I'm sure he won't mind. I mean, he'll want the thief caught.'

Jack thought this through. She hadn't agreed to take on the case. The case report, despite being written by a couple of constables, was clear and informative. But there were things that she might spot that they wouldn't know were significant. Of course, she could just take on the case and be able to access the crime scene for a legitimate reason. 'Let's look up on the roof and see.'

They reached the roof level a few moments later. The caretaker exited first and led the way to a grey steel door, reaching for his key bunch with his left hand and unclipping it from his belt. Jack noticed how similar it was to her climbing harness. He had hammers and wrenches, whereas she had ice axes and carabiners.

Pete hooked the large keyring over his plastered wrist and checked each key.

'You know which one's for the roof, do you?' Jack asked, as she leant back on the wall, just stopping herself from tapping her foot on the concrete step.

Pete found a key marked with red duct tape and held it in front of her. 'I know all my keys.' He tried it in the lock, but it wouldn't turn. 'Maybe it's the one with the orange tape.'

Jack frowned whilst he searched through the ring again.

'Got it this time.' He turned the new key in the lock and the door swung open. Bright light filled the hallway from outside, making them both squint for a moment.

Once on the roof, Jack sought her bearings, trying to work out which side of the building the apartment's balcony was on. Pete nudged her. 'That side, I reckon.' He pointed to the area facing the Bullring.

'Thanks,' Jack muttered, heading for the metal rail that circled the top of the building.

She knelt to inspect it, not expecting to find anything of any significance since surely whoever had been on the roof would have needed a key. The door itself was sturdy enough and bore no signs of damage. It was unlikely the thief had broken in unless, of course, the burglar was a good lockpicker. She certainly couldn't rule that out.

The white painted steel of the rail was speckled with layers of dirt. Jack was looking for any sign that a rope had rubbed against it. Ropes were never clean. They trapped dirt and grease in their fibres but could also scratch paintwork as they were held taut. The climber may have used ropes, particularly if he wasn't alone. Someone could have belayed for him, lowering him down and up to the apartment. Or he could have used ropes to abseil himself down or carry what he had stolen up to the roof.

All this begged the question: why didn't he just break in through the front door of the flat rather than the balcony?

'There you go.' Jack spotted a telltale patch on the offside of the rail. It was in line with a thin chimney about a metre high. 'We need to get our SOCOs up here.'

Jack stepped back, careful not to disturb any other evidence in the area. Pete didn't move, so Jack directed him to the stairs. 'Let's go back to the lobby and wait for the forensics team, yeah?' The last thing she wanted was the guy stepping every-where with his size tens.

It was a difficult phone call to make. First, she had to explain to Sergeant Travis that she wasn't taking over the case and that she'd just taken a look as a favour. It was still just a robbery, after all, and one of his constables could easily continue to investigate. Then she decided to ask if she could have access to the flat. All she wanted to do was check the balcony for any further signs of rope use.

She knew that she was just helping them out. They, of course, had other ideas. If they could get a detective to take on the case, they could concentrate on other work. Eventually, the sergeant gave in. By then, she'd kept him on the line for ten minutes listing all the reasons why she couldn't lead the investi-gation. An agreement was reached; she could inspect the apart-ment before SOCOs arrived, just to check if they needed to go in again to collect further evidence.

Jack smiled as she relayed this information to Pete. He seemed more than happy to take her to the flat and started to locate the relevant key while they were in the elevator. Jack only hoped it was the right one this time.

The hallway on this floor was remarkably light and airy. A number of residents had placed brightly coloured plant pots outside their doors, but not the resident of Flat 106. His entryway was unadorned and bereft of even a welcome mat. Pete opened the front door and Jack was greeted by the musty smell of prolonged non-habitation.

The walls of the hallway were as empty as the entrance. There were no personal effects or carefully chosen pictures. Jack shivered as she entered the front room. The living room area led directly onto the kitchen. She never really rated this arrangement. Who wanted to smell their dinner while watching the television or wanted to see the piles of unwashed plates while trying to relax?

The balcony could be accessed through a door in the living room. The windows and door were floor to ceiling, giving the occupier a most impressive view of the city. The only thing ruining the line of sight was a mortice lock. Jack glanced at the caretaker.

He shook his head. 'It wasn't locked.'

Of course, you wouldn't expect anyone to break in via the balcony on the tenth floor. The door still showed the telltale sign of fingerprint ink, so Jack didn't glove up to open it. It still wasn't locked, mind.

It was windy up here. Downstairs, it was a calm spring day. Up so high, it would always be blowy. The other apartments on the floor had carefully placed garden furniture adorning them. No cheap plastic chairs in this building either – these were all solid wood, and fairy lights bounced in the breeze.

Any print dust that the forensic officers had used on the outside would have been blown away. So, Jack assumed that they'd dusted but was quite prepared to call them back if she spotted any area that had been stood on by the intruder's boots or handled. Being careful not to touch the rail, Jack glanced over the edge. Heights never bothered her, but it wasn't hard to see that a fall from this floor would be deadly. She'd need to lean on the rail to get a good look up to the roof. A drone might help her to pick up any marks higher up on the wall.

'Do you know what was taken?' Jack assumed the caretaker would know everything that had happened that night. He was the eyes and ears of the building. 'Did you get an inventory?'

Pete took a step back, but didn't answer.

'Where is Mr Hunani based?'

'Dubai.'

So, someone had to write the inventory for him. 'Did he describe to you what was supposed to be here?'

'Listen,' Pete's voice raised a fraction but wasn't intimidating, 'if you're suggesting—'

'Suggesting what?'

'That it was me.'

'I wasn't. I was just asking if it was you that wrote the inventory on Mr Hunani's behalf?'

Pete mumbled, 'Yes. I did. He asked me to, and I wanted to be helpful. I knew the police would want it. Sorry, I wasn't trying to be difficult.' He held up his plastered arm. 'It's been a hard week. I fell down the stairs on Monday, and, d'ya know, no one came to see if I was okay and I've worked here for years.'

Jack frowned. 'I'm sorry to hear that.' Then she brought him back to the issue in hand. 'So, you know what was taken?'

'I guess.' Colour rose in the caretaker's cheeks.

'Could you tell me then what was missing and where it was taken from?' Jack was starting to lose patience. The caretaker clearly meant well, but was slowing her down.

He led her to the bedroom first and opened the top drawer in a large bureau. Jack expected it to contain underwear or other items of clothing, but it held fitted jewellery cases instead. Nothing was left of their contents.

'What did these contain?'

Pete tapped his chin with a finger. 'Watches – expensive ones, twenty-two-carat chains and rings. That kind of thing.'

The inventory should list the full contents and value. She knew the overall figure as she'd checked it last night. Approximately £18,000 worth of jewellery and £5,000 in cash had been taken.

'Where was the cash kept?'

The caretaker moved towards the foot of the Pullman bed, pulled on the large tab and the bed frame slowly rose. Underneath the bed were a number of vacuum-sealed bags of bedclothes. On the right-hand side, Jack spotted a small keypad-protected safe. It didn't look tampered with. Jack was surprised that forensics hadn't removed it. She stood and turned to face Pete. 'How was the safe found, do you know?'

Pete shrugged. 'I'm not entirely sure.'

'What did you see when you first came in?'

'The cleaner realised there'd been a break-in. I just called the police and Mr Hunani. He told me what valuables he had, and I checked them... that's it.'

'Then you didn't see how the safe was found?'

'Nah. He told me it had cash in it. When I checked, it was open.' Suddenly, he grinned and winked. 'I did wonder what it was all for.'

Drugs, sex workers and other illegal activities, probably, thought Jack.

A few other smaller items had been taken, but everything would have fitted in a backpack, so Jack could scrap the idea that the climber needed ropes to move his haul. It just wasn't necessary.

All she had to do now was contact the constables that had first entered the flat and get a good picture of what they found. There were still many unanswered questions. The main one she had was: why go to so much trouble and not just break in through the door? Maybe this guy was just a thrill seeker? Assuming it was a man, of course. There was no reason why the heist couldn't have been pulled off by a woman.

The caretaker drummed his fingers on his elbow impatiently. Jack glared at him. 'One more thing. CCTV – do you have any?'

Back at the station, Jack planned to take another look at the burglary case files. There was something nagging at her that she couldn't quite put her finger on. DS Begum sat hunched over her laptop, not appearing to notice that Jack was there.

'How are you getting on with the surveillance tapes?'

Nadia jumped. 'Boss?'

'The tapes I emailed you from the reception area at Sheriff Tower.'

'I didn't spot your message, soz.'

Didn't spot it – or ignored it?

They had a couple of Detective Constables who worked opposite ends of the week. One of them, Georgia Steele, entered the office at just the right moment. She was balancing a white paper bag on top of two coffees. 'Sorry... didn't know you'd be back, boss.'

'No worries. I'm just forwarding you some surveillance footage. Can you take a look at it and note down if anyone enters the building on Tuesday, 5th of May between 7 p.m. and 6 a.m. the next morning?'

Georgia placed the drinks and bag down on the desk next to her laptop. 'Sure. Are we looking for anyone in particular? Male, female... young, old?'

'Anyone.' If the caretaker hadn't been so bumbling, she might have sat with him to go through the tapes. Mind you, trawling through nine hours of tape would probably be pushing it for anyone.

Nadia still had her head down, engrossed in whatever was on her screen.

'Anything from the CPS about the Jacobs case?' Jack asked, not that she expected a positive response.

Nadia looked up then. 'Nope, not yet.'

'It's early days, but I'm so looking forward to arresting the bastard.'

Georgia strode across to her colleagues to place a sandwich carton and one of the coffee cups in front of Nadia. 'You know what would be good?' No one responded. Georgia continued. 'If you arrested him at the mayoral inauguration ceremony in front of all his dad's mates... I'd pay to see that.'

Jack must have looked confused.

'It's next Friday. Saw it on the council website... 2 p.m. in the Council House Banqueting Suite.'

Only two people had entered Sheriff Tower during the key times, both of them cleaners. They'd entered the building at 5.30 a.m., chatting nineteen to the dozen, and gone over to a cupboard to fetch their equipment. Then at various intervals over the next half hour, they appeared and disappeared on the footage, scrubbing as they went. This presented Jack with another puzzle: if the burglar didn't come through reception to get to the roof, then how did he get there?

It was midnight. Jack was eating a large slice of carrot cake when she suddenly remembered what else was bothering her. She opened up the lid of her laptop and found the document that listed the value of goods stolen from each of the flats. One stood out. A robbery had taken place at Sherborne Wharf. The amount stolen was valued at approximately £12,500. It couldn't be a coincidence, surely?

Jack searched for her mobile, which had slid down the back of her sofa cushions. She found Shauna's number in her contacts and dialled. Shauna didn't answer straight away. When she eventually did, Jack asked, 'Did they find out anything more about that money? I mean at the Pride Centre?'

Shauna answered with a yawn. Jack just about made out a muffled, 'Come back to bed, hun.'

'Sorry, is it a bad time?'

Shauna laughed. 'She'll wait.'

'The money?'

'Haven't heard a bean. But I'm not back there till Monday. Want me to check?'

'Yeah, please.'

Jack was just about to cut the call when Shauna muttered, 'Ring Klaudie. You know you wanna.'

'Go to hell,' was Jack's quick retort. Grinning, she ended the call.

Of course, she then spent the next half hour thinking of Klaudie. She slipped into sleep sensing the softness of her lips on her own, tasting of strawberries with a hint of mint.

But it wasn't long before her mind returned to Annapurna, the mountain goddess holding her in a frozen embrace, teasing her with images of a smiling Hannah, her face flushed from the final day's hike to base camp. In the next dream scene, Hannah's smile turned to a look of pure horror, eyes pleading with Jack for help as she was wrenched from the mountain, battered by plunging shards of serac.

Jack awoke with a start, wrapped in soaking sheets. Tears came hot and plenty as she hit her head with her palm. It was her fault for thinking that she could forget Hannah for even a second.

THREE

1993

If only someone had taken me under their wing. Instead, the day my mother died, they put me in a taxi and dropped me at a strange home filled to the brim with feral kids. I'd spent every hour ignoring them, barely speaking, as I had nothing to say. At night, I'd climb out of the dorm window and up to the roof. I'd stare up at the stars searching for Mum. I never found her there, but I did find a kind of peace.

During the day, I tried to study, my nose firmly in a book, trying to ignore the chaos of the classroom. The other kids didn't bully me, probably because they'd get no response to their jibes and punches. They were met with silence and still-ness. Then, at school, I met Joseph, the maths freak and a real-life friend. We became inseparable, speaking in code and sharing sweets that I'd pinched from the night matron.

Joseph taught me many things: that kindness didn't cost a penny; that sometimes you could sit next to a person and not speak, and that was okay. So was telling them that you were sad or that memories of your mother caused you pain right where your heart was supposed to be.

I thought we'd be friends forever. I thought he'd be best man at my wedding, even though I found girls quite odd and couldn't imagine that ever happening. I thought that no one would come between us, until one May afternoon when Joseph fell from a tree and broke his neck.

The head teacher led a special assembly the next morning. He told us about Joseph's death while staring at the floor. He seemed strange, upset, as though Joseph was *his* friend. Usually, Mr Bryant made silly jokes in assembly that made the other teachers laugh. But there were no jokes today. Just a message: do not climb trees! He didn't say we couldn't climb guttering or over walls, just trees. I promised myself; *I will take this to heart.*

I often think about my friend. We had some good times, but he shouldn't have ripped my *Batman* comic. Why can't people be more careful with precious things? I had to throw it in the bin, it was unreadable.

After that, there was little point seeking out new friends. They would never climb as high as Joseph.

FOUR

Uncle David. The person Jack turned to when her world fell apart. His advice was always blunt: 'Just choose the simple route and get up the damn mountain!' and sometimes caring: 'There's a bed here if you need it, lass.'

At 6.40 a.m., she called him, letting it ring. He always took an interminable time to answer the phone. Jack imagined him moving aside magazines, maps and dirty plates, searching for the wretched thing, until finally he answered with a firm, 'Yes?'

'It's Jack.'

He'd have picked up her mood in those two words.

'Ah, Jack. Get your gear together and meet me at...' he paused, then read off a set of coordinates. Jack grabbed a pen and jotted them down.

Before she could say anything more, he cut the call.

Smiling, Jack typed the coordinates into the search engine of one of her few saved sites. She now had the location and grading of the climb in the Peak District. Curbar Edge – renowned for extreme-rated routes. She muttered, 'Good choice, Uncle David,' then headed for the cupboard in the hall that had sold her on taking this flat. Inside, on hangers and metal shelves, sat all her climbing gear. She picked up a thick pair of leggings, base layer and fleece, her outdoor climbing harness and a pair of soft climbing shoes. The shoes were beginning to split and only had a few months of life left in them, but she trusted them and was in no rush to buy a new pair. Out of the corner of her eye, she spotted a flash of red – her snow jacket, which she'd last worn on Annapurna. Hannah had chosen a blue one. She'd picked hers first and paraded around in it at the specialist climbing shop in Nepal. The other jackets were more muted tones and Jack wanted to stand out. The brighter the jacket, the more likely you were to be seen against the stark white canvas. That could be the difference between life and death in an avalanche. At that moment, all Jack wanted to do was to bundle that red jacket into a bin liner, burn it, or hide it away forever. But it was better that it reminded her of her fatal choices. She slammed the door on the cupboard.

In the kitchen, she boiled a kettle, then poured the water into a plastic pot of porridge, a flask of powdered Thai chicken soup, and a second flask of coffee. She stood by the sink, eating the porridge, staring across the fields, watching the mist burn off in the early morning sun. As soon as she'd finished eating, she grabbed a banana from the fruit bowl, her backpack, the flasks and harness, and headed for the car.

The ninety-minute drive allowed her time to collect her thoughts. She called each of her team, giving them instructions for their day's tasks. Georgia first. 'Hey, I'm heading out to interview a mountaineer.'

'Boss.'

'Can you ring as many local charities as you can and ask them about any considerable donations they've received in the last few months?'

'Sure.' Georgia never needed a job explaining twice.

Next, DS Begum. Jack started the conversation on the same note and was met with, 'Are we taking this on then?'

It was a fair question. 'For now. While we wait for news from the CPS.'

'I've been speaking to Sara and—'

Jack glanced down at her dashboard and noticed she was speeding. She took her foot off the gas. 'Okay, but I need you to organise some door-to-door. The original team only spoke to the immediate neighbours of the burgled apartments. I want to speak to the entire block.'

Silence. Then, 'She's scared, boss – Sara. She reckons she'll be outed by the press.'

Jack sighed. 'I hope you explained how anonymity works in a rape case?'

''Course, but—'

'She doesn't want to pull out?'

'No... don't think so.'

Jack mentally counted the beats as her car ran over the concrete blocks of a bridge.

'If I could just work with her a bit...?' Nadia was verging on pleading, her voice becoming a squeak.

Grasping the steering wheel a little tighter, Jack answered, 'Do this first, then you can work with her.' She didn't wait for a response.

Up ahead in a lay-by sat David Cavendish's jeep, just where she'd expected it to be. When she touched the front, it was still warm. 'Not far behind you, Uncle.'

Dusty footprints occasionally marked the route. It could have been breadcrumbs, as Jack felt the tingling, childish excitement rise. This was what she lived for. From her first ascent of Snowdon at the age of three to the queue to the top of Everest. Every mountain etched a mark in her heart.

David stood at the foot of the crag, rope in hand. As she drew nearer, he waved. Up close, his scraggly hair and beard and broad smile took her straight back to joint family holidays. Four adults and three children, wild camping, hiking and climbing with not a care in the world. It felt like a lifetime ago.

'You want to lead?' he asked. 'Only, Danny said that you were losing your touch.'

Her voice rose in protest. 'What?! He didn't—'

David laughed, his head rolling back on his shoulders. 'It's just too easy.'

They climbed for an hour, only speaking to discuss the route. He belayed, she led, enjoying searching for comfortable handholds. The natural bands, ridges and sharp edges of the rock face dug into her skin with the same familiarity and comfort as the contours of her bed. Tapping in a bolt felt natural and rhythmic, almost hypnotic. She could take her time attaching the rope, knowing that her toe and handholds were safe and secure since this was the straightforward part of the climb.

Soon, they were both resting on a ledge, mentally preparing a route for the challenges that were to come. Jack opened her flask of coffee and offered a cup to David. He declined, preferring water. As she took a sip of the warm, bitter brew, she said, 'I've got a new case. We think the suspect's a climber, but it's, well... odd.'

He listened as she told the thief's story.

'He sounds like Robin Hood.' Jack must have looked blank, because he added, 'Takes from the rich, gives to the poor?'

Was it that simple? 'Maybe. In my experience, someone always gets hurt.'

'Not like you to side with the privileged. You never shut up about the mountain tourists and their bottomless bank accounts.'

Jack stared across the valley and its undulations. Tiny specks of white bothies and farmer's cottages glinted in the green waves with the odd family of houses grouped around a village church. She shrugged. 'Seeing both sides is my job.'

'I guess.' He took another sip of water as they breathed in their shared view.

Turning sharply, sending a river of loose shards to the ground below, Jack said, 'I just don't get it. This guy uses rope when it's unnecessary. He either climbs up the side of buildings or rappels down, then breaks in through balcony doors and, at some point, heads for the roof. The roof access is locked, so why bother? It makes no sense.'

'Describe the climb.'

Jack chose a couple of the apartment blocks and talked through the likely routes, the exterior features like drainpipes and the building structure. David nodded occasionally. Eventually, he muttered, 'He climbs it cos it's there.'

No Limit. A modern climbing centre in the heart of the Potteries.

That's what it said in all the magazine adverts. For Jack, No Limit was simply a minor detour on her way back to Birmingham. Jack spotted Suzy straight away, with her long, black hair swept in a ponytail and a harried look on her face.

'Can you go in through the doors and not block them?' Suzy shouted. A group of blazer-clad schoolkids shot her a look but complied.

Jack waited until the queue in front of the desk had dissipated before striding up to it. Suzy grinned when she spotted her. 'Hey, look at you, long time no see. I'm so sorry if you wanted a climb. As you can see, we're chocka this evening.'

Jack ignored the counter between them and pulled her friend into a hug. 'It was you I came to see.'

''Ang on.' Suzy motioned to a young blonde woman who was emptying the bins. 'Anya, take over the till, there's a love.' She then turned back to Jack. 'Coffee, or summat stronger?'

Leading her friend upstairs to the office, her ponytail bobbing as she walked, Suzy hummed a tune that Jack couldn't place. As soon as they reached her sanctuary, Suzy took off her shoes and grabbed a bottle of Scotch and two tumblers from a drawer. She poured a finger of the amber liquid into each glass, passing one to Jack without ice or water.

Jack took a slug. 'Only the one or I won't get home.'

As they both sat down on the threadbare sofa in the corner of the room, Suzy tapped her friend's knee. 'You can stay at ours, you daft beggar.'

Jack didn't answer. She'd remembered on the car journey back that she had photos of the apartment buildings on her phone. Now, she scrolled through until she found the right picture. Passing her phone to Suzy, she asked, 'If I wanted to climb this building, what skills would I need? It's for a case. Guy is breaking into apartments from the outside and stealing from the occupants. It's... odd.'

Suzy sat forward on the settee, throwing her ponytail over her shoulder with her hand. She scanned the photograph. 'It's actually quite an easy climb. Anyone with amateur level parkour skills, I reckon.'

Jack took the phone back and found a photo of the higher tower block. 'And this one?'

'Umm... that one's a little tougher as there are fewer possible holds.' She stood and went over to her desk to pick up her iPad. 'Have you heard of Hazal Nehir?'

Jack shook her head. Suzy found a video and pressed play. 'This is her. She's just an average Turkish teenager who learnt parkour from videos and trained in her backyard.'

Effortless. There was no other word to describe her moves, and Jack saw how easy it might be to traverse an apartment wall. A climber would take their time, a freerunner relied on speed and dexterity. 'Do you know anyone? Anyone you think could do it, I mean?'

'We've had kids here who'd steal your phone if you put it down for two seconds, but they wouldn't bother to scale a building.'

'I meant in the climbing community.'

Suzy frowned. 'Come on, Jack. I know it's your job, but you really think it's one of us? You and your stupid conspiracy theories.'

'I wasn't trying to cause offence.'

'You haven't. I meant the stuff with your dad and that. It's just... you've upset a few people over the last fifteen years. No one's blaming you, but climbing people? Well, you know they don't like to be questioned.'

Jack stared at the tiled floor and muttered, 'Dad shouldn't have fallen.'

'You were fifteen when it happened. You were bound to feel like that. But you must know now that climbers die on mountains. It takes just one slight mistake. And God knows we've all tried—'

Jack stood, banging her glass down on a side table. The remaining liquid slopped but didn't spill. 'Thanks for your help, Suze.'

'Don't be like that.'

Jack slammed the door as she left.

There was no point dwelling on it. Getting angry hadn't helped, and she was supposed to be on the job. Nothing seemed right. No aspect of work, home, or social life. Jack had thrown herself into her work since returning from Annapurna and now, like the ends of her favourite jumper, everything seemed to be fraying.

She pulled up outside Danny's house. The lights were on, and his car was parked in the drive, so hopefully he was at home. After knocking at the door, she dropped her head onto its glass, relishing its coldness, suddenly realising how tired she was.

Danny answered and ushered her in. The door to the living room swung shut as she entered the hall, but not before Jack noticed Gemma pacing the floor with the youngest on her shoulder. 'Sorry, am I disturbing you all?'

Danny's eyes darted to the lounge. 'It's okay, Molly's teething.' Jack nodded as if she had any clue what that was like.

In the kitchen, Danny popped the kettle on. 'How was the climb?' So, he'd spoken to his dad.

'Great. Just what I needed.'

'He said, as long as Sally's okay with it, you can stop by to chat anytime.'

It took Jack a moment to realise that Sally was Uncle David's border collie and not a new girlfriend. As far as she knew, he hadn't dated anyone since Danny's mum walked out.

'Coffee or tea?'

Danny had clearly forgotten that she only drank Sherpa tea. And no one other than Sherpas could make tea. 'Coffee. And biscuits, if you have any.' She was starving.

'Gemma made lasagne. I can warm up some leftovers?' Danny always knew what she needed.

'Would you?'

Between mouthfuls of food, Jack recounted the climb, high-lighting some of the more difficult transitions. Her climbing style and Uncle David's were different. They had to be. She was short and slight, whereas he was tall and muscular. It always interested her how thoughtful and strategic climbing was. She could talk about that for hours. It was eleven thirty before she got onto the subject of her case. 'I need help finding a climber. Someone socially conscious... or maybe just with a strong sense of justice.'

'You mean someone who's into politics?' Danny cleared her plate, putting it straight in the dishwasher.

'Maybe.'

'Most of us are opinionated... but it's not a usual topic for climbers, politics.'

That was true. Most climbers had opinions on the commercialisation of climbing —Jack wasn't alone in hating the idea that you could spend tens of thousands and climb Everest with very little experience. But that was mostly about the danger that posed for everyone. She'd lost a toe due to having to queue for her turn on the summit. Frostbite had turned it black, and it had to be amputated in a Nepalese hospital.

'So, there's no one you can think of that comes to your centre? No one who's a bit different that way?'

Danny drummed his fingers on the kitchen table. 'Only the usual loners, narcissists and thrill seekers. No one that stands out.'

Sighing, Jack rubbed her face.

Danny touched her arm. 'You're knackered, Jack. Go home.'

'Maybe I shouldn't even be searching for him. Let's face it, there are some dreadful crimes being committed... but stealing cash and donating it to charity? He's basically a modern-day superhero.'

Jack arrived at the station early the next morning. DS Begum had beaten her to it and was catching up with emails. Without looking up, she said, 'Super wants to see you.'

'He's in already?' Jack placed her backpack on her desk.

'Yeah.'

'That's keen of him.'

'Must have a golf tournament this after.' Nadia smiled.

Jack smiled back at her. 'Yep.'

Instead of knocking and waiting, Jack tapped on the glass door of DSI Campbell's office and strode in. He closed his laptop, took off his spectacles and glared at her. 'Take a seat, Jack.' He waved at one of the metal chairs in the corner.

No plush luxury today. She grabbed a chair and sat down opposite her boss. 'What's up?'

He leant forward. 'Nadia's been telling me that Sara Millings is having second thoughts.'

'She's obviously worried about the trial. Who wouldn't be?' Jack rubbed her fingertips together; they were still rough and sore from the climb.

'I think it's a good idea for you both to visit her and check that she understands what's going to happen.' He pointed at her then, making Jack clench her jaw. 'And another thing: where were you yesterday? It might be better if you spent more time with your team. They'll benefit from your coaching and direction.'

Jack took a moment to calm herself. 'I'm not sure they'd have managed that interview; it was halfway up a mountain.'

DSI Campbell tapped his glasses on the edge of his desk. 'So, you've definitely taken this case on?'

Of course she had. Her curiosity had eaten away at her until she couldn't resist investigating. 'It would seem so, sir.'

'I'm glad.' He put his glasses back on. 'You can go now.'

Jack took a detour back to her office mainly because she needed to calm down before speaking to Nadia. Snitching to her boss wasn't cool, even if Jack had been dismissive of her yesterday.

A few minutes later, two coffees in hand, Jack entered her office. She placed a coffee in front of Nadia, next to her last empty cup. 'Black, two sugars.'

She put her cup down, opened her backpack and took out her laptop. Nadia was staring at her expectantly. She said nothing. Instead, she opened her laptop, logged in and browsed through her emails, answering one of two. DC Harry Martin arrived a few minutes later, reminding Jack that it was Thursday.

Nadia broke the ice. 'I've got two groups going door-to-door today and tomorrow, so we should be able to get all four blocks of flats done.'

'That's great. Thanks. Will they need us?' Jack nodded towards Harry.

Nadia shrugged. 'I think they'll be okay. The sergeant was very cooperative about providing officers when he knew which case it was.'

I bet he was, thought Jack. 'Did you want to speak to Sara today then?'

Looking up, Nadia smiled at her boss. 'Please.'

Jack sighed. This wasn't over, but there were other ways of reminding the DS who was in charge. She looked back down at her inbox. At that moment, an email arrived marked urgent. It was a response in the Case Management System from Marcus Barnet, QC.

Jack didn't need to say anything other than, 'It's here,' for the others in the room to be drawn to her screen. She opened the email and quickly scanned to '...decision has been made to charge..." Jack banged her hand down on the desk, instantly regretting it as a wave of pain raced through her sore shoulder, still raging from the tough parts of yesterday's climb. Behind her, Nadia and Harry high-fived each other. Tomorrow was Friday – the mayor's inauguration. It was so tempting to make the humiliating arrest in such a public arena... arguments for and against flew across the room. The press coverage would land the mayor and his son front and centre in the rape allegations, but they still needed to protect Sara. The pure beauty of it, though – handcuffing the arrogant bastard in the middle of the ceremony...

.   .   .

Sara Millings lived in one of the many student blocks along the
canal between the city centre and Birmingham University.
Jack's main recollection of student accommodation was of
concrete and the smell of boiled cabbage – Ryton Police College
didn't offer luxury, just a bed, a desk and a cupboard in a shared
room. If you wanted a bath, you had to queue with a towel in
the corridor. Here, Sara had her own room and en-suite. The
living area for the three flatmates had a comfortable sofa that
Jack and Nadia perched on, and a matching bucket chair where
Sara sat, legs folded under her.

Nadia did the talking, leaving Jack free to observe and take
notes. Sara made herself as small as she could, but at least today
she didn't tremble as she spoke. When Jack had first met her,
she could barely speak. She must have said sorry a hundred
times. 'Sorry, I didn't fight. Sorry, I didn't scream out. Sorry, I
had a shower after. Sorry, I didn't call the police for six hours.'
All completely understandable.

'—and the good news is that the CPS have agreed that we
can formally charge Jacobs and bring the case to trial.' Nadia
spoke slowly and with clarity, pausing to allow Sara to consider
what she was saying.

Sara took hold of a strand of her long, blonde hair, twisting
it tightly to the root, then letting it fall. 'Will he stay locked up?'

They'd failed her last time, or at least the system had. At the
initial hearing, the magistrate had decided that Steven Jacobs
could be bailed to stay at his father's address. The expectation
was that this time they'd be able to remand him until the trial,
but you could never promise this.

'Of course he will.' Nadia rubbed her hands on her trousers.

Jack sat forward, holding her notebook shut in both hands.
'Sara, I'm sorry, but we can't be certain of that. It's extremely
unlikely that he'll be granted bail as this is a serious crime and
must be treated accordingly... but there is a possibility that the
judge will assess him as not a risk to others or not a flight risk.

That said, he used a knife, and we have proof of that. In my experience, that will swing it and they'll hold him in custody.'

Sara nodded, not looking either woman in the eye. 'Will I have to speak?'

'At the magistrates' hearing?' Nadia asked.

Sara nodded.

'No. We'll arrest him, charge him, then keep him in custody. Then he'll attend the Magistrates' Court where we hope they'll remand him – keep him in prison until the trial.' Nadia rubbed her hands as she spoke. Jack smiled at Sara, hoping that she'd keep it together, afraid that she might bolt before the trial.

Sara started chewing the hood of the oversized jumper she was wearing. 'I don't want to talk about this ever... I just wish I never had. It would be easier to walk away. Pretend it never happened.'

'You've got to—' Nadia began, but Jack touched her arm.

Jack let Sara's comment hang in the air for a moment. 'I understand. But you've come this far. Let's take one step at a time. Can we come by again after the Magistrates' Court date?'

Sara nodded.

'I'll call you—' Nadia began again.

Jack interrupted. 'There might be some publicity around his arrest, but the press know they can't publish anything that could possibly identify you. This period will be hard and there may be gossip on campus, that kind of thing. Do you have some support... family, friends, the university?'

'I want to stay here. My flatmates know. And my tutor.' She looked down at her feet. 'My mum wants me to come home, but I want to finish the year.'

'Of course. I'm sure your mum's anxious. And you must remember to ask for help when you need it.'

This was going to be a long process. They needed to break it down into small steps for her. But Jack knew Marcus Barnet QC well as a colleague, friend, and past lover. He was intelli-

gent, kind, and knew when to deploy humour to ease the
tension. He was also a determined campaigner for justice and a
wonderful ally to have. She hoped that he'd also support Sara
from now until the case concluded and not be too distant.

The next day, Jack and her team walked to Victoria Square,
making the most of the glorious sunshine. Nadia had arranged
for a squad car to meet them there, as the hope was that they'd
have a passenger in the back on the return journey. Near the
steps by the Floozy in the Jacuzzi – the local nickname for the
fountain in the middle of the square – Jack spotted Georgia
pushing her youngest in a pushchair. She waved and the toddler
waved back. Georgia just half smiled. It was her day off, and
perhaps she hadn't thought this through. It could be a while
before they left the Council House with Jacobs in handcuffs.
Keeping a two-year-old amused might not be that easy, but Jack
understood why Georgia wanted to try. Of course, the boss in
her considered telling Georgia to go home, but there was no risk
to them in watching the bizarre spectacle from a distance.

The Banqueting Suite felt dark and damp despite every
light being switched on. Its chandeliers were heavy, gilded
metal and what charm and splendour the hall may have once
possessed had long since vanished. Jack sat at the back, urging
DS Begum and DC Martin to the front. 'It's your collar, Nadia.
You deserve it.'

It was hard to get comfortable on the plastic chairs in the
cheap seats. The rows in front were the plusher variety, made
for an event. Jack concentrated on the sporadic groups of people
entering the hall. Some of them seemed to have dressed for a
wedding or a day at the races. No sign of Steven Jacobs. A
pompous high-pitched chatter signalled the arrival of another
councillor and his wife. The large, overbearing man, who Jack
recognised as Councillor Mahmood, the Majority Opposition

Party leader, shook hands with everyone in the front rows. He paused when he reached Nadia with a look of confused recognition on his face, then moved on to DC Martin. Maybe he'd spotted her police lanyard. The white lettering was a dead giveaway.

Still no sign of Steven Jacobs. It was coming up to 2 p.m. The ceremony would start soon. Surely, he wouldn't be late for his own father's inauguration? Jack stood up. There wasn't much time. She strode towards the nearest door leading back into the corridor. She recognised the mayor and his entourage shuffling towards the hall. Jack half ran towards him, pulling at her lanyard as she did. As she approached the mayor, she waved her warrant card at him. 'We need to talk – now.'

Frowning, Christopher Jacobs ushered the others into the hall. 'I'll just be a minute.' He stepped back and turned, leading Jack back towards his office, muttering. 'This had better be important.'

As soon as he'd shut the office door, Jack demanded, 'Where's your son? Where's Steven?'

The mayor didn't answer. He leant back on his desk, folded his arms, and stared at Jack. He was much smaller than she'd expected. Even his square jawline had lost its sense of entitlement in the last few seconds.

Jack continued. 'Steven needs to present himself at Birmingham Central Police Station by four o'clock this afternoon or I'll issue a warrant for his arrest.'

She wasn't sure what the plan had been – whether the mayor still expected his son to be here on his big day, or if they'd decided together to keep him out of the limelight. Either way, Steven's father clearly knew that this was the end of the road. No more bail and no more pretending that everything was going to be fine. Eventually, Jacobs nodded and swiftly moved towards Jack. He almost took hold of her arm, but thought better of it and motioned her out of the office. Leaving her in the hallway, he strode off towards the Banqueting Hall, his mobile now pressed to his ear.

Disappointed, Jack messaged the rest of her team. They might as well walk back to the station to await the arrival of Steven Jacobs. The gathering press in the Council House would never know how close they'd come to a sensational front-page photograph. Jack was tempted to whisper in the ear of the local reporter she knew to brief her about what would take place later but, in the end, decided to leave them be. Let them get the shots of Christopher Jacobs in his splendour before his downfall. Nadia filled Georgia in as they left the building. She looked disappointed and sighed audibly as she pushed the buggy in the direction of New Street.

Jack watched Georgia leave, knowing her colleague was well on the path to becoming a first-class detective – keenness shone from her. In the distance, Jack spotted a tall, bearded man who was vaguely familiar. She shook her head. It almost looked like Teddy, a climbing friend from her younger days. He wouldn't be out and about on a weekday – he taught kids in an Outdoor Education Centre in Wales. Whoever it was turned away from her, following in the same direction as Georgia to the train station.

At 3.58 p.m., Steven Jacobs arrived at the station with his lawyer. Nadia read out the charge and the custody sergeant took him to a cell. He would appear before the magistrates in the morning.

Jack left Nadia to fill in the paperwork and found a quiet spot to call Marcus Barnet.

Her quick 'Hi' was met with, 'Jack, good to hear from you. I presume you now have Jacobs in custody.'

Jack filled him in on the arrangements for the Magistrates' Court in the morning, knowing that Marcus would have a full army of arguments prepared to oppose bail. He laughed as she told him about her meeting with the mayor prior to his inauguration. Then he said, 'I'll get my hair cut ready for the photos, shall I?'

Jack had noticed when she last saw him that he now shaved his head. When she'd first met him, he'd worn his afro with pride. Maybe now he'd settled down and married a fellow lawyer, he'd ditched his rebellious side. She muttered, 'Right.'

There was an awkward silence, followed by, 'You okay, Jack?'

Jack opted for the expected. 'I'm fine.'

'Why don't you come round to dinner sometime? I'm sure Rosa would love to meet you.'

I'm sure Rosa wouldn't, thought Jack. There was no questioning Marcus's faithfulness and Jack had no intention of testing that, but she couldn't imagine his wife would want to be confronted by one of his exes over dinner. That's if she even knew, which she may not. 'Yeah, that'd be nice, but I'm busy with work, so maybe in a few months. I should also tell you that DS Begum is the case officer for Jacobs.'

'Oh, okay. I thought—'

'It's time she took on more responsibility.'

'Sure. Makes perfect sense.'

Maybe he was a little disappointed. Jack couldn't tell. In some ways, she hoped he was.

FIVE

1993

Every Thursday evening was the same. I just sat on the hard metal chair, held her hand, and waited for each whoosh of the pump. The counter moved round to six. I couldn't look at her face anymore. The papery skin stretched across her skull gave me night terrors. So instead, I stared at the machine with its various dials and switches.

My mum's body lay now curled in the foetal position. I'd read that phrase in a school textbook on making babies. That was before the teacher took the book off me and hid it in a cupboard, muttering, 'It's not appropriate.' Another whoosh. Seven rounds of morphine.

I heard laughter coming from the room across the hall and the nurse saying in a hushed voice, 'Martha is improving by the day.' I didn't care. I'd rather she was ill and Mum was better, but, of course, it wasn't my choice. I didn't think it was God's either. I was watching Mum disappear before my eyes. For the last few months, I'd lived on this ward at the hospital. After school every Thursday, the social worker would drop me off and then Poppy would cheerfully pick me up two hours later with the promise of something nice for tea. It was usually a pasta bake. In the past I'd have preferred pie and chips, but now I wasn't sure I'd be hungry enough to eat it. Something about the smell.

No one cared about me at the hospital. They didn't spare a thought for what I heard, felt, or saw. Maybe I'd become the chair that I sat on, metamorphosed into the heart of its steel legs. My mind drifted to the superhero figures imprisoned in my bedroom, the ones that the social worker had refused to let me take to the temporary foster home. 'You're a big boy now. No need for toys.' I drew myself as a shapeshifter in my head, with skinny, flexible legs. Then I tried to think of a new, suitable name for myself.

Another giggle from across the way.

I knew, because I'd overheard the old doctor say it, that Martha had been given special medicine. My mum had the same illness as Martha: Non-Hodgkin lymphoma. I said the name over and over in my head until I knew it.

'Can I go to the toilet?' I asked the nurse, as she adjusted Mum's drip.

She smiled and nodded. 'You don't have to ask, silly. This isn't school.'

It was just an excuse to walk past Martha's room. I peeked in. She had vases full of flowers standing healthily upright and rows and rows of cards on her nightstand. My mum had one card on hers. Poppy had helped me make it. After she glanced at it, she let it fall from her hand and onto the bed as though it was made from lead. I wondered if Martha was a nicer person than my mum, if people liked her more.

Martha's satin dressing gown lay across a chair. It looked brand-new, as did the slippers under her bed. Not a speck of dirt on them. She'd never worn them in a run to the corner shop for milk. Mum didn't need a dressing gown or slippers here. She hadn't been out of bed for weeks.

Martha laughed again; her eyes glued to a programme on the new television set that I'd spotted her husband bring her last Thursday. Her yellow teeth exposed, head tilted back, she roared with laughter. We didn't have a spare television to give Mum, and anyway ours at home was so heavy that it always took two of us to move it across the room. Mum didn't need a television anyway. She was rarely awake.

It was strange, and no one bothered to explain. How they both had the same disease, yet they were so different.

Then it struck me: Mum was dying, Martha was not.

SIX

Another apartment. Another caretaker. He hobbled towards Jack, cap pulled down leaving just a hint of grey fringe, and handed her a key. 'It's number 405,' he said in a broad Black Country accent. Jack was about to ask him what floor it was on, but he'd already turned back to his mop and bucket; leaning over made his dowager's hump even more pronounced.

A pair of SOCOs arrived just at that moment. They were already dressed in white overalls, so Jack passed them the key. Let them work out which floor. She needed to get her pack from her car and get suited and booted or she wouldn't hear the end of it.

Ten minutes later, she entered the apartment. Her colleagues had already started their sweep by identifying key areas to dust. Jack was initially surprised that so few things had been moved. On the surface, you wouldn't have known that there'd been a break-in. Janice, one of the forensic officers, nodded towards a bedroom.

In here, it was more obvious that a robbery had taken place; watch boxes were strewn over the bed. Jack counted at least twenty of them. The cartons would have taken up unnecessary room, so they'd been discarded. She didn't touch them. Forensics needed to do their work. It was easy to spot and recognise some of the brand names. All expensive models, and yet there was no sign of a safe. By the look of it, the flat owner had kept them out on show.

Jack returned to the living room where Janice was dusting the door to the balcony.

'Did he come in this way?'

'Looks like it.' Janice pointed to the lock and the twisted plastic frame of the door. 'They must have forced their way in. The door was locked but not alarmed and, to be honest, it wouldn't have taken much to bend the frame.'

'Have you finished in the bedroom? Mind if I take a proper look around?' It was Janice's scene, not hers, but Jack wanted to see what the climber had chosen to leave.

Janice stretched, then rubbed her lower back. Her pregnancy bump was now more pronounced. 'Sean, can you collect up the watch boxes and dust the shelves that they came off?' Then she turned to Jack. 'Just give him a minute. I doubt we'll get anything off the boxes, but you never know. To be honest, our perp hasn't really handled much. Looks to me like they were in and out in a flash and knew exactly what they wanted.' Janice raised her eyebrows.

He knew exactly what to take, which implied he had somewhere to sell them on. While she waited, Jack rang Sergeant Travis and explained that she needed some officers to trawl the known local fences who dealt with expensive jewellery. After some prevarication, he agreed to her request. Then she concentrated on the scene. Starting in the bedroom, she opened drawers and doors. This flat owner had expensive tastes. She could only find formal wear and the odd item of gym wear.

The rest of the flat showed little sign of use. The kitchen cupboards just held one matching set of crockery and some crystal glasses. The fridge was empty except for a few bottles of beer. There were a couple of upmarket ready meals in the freezer. In the bathroom, she found six bottles of cologne and a wash bag, but this was all that gave any clue that anyone lived here.

Jack looked again at the crime report. A neighbour in the flat opposite had spotted the balcony door hanging off its hinges. Otherwise, they may well have been waiting for weeks or even months for the homeowner to return to Birmingham to complete another business deal before the crime was reported.

Janice had finished with the door, which gave Jack the opportunity to check out the balcony. It was easy to spot the access – drainpipes ran up the side of each of the flat's balconies. It would have been a quick hop from that and straight in. Still, Jack felt drawn to the roof and went in search of the caretaker.

He wasn't in the entrance hall, and neither were his mop and bucket. She was about to ring the station to see if they could contact him again when the elevator pinged. A young woman stepped out, her stiletto heels clicking with each step.

Jack approached her. 'Have you seen the caretaker, by any chance?'

'Joe, you mean?' The woman looked puzzled. 'Oh, he just cleans once a week. We have nothing as fancy as a caretaker. I wish we did. One of my taps has been dripping for a month. The management company don't give a damn.'

'Do you have the company number?'

The woman tutted, reaching into her shoulder bag for her mobile. Jack was clearly keeping her from something important. Eventually, she found her phone, scrolled down, and rattled off a number that Jack tapped straight into her mobile, muttering, 'Thanks.'

The bored-sounding woman who answered her call didn't think she could help; Jack would need to speak to the Birmingham office, and she couldn't just hand out their number because of data privacy. Jack reminded the woman that she was a police officer and that the operator was now obstructing her in her line of duty. Finally, the gatekeeper reeled off a number that Jack wrote on the back of her hand while cradling her own phone under her chin.

Ten minutes later, she'd finally got someone to agree that they'd drop the roof key into the station at some point that afternoon. She hoped that all the fuss it had taken was worth it.

Back at the office, Jack settled into checking emails and reviewing paperwork. She relished the quiet of Saturday working. After a short while, she received a welcome text from Nadia:

> They've remanded Jacobs in custody.

Jack leant back in her chair and smiled. Hopefully, Sara would now feel a little safer. It might take a while to come to court and, without her, they had no case.

In the meantime, Georgia had dug up a list of charities – fifteen in all – that had received substantial anonymous donations in the last six months. All of the cash had been left in a carrier bag at a local centre or shop. Jack recognised some names: the Pride Centre, Hands Together for Birmingham Youth, Young Brum, and Shard End Youth Cooperative. There were other national charities, all mainly for youth projects.

Jack found some sticky notes and started to match up the amounts given with the estimates of the amount stolen. The dates and figures were remarkably close to each other. Young Brum had received £12,380 on 3rd April. A robbery two days before had netted goods to the estimated value of £13,000. Uncle David was right. Sherwood Forest wasn't the only place that had a Robin Hood.

·   ·   ·

A call came in from the desk downstairs to tell Jack that her key had arrived in the station reception. She took the stairs. She expected just to be collecting a key and was surprised to see the imposing figure of Teddy Garson waiting for her. *So maybe it was him near the fountain? Why didn't he say hello at least?* Teddy wasn't his real name, and Jack had long since forgotten what it was. He'd earned the nickname Teddy because he was a bear of a man, tall and broad, not the usual shape for a climber. They wouldn't see each other for years on end, but he was the kind of friend that would continue their last conversation as though they'd never been apart.

'Jack Kent, I couldn't miss the chance of coming to see you.' He strode right up to her and wrapped his arms around her in a hug. When he finally let her breathe, he said, 'I've got that key you wanted.'

'Wait... *you* work for the management company?'

He looked at the ground. 'Yeah. Things are tough, so I've left Outdoor Education. I do maintenance now for a number of businesses and a few other bits and pieces.'

'That's a shame. You loved working with kids.'

'It just doesn't pay enough, and they were selling the centre to a private company so offered me redundancy.'

Jack nodded. 'That's the public sector for you. Still climbing?'

Ted rubbed his stomach. 'Not as much as I'd like... listen, why don't I pop over to the flats with you? We can take the van and catch up as we go.'

As Ted drove, Jack filled him in about the case. 'So, I think we're looking for a climber. Although, talking to Suzy, I guess anyone with freerunning skills could manage it. Why do they make these new apartments so simple to break into?'

'Money. If they had to pay for an alarm system throughout

the block, it'd cost them a fortune and they'd need to have a
security company monitoring it to be effective. That's why they
just focus on the entrance. Maybe they put in a few security
phones or CCTV, but that's about it.'

'You'd think the tenants would complain.'

Ted nodded, still staring ahead in case a shopper foolishly
stepped into the road. 'I guess they assess the risk and think it's
worth it. Same as we do every time we set foot on a mountain.'
Ted brought the van to a halt. 'We're here.'

As they made their way up to the building's roof, Jack
thought about what Ted had said. He was wrong. If climbers
truly assessed risk on level ground, then they wouldn't climb
anything higher than Scotland's Ben Nevis or more difficult
than a D-graded climb. But every climber had their own
threshold for risk – had their own method for assessing danger,
made their own mistakes. The 1996 Mount Everest Disaster
was proof of that. And then there were the climbers who accu-
rately assessed the risk and still fell at the will of the mountain.
Like Hannah.

The roof was far flatter than the last block. Apart from the
maintenance room for the elevator, there was very little up
there. There wasn't even much of a railing to stop you from
falling off the edge. Jack took a deep breath. She needed to stop
Ted from contaminating a potential crime scene as he seemed
intent on scrutinising every inch of the roof. The sun reflected
off the white surface beneath them, causing a momentary blind-
ness, and on the edge of her consciousness, she was back on the
icy slopes of Annapurna.

It started with an annoying buzz near her ear. Jack flapped
her hand in its general direction. She knew what was coming.
She'd experienced panic attacks too frequently lately. The
buzzing grew to a roar, practically throwing her off her feet. She
clutched her head, fearful it might shatter into tiny pieces. The
air rushed past her with the strength of a tube train speeding

past a station. The roar grew and grew in intensity, forcing her to her knees. Blanketed in ice. Air froze in her lungs. She couldn't breathe. *The pain...*

On the periphery of everything, she sensed she was still alive. Swaddled and comforted.

'It's okay... you're safe. I've got you.'

Slowly, Jack opened her eyes, aware now that she was on the ground, Ted holding her. Deeply ashamed, she pushed him away, dragging herself to her feet. 'I must have—'

'It's okay, Jack.' Ted held his arm out. 'How long have you been suffering from PTSD?'

She stepped further away. 'I'm not sure what happened... I'm alright now.'

Ted looked to the floor, his cheeks reddening as though soaking up her embarrassment.

'You won't tell anyone, will you?' Jack implored.

Ted shook his head. Then he looked back up at her and smiled. 'I found something.'

Jack went where he pointed. She still felt shaky, but hid that from her friend by concentrating on taking each step. Near the edge of the roof lay a carabiner. There was absolutely no reason for it to be there. The climber was taunting them.

Teddy insisted they went for a meal after she'd handed in the evidence bag containing the carabiner. He chose the restaurant, an independent Italian. Jack had to admit from the first taste of her ragu that he'd made an excellent choice. Neither spoke as they ate. Every time Jack looked up from her meal, she met Ted's concerned gaze.

Eventually, she said, 'I'm fine. It's getting better anyway.'

'Are you getting help?' He broke off a large piece of garlic bread to mop up the last of the pasta sauce. 'I know someone, if not.'

Jack nodded. She wasn't getting help. Never was. Never would. She was dealing with it.

Ted chewed on the bread, still staring at her. She looked down at her meal. Ted continued. 'I saw your sister the other day. She's changed.'

'Has she?' Jack grinned. 'When did you last see her before that? When my dad was alive? She owns a boutique in Moseley now. And Mum helps her when she's not going out for lunch with her friends. I can't believe you've given up the mountains to live *here*.'

'Not like I had a choice. Unlike you.' He waved his knife at her. 'Don't they have police forces in the Peaks? Can't believe that you're not up a mountain every weekend.'

Climbing had always been something she'd done with her dad. He was larger than life and tried to make it all fun. Even when she, or even her sister, was soaking wet and holding on to rock edges for dear life, he'd just shout out an instruction and pull the rope tight to remind you he was there if you should fall. Until, of course, he wasn't.

Ted sipped some of his wine. 'You ever go back there?'

Jack didn't need it explained. He meant where her dad had died in the Peak District. She shook her head. 'Nope. Never that rock face.'

'Maybe you should. Expel some ghosts. I'll come with you if you like.'

Jack shuddered. 'If I was ever going to go, I'd go alone, just like Dad did.'

'Alone?' Ted looked puzzled.

'It was a solo climb, without ropes.'

'No... surely not. I mean...'

Jack stared at Ted. 'You didn't know?'

'But he *never* climbed solo. Not your dad.'

For the first time, Jack felt vindicated. It's what she'd been saying since she was fifteen and not one other climber had taken any notice.

Ted continued. 'I'm sorry I wasn't at the funeral, so I didn't pick that up. The damned Outdoor Education Centre had a booking that day' – he slammed his hand on the table, making the glasses shake – 'and I don't do gossip.'

Jack pushed the remains of her pasta around the plate. 'Dad died alone on that crag... but I don't think he climbed alone.'

SEVEN

1993

Michael arrived at the house three weeks after I moved in. A regular visitor, who I assumed was Poppy's boyfriend. He only ever visited at night when I was tucked up in bed. 'Lights go off at nine,' was Poppy's rule, and I tried to stick to it. She could be kind sometimes, and I wanted to please her. But then I'd always had good night vision and excellent hearing. It was only natural that I'd want to see who visited during the night.

I wondered why Michael wasn't allowed to stay over. I thought it might be nice to have a father around. We could have talked about astronomy and superheroes. Mum had never really got it. And soon Mum would be gone. I'd be alone. Just me. 'It could just be days now,' I'd overheard the nurse, with the tiny hole in her nose, say to Matron. That was on Thursday. Three days ago and counting.

I could hear Michael laughing downstairs and the clinking of glasses. I crept out of bed and found a spot on the stairs where I could see Michael's shadow through the tinted glass of the living room door. I listened for ages as he chatted with

Poppy. He had such high hopes for their future together. It was so unfair. What future did I have?

My back began to ache sitting on the hard step, I stretched to ease it, causing it to creak. I froze. The living room fell silent. I couldn't be caught on the stairs. I turned and crept back up them slowly, trying not to make a sound, only breathing when I reached my bed and pulled the duvet over my head.

Later that night, Michael came upstairs just as I was dropping off. I heard the toilet flush. It made me jump. I burrowed deeper. I felt Michael's presence as he sat down on the bed next to me. I didn't turn away from the wall.

His hot, stinky breath tickled my ear as he whispered. 'I want you gone. I know you're listening. It should just be me and Poppy in this house. No one wants you around.'

The bed creaked as he stood, the weight gone from the mattress. I waited and rolled over so I faced the door. I imagined I was following him, creeping up behind him and stabbing him in the back with one of Poppy's knives. Just under the shoulder blades, I'd twist the knife until he squealed like the neighbour's puppy did when I twisted its tail.

Each day was a day closer to my mum's death. It hung in the air like cigarette smoke. I could almost smell it.

They could never hear me crying. I was supposed to be a man now. At just ten years old.

Poppy made it clear the last time I woke up screaming. 'You need to grow up. There's no point in getting yourself in a state. There's nothing you can do. There's nothing anyone can do.'

It was going to be just days now.

EIGHT

Warm light spread slowly up from the edge of her bed. As each half-hour passed, it crept higher and closer to her head. Jack ignored it. It was so unusual for her to lie in. She wanted to be lost in her thoughts, giving them permission to run wild to see where they led, not thinking of work. She pushed the climber case to the back of her mind. That could wait until Monday.

The meal with Ted had awoken her fears. Someone else had been on the mountain that day with her dad. Maybe they felt guilt over his death and for that reason never came forward? She could relate to that vile gnawing feeling that consumed you and never gave you peace, that penetrated even happier memories, turning them to dust, until all that was left was the heavy weight of fear and anxiety. Someone could have run away after her dad fell and could still be running.

The sun's rays reached her forehead, making her feel hot and uncomfortable. It was time to get up and face the day.

Jack's mother lived a fifteen-minute drive away, half an hour in traffic if you were unlucky. She'd received a summons by text on Thursday evening:

Sunday lunch, 1 o'clock. Bring wine.

The wine sat on the passenger seat in a plastic Co-op bag. It was only a cheap rosé, but Clare, her sister, had once said this brand was her favourite.

Part of Jack wished she had an excuse not to go. She'd willed the climber to break into another flat overnight. Maybe he had, and no one had realised it yet. Before she could contemplate driving back home, she reached her destination. As ever, there was no room to park her Range Rover on her mother's street. She drove around the block three times until she eventually found a space a few streets away.

They had converted most of the houses in the street into flats. These were once imposing villas, but years of landlord neglect had removed their grandeur and left them with flaking masonry. Jack noted that her sister had found a parking space right outside. Maybe her sister had stayed over? She might even have moved in for all Jack knew or cared.

Clare opened the door and stood at the top of the steps with her arms folded. 'Dinner's ready.'

Jack passed her the bottle of wine, muttering, 'I couldn't find a place to park.' She ignored her younger sister's glare and went straight through to the kitchen.

Their mum was stirring the gravy. The gas under the rest of the saucepans was turned down low, while the meat sat on a plate ready to carve. Jack kissed her mum on the cheek. 'Sorry I'm late.'

Her mum smiled. 'Pour the wine, there's a love.'

Once the roast beef was served, the room fell quiet apart from the clatter of cutlery and the crunch of the first bite of the

Yorkshire puddings. Jack couldn't help but spot how quickly the bottle of rosé emptied. She was on her first glass, while her mother and sister were now on to a bottle of red.

'How's work?' her mum finally asked, no doubt expecting the usual response.

'Fine... busy.' Jack chewed on her beef.

Her sister grinned at her. 'I showed Mum that photo of you in the paper.' Jack put her knife and fork down for a moment. *What photo?* When she didn't respond, her sister poked her fork in Jack's direction. Clare's cheeks glowed, probably as a result of all of the wine. 'She said you look like a boy... or a lesbian.'

Jack hadn't a clue what Clare was talking about until her sister leant back and reached for a paper from the dresser. She threw the *Sunday Mercury* in her direction. On the front cover was a large photo of the mayor and his son at some black-tie event. There were also smaller photos in the top right-hand corner of her and Nadia. The headline stated: 'Mayor's Son Held on Rape Charge'. She scanned the article as her mother glared at her. No mention of anything new, just that Steven Jacobs had been arrested and charged after voluntarily attending the station. He was now on remand, awaiting trial. The mayor described this as a 'travesty of justice'. His son would be 'proven innocent', and this was all 'a storm in a teacup' and, 'just the case of a young woman regretting it in the morning'. There was no mention of the knife. Apparently, she and DS Begum had 'declined to comment on the case'. That much was true.

'Jacqueline, do you have to cut your hair so short?' Her mum set her knife and fork down on the side of her plate before taking another large gulp from the quickly emptying glass.

There wasn't really an answer to that, so Jack didn't bother giving one. It was the usual Sunday. Her mum and sister would get tipsy and use that as an excuse to be rude. Of course, she could just leave. She'd tried that and it just led to them being

cloyingly nice the next time, which was worse, so she changed
the subject. She turned to her sister. 'How's the shop?'

'The boutique's doing really well, isn't it, Mum?' Clare
smiled. 'We've branched out to soft furnishings and home
accessories.'

Jack imagined a few cushions and candles strategically
placed on shelves. In her sister's case, 'boutique' apparently
meant not having much to sell, just a few lovely things. 'I'll have
to pop in.'

Clare piled up the dishes. 'We don't do menswear.'

Jack looked down at her black jeans and plain black T-shirt,
then looked back up at her sister, who was now leaning down to
load up the dishwasher, her long dress rising, leaving a gap that
revealed the top of high-heeled sandals. Her mum poured
herself another glass of wine, emptying the bottle of red. Jack
gulped the last of the rosé in her glass and wondered if it was
too early to leave without consequences.

Her sister walked back to the table. 'Shall we have dessert in
the lounge?'

Jack could, of course, text Shauna and ask her to ring her.
Then she'd have the excuse to leave because of a work issue.
Instead, she rose and headed for the living room.

In the hallway, she spotted her favourite photo: her dad was
standing between his two daughters, all three in harnesses and
helmets, grinning. Her mum stood slightly to the side in a Helly
Hansen dress and walking boots. In the background was the
mountain they'd just climbed. Mum had taken the easy path to
the summit, lagging behind a group of hill walkers. Everyone
else had climbed up the rocky sheer wall. Jack remembered the
day very well. Clare had lost her footing, sending a train of
gravel towards their father. She'd clung to the rope as her father
tightened it steady. Jack was already on the ledge above.
Reaching down, she'd grabbed her eleven-year-old sister's hand,
helping her up to sit beside her. She remembered the pull on

her shoulder as she took Clare's weight. No damage done, mind.
Once they reached the top, they tucked into sandwiches and
cake, then all descended together. It was an average Sunday
when Dad was alive.

For an hour, Jack sat in her mother's lounge watching a
black-and-white film that seemed to be some kind of murder
mystery. It involved a lot of running up to the edge of cliffs and
crashing waves. It was starting to annoy Jack that the camera
didn't linger long enough on the cliff face for her to plot a route
up, but her mum and sister seemed to enjoy it. Her sister lay
stretched out on the sofa with her head in their mum's lap. Jack
sat on the chair. Eventually, she took off her shoes and pulled
her feet up under her. Every time she attempted to start a
conversation, the main female actor began shrieking and crying
for no discernible reason. Jack started picking at a small area of
rough skin on her fingertip until she could take it no longer.
'Anyone for tea? And do you want me to serve dessert?'

'There's a bowl of trifle in the fridge.' Clare sat up. 'Ta.'

Jack popped the kettle on and added tea bags to the teapot.
While she waited for the kettle to boil, she reached for the
newspaper. Ignoring the front page, she scanned various articles
inside the paper until one caught her eye: 'Anonymous Donation Changes Lives'. The kettle boiled, so Jack filled the pot and
her coffee cup before turning her attention back to the article.
'A large anonymous donation of money left in a carrier bag at
Small Heath Youth Collective will support a group of
teenagers. The cash, according to the charity, was a substantial
amount and will enable three young people to attend university
to study sound engineering.' Jack wondered if there'd be a
future article about the money being sequestrated by the courts.
How many would think that the climber was doing good,
leaving the police and prosecutors to be seen as the bad guys in
the case?

Jack returned to the living room with the tray of tea and

trifle. The film approached its climax with another round of wailing and howling. Jack ate her trifle; she'd only given herself a small portion. She searched the Internet on her phone for the digital version of the *Mercury* article, including its Facebook group. There were several comments relating to the mayor's story, which Jack ignored, looking instead for comments about the climber's donation. She found these eventually. Although they were few in number, they were all positive. One stood out. It was only on the website and it said: 'What a lovely way to redistribute wealth'. It was signed 'Robin'.

Of course, it could have been a complete coincidence. Whoever Robin was may have not known that it was stolen money. The credits rolled on the film. This was her chance to leave. Jack stood.

'Are you off?' Clare didn't look surprised.

'Yeah, I've got work to do.' Jack went to the couch and hugged her mother and sister. 'Thanks for lunch.'

She reached the door and turned. 'Mum, can I borrow you for a second?'

Her mother took a moment to get up, reminding Jack that she wasn't as fit as she had been. Jack moved out to the hall, so they'd be out of earshot of her sister. She took a deep breath. 'I saw Teddy yesterday. You remember him?'

Her mum nodded. 'The one that worked with kids.'

'Yeah, that's him.' Jack continued. 'He said that he never knew Dad to climb solo. Is that what you remember?'

'Jack, not this again, please—'

'It's important.'

'Fine. Your dad never climbed solo... is that what you want to hear? He never climbed solo until the day he died.'

Jack turned to leave. Her mum caught her arm. 'But then, he'd had some shocking news that week... you'd told him you were... well, you know.' Her mum took in a sharp breath. Maybe she realised what she'd said.

Surely, she wasn't suggesting...

Jack's legs felt like lead as she returned to her car. Her father had shown no signs that he was upset about her sexuality. His mantra had always been 'each to their own'.

But so much of that weekend had been strange, as unreal as the film she'd just watched. Could it possibly be true? No, surely there must be another reason for the solo climb... if it was ever a solo climb? As for her mother, Jack knew she pretended to be fine with having a queer daughter in public, yet berated her in private. Jack would always be her father's daughter, and he'd had the audacity to die and leave her mother alone. At least that was her mother's view of the situation.

Jack found her car and took out her phone. She swiped Shauna's name and waited. Shauna answered, 'Hey babe, what's up?'

'Are you free? Can I stop by?'

Shauna was silent for a moment. 'Just checking the bridge number, hang on.'

A few seconds later, she said, 'I'm just next to the bridge on St James Road, by Five Ways Station. Oh, and I'm out of coffee. And milk.'

Jack stopped at the first corner shop she found and bought a bag of supplies for her friend. There was a lay-by next to the bridge, so she pulled in and parked. She spotted Shauna's lavender narrowboat from the bridge and walked down the towpath to reach it. After stepping into the well deck, steadying herself as the boat rocked gently, Jack rapped on the wooden door. Shauna opened it, greeting Jack with the smell of fresh basil and wood smoke. She was still in a silky dressing gown and pyjamas and took the carrier bag from Jack, smiling. 'Thanks, mate. I'll pop the kettle on.'

Jack sat down on the sofa, which was covered by an assortment of hippie-patterned fabrics. She realised she was sitting on a book and stood up. The front cover image was the outline of a dead body. A crime novel then. Jack moved the book to the top of the cupboard next to her, mumbling, 'I can't believe you read that crap.'

Shauna filled the empty kettle and positioned it on the hob. 'Sorry, should I get dressed?'

Jack glanced at her watch. 'Not much point now, to be honest.'

Shauna giggled and sat down next to Jack. 'I had a late night. Deanna stayed over.'

'Deanna?'

'The one I met on Her the other day... remember?'

Jack opened the door to the well deck and peered outside.

'What are you doing?' Shauna asked. 'I didn't hear anyone knock.'

Jack grinned. 'Looking for the removal van.' It was a long-standing joke with her friend. Everyone knew that the women Shauna fancied were always looking for more than just a one-night stand. Everyone, that is, except Shauna.

Shauna slapped Jack's arm. 'Ha ha. We've only had a few dates. She's Australian.'

'That explains it then.'

Shauna looked puzzled. 'Explains what?'

'Australian lesbians are a little more flighty than British ones. She's probably booked the removal truck for next weekend instead.'

The kettle whistled. Shauna stood and stuck her tongue out at Jack. 'Isn't it time *you* settled down a little, old maid?'

Of course, if Hannah was still here, maybe she would have. Jack shook her head. There were enough demons floating about without adding to them.

Shauna carried the coffees and nodded towards the door. 'Shall we sit outside? It's such a lovely day.'

'In your PJs?'

'Believe me, boaty people don't care.'

'I was thinking of some poor guy taking a shortcut to the station.'

'I'm perfectly decent. Get your arse outside and take these cups off me.'

Most continuous cruisers stored as much as possible on their outdoor well decks to allow for more space inside. Shauna filled hers with plants, so you were always sharing a seat with a pot of fresh herbs or a succulent.

Shauna tipped her head back and closed her eyes. 'This is nice.'

Jack had to admit that, now she was outdoors, it was a lovely spring day. The blue sky was punctuated with just the odd ball of fluffy, white cloud. She wished she was up a mountain, but this could be second best.

Shauna stared at her. 'What brings you here then?'

Jack leant forward, running her hand through the soft spikes of her hair. 'Bloody mother and the dragon.'

'Sunday lunch again? Do you never learn?' Shauna covered her knee with the silky dressing gown.

'Best one yet. Mum reckons Dad died because I came out to him.'

Shauna spat out a mouthful of coffee. 'What the actual fuck?'

Jack rubbed her face. Biting her tongue, just stopping herself from showing how upset it made her.

Shauna reached over and touched Jack's knee. 'That's just bollocks and you know it.'

'You never met my dad. But you're right, that just wasn't him.' If she said it enough times, then she might fully believe it.

'Let's talk about something more pleasant.'

'Like what?' Jack smiled. She picked at the leaf of a herb she didn't recognise, rubbed it between her fingers and then smelt them. *Mint. Possibly.*

'Tell me about Hannah.' Shauna waited like a priest in a confessional.

Jack bit her tongue. 'Why are you asking me about her? Now, I mean?'

'Your parents can't make you straight and only you can decide who you're in love with. I know, Jack, how you felt about Hannah.'

'It was probably one-sided.'

'I don't believe that for a minute. I saw the two of you together before you left. You are an idiot sometimes.' Shauna laughed so hard she made the boat rock.

Jack could feel the heat rise up her neck and cheeks. 'We never—'

Shauna stopped laughing and sighed. 'I know.'

They both sat in silence for a moment. A loud tapping behind Jack made her suddenly jump and turn. The orange beak of a swan rose up in front of her face.

Shauna headed towards the galley. 'There's some stale bread in the bin. Better feed it or it might snap your head off.'

Jack did as she was told. 'I thought swans weren't supposed to have bread.'

Shauna shrugged. 'I've never cut one up to see the damage.'

The menacing swan quickly consumed all the bread and swam off.

Shauna sighed again. 'Do you know why I live on a boat?'

Jack sat back down and shook her head.

'When I was sixteen, Dad caught me kissing my best friend in my bedroom.' Shauna pulled her knee up and leant her head on it. 'He threw me out that night. My cousin Gerry had a boat moored nearby, and he took me in. To be honest, I loved living on that old rust bucket.'

'Go on.'

'I never went back home except to get my stuff. I got benefits, don't ask me how. And some support from the local lesbian and gay group, or I'd never have got to college.' Shauna smiled. 'I had to learn quickly to look after myself. I went to uni and was probably the only person on the block who could properly cook. First thing I did after starting work was to get my own boat. I've never seen my parents since... never wanted to.'

Jack wondered why she didn't already know this. At least she still had a family, even if they acted like she was an interloper.

'Oh, and I should say that Gerry died soon after I left for uni. He wasn't in a good place... never really was.' Shauna wiped away a stray tear. Jack moved a plant from Shauna's side of the deck, then sat next to her friend and held her, muttering, 'Bloody families, eh?'

NINE

The doctors and nurses never noticed me when I followed them around, just as my teachers never had. Mimicking their gestures, stride and facial expressions came easily. At school, before Mum got ill, I was the class clown, raising laughter from the other students and scowls from the teachers. Then Mum collapsed and ended up in hospital. I stopped copying the teachers and, instead, copied the medical staff. Sometimes the visitors spotted me and smiled, like it was our shared secret.

Martha's husband used to give me little presents of coins whenever I followed a doctor into his wife's room, usually a shiny fifty pence or five tens. I'd grasp them, rubbing them between my fingers – I loved the feel of them – before feeding them into the vending machine by the entrance in exchange for crisps or chocolate. Then I'd scoff the lot before Poppy arrived. She didn't let me eat junk food. 'It isn't what they pay me to feed you,' she'd say. The other kids used to laugh when I opened my lunchbox in the canteen. No one else had hummus and

carrot sticks in place of a Club biscuit or a chocolate Penguin.
By then, I'd stopped playing the fool. Life had become serious.

I heard Martha's husband crying last night. I sat behind the
cupboard where they keep the vases for flowers. I scrunched
myself in the corner; I didn't want anyone to notice me. My
body heaved as his did. If I squeezed my eyelids together hard
enough and thought of Mum, I could make real wet tears too. I
licked them as they reached my mouth. They tasted salty. Soon
I was sobbing in time with him.

Then I bit my lip. How dare *he* cry? *He has nothing to cry
for*, I thought. *Not yet anyway. Just wait until his wife suffers
like my mum, then he'll have a reason to cry.*

TEN

Jack had called a case review for 9 a.m. She arrived early to set up the board ready for her team. Like many of the office spaces at the new police station, they had access to a smart board. Jack had spent a few hours the night before compiling a presentation on the burglary cases, but she never felt comfortable until she knew her laptop had connected with the board properly and she'd done a run-through without her team being present.

Jack had just reviewed each slide when Nadia walked into the office. Without speaking, she sat in her usual place and took out her laptop. Her lack of usual enthusiasm was noticeable. Jack wondered if her DS had had as trying a weekend as her own.

'Why don't you see if you can rustle up an urn of coffee and some mugs?' she suggested. Nadia might as well make herself useful. They were expecting the team of door-to-door police constables to join them.

'Sure.' Nadia stood without complaint and left the room, leaving Jack feeling more worried.

Before long, everyone had arrived and seated themselves facing the screen armed with tea or coffee and biscuits.

Jack coughed. 'This morning I want to review what we know so far about our urban climber.'

One of the police constables chimed in, 'Hey! I thought his name was Robin Hood?' which was met with laughter from the rest of the team.

Jack scowled. 'Let's stick with the Urban Climber or UC for short.' It was an easy enough name to remember, and it stopped anyone from thinking that their thief was doing some good. To be honest, she was getting sick of the comparison.

The room fell silent, and Jack continued. 'You have a list in your pack of all the locations that we know have been burgled that fit the profile and timeframe. Have we completed the door-to-door for all the flats on the list?'

The room stayed silent until Nadia chimed in. 'There are still the couple of blocks that we've just added. I'll send out assignments for today.'

'Thanks.' Jack tapped the screen. 'Anything relevant come up so far?'

A young PC spoke up. 'PC Jayden Brown, ma'am. One resident in Sheriff Tower said that they'd heard a noise outside their bedroom window at around 3 a.m. They looked out and couldn't see anything. It only took them a few moments to get out onto their balcony, they reckoned. Looked up and down but didn't spot a soul. They thought it might be a neighbour's cat that sometimes gets stuck outside.'

'How many floors up?' Jack smiled. Jayden reminded her of Georgia, a young and conscientious officer.

PC Brown checked his notes. 'Sixth floor.'

This guy moved fast, if it was him, thought Jack. The burglary had taken place on the tenth floor. If he was still climbing when the sixth-floor resident looked out, then he or she would probably have been spotted.

Jack turned to the next slide. 'We've matched the break-ins to the amounts given as donations.'

She'd used the details from her comparison exercise and added them to a simple table. There were more donations than known hauls from robberies. Jack would have expected it to be the other way round. The proceeds would be far less than the amounts stolen as homeowners notoriously overcompensated the value of goods taken and fences would want their cut. 'I think we can safely say that there have been other burglaries that we're not aware of.'

One of the PCs had his hand up. He introduced himself as PC Simon Hollis. 'Shall I look at further locations? Outside Birmingham City Centre, I mean.'

Jack nodded. 'Good idea.'

PC Brown then added. 'Also, they might not have reported a break-in.'

'That's true. They might be away or might have something to hide.'

Another of the constables quipped, 'Some of these business owners might not be legit. Who'd have thought it?'

Jack turned to Georgia. 'Can you look at CCTV for the charities and the areas local to them? You never know, we might capture an image of him.'

'Will do, boss.' Georgia smiled. She was one of the few people that never seemed to mind doing the donkey work. It was something she could finish up at home on the days she wasn't on the rota.

Jack then turned her attention back to the constables. 'Any luck with the fences? Did you find any of the stolen goods?'

PC Hollis spoke for the group. 'Nothing, ma'am, although we managed to catch a few with stolen goods in their possession, so it wasn't a wasted day.'

'He's got to be fencing them somewhere. Maybe we should look outside the city? Or see if there's anyone new on the scene?'

'I can use that as leverage with the dealers we've charged –

if you're happy for me to do that.' PC Hollis sought Jack's agreement. She nodded in response.

Jack noted that DS Begum had barely said anything during
the briefing. When she glanced over at her, she was playing
with her pen, screwing and unscrewing the barrel. 'Anything to
report on the Jacobs case? Have you contacted Sara since we
remanded Steven?' DS Begum didn't answer. 'Nadia?'

She looked up when she heard her name. 'Sorry, what?'

Everyone in the room now looked at Nadia, who blushed.

'Late night, was it?' PC Brown asked. One or two laughed,
making Nadia blush even more.

'Right, that's all I have,' Jack brought the room to heel. 'Any
questions?'

PC Hollis stuck his hand in the air. Jack nodded to him. 'So,
he's definitely a climber, then, this Robin Hood guy?'

'I think so.' Jack switched off the screen. 'And he's playing
us, or at least that's how it seems.'

'Do you think he knows about you then?' Hollis asked,
causing the entire room to stare at Jack. She paused. *Was this
personal?* 'I mean, you're a famous climber. You've done Everest
and all that—'

Brown butted in. 'And you're out of breath climbing the
stairs, Hollis.'

'Go to hell, Jay.'

Jack sat down, not willing to engage in a discussion about
whether this was someone's way of getting her attention. 'We've
all got jobs to do. I expect to be fully briefed, so fill in your daily
logs and tag me, please.' The lads soon stood and left to resume
the door-to-door. That just left Jack, Georgia and Nadia in the
room. Georgia had already begun ringing the charities to ask if
they had CCTV. Nadia was staring at her laptop screen. Jack
considered taking her to one side to see what the problem was,
but then decided that she'd have come to her if it was anything
serious.

While the other two detectives were engrossed in their work, Jack opened the case folder on the first burglary. One thing they hadn't done was a pattern analysis. She'd picked up a map of Birmingham City Centre on the way in. Laying it out on the table, she marked out where each of the robberies had taken place. For each location, she also created a digital card detailing who owned the block, who they employed to manage and clean the block, and anything else of interest. She also checked where the residents were at the time of the burglary. It was painstaking work and, by four in the afternoon, she'd only completed half of the burglaries.

Just before five, Georgia called out, 'I think we might have someone on CCTV.' She stood and connected her laptop to the screen. The video started with a grainy picture of the distinctive graffiti on the walls of the Small Heath Youth Collective building. The clock on the right-hand side of the screen showed the passing seconds until a figure, probably a man, shuffled into view. He was wearing a cap pulled down on his head with the peak covering his face. The collar on his long, grey coat was pulled up so that very little of his facial features showed. He walked with a slight stoop and a short gait. If this was their climber, then the chances were that this was all for show. Jack doubted that he'd trust someone else to make the drop, and this guy was carrying a large plastic bag the same colour and size as the one found on the doorstep of the youth centre that morning.

'My guess is that's him, but he's disguising his normal walk. We can't see his features in these shots.' Jack turned to Georgia. 'See if you can pick him up from any other nearby cameras. We might be lucky and get his car.'

Georgia nodded. 'Do you want me to do that before I look at the other charity sites?'

'What have you got left to do, Nadia?' Jack stared at her colleague, who'd already returned to her laptop screen. 'Can you do the wider search so Georgia can concentrate on the other sites?'

DS Begum shrugged. 'I guess.'

Georgia didn't return to her desk. 'Is it okay if I continue at home?'

'Sure. I'm stopping here for a while. Nadia, do you want food, or would you rather also work from home?' Jack hoped Nadia was staying, then she might get to the bottom of her mood.

'I'm not hungry.'

After Georgia left the room, Jack continued with her pattern analysis. Now she'd plotted all the known break-ins, it was clear that the UC had only targeted flats in a small area. Each site fitted within a three-mile radius. Most of the locations were within a mile's radius of The Mailbox Shopping Centre. Of course, this was where most of the new central apartments had been built over the last twenty years, and it could just be that. But he was taking a risk too. If he'd want to reduce the possibility of being seen, then he'd have been better off targeting flats in the suburbs of Birmingham, not slap bang in the centre. There were people around at all hours in this area – revellers until three in the morning, then cleaners, hotel workers and other early risers, not to mention all those who lived there, including the homeless.

'Do you think it's worth going public with our first shot of the guy?' Jack asked.

Nadia glanced at Jack; her threaded eyebrows scrunched up. 'To what end? He's not identifiable.'

Good point. 'There are so many people around the centre of Brum, someone will have seen him. We might get a witness who saw more of his face, or his car. Unless you're getting somewhere with the CCTV?'

Nadia bit her thumb. 'Not yet. Just finishing something off first.'

'Is everything okay? Only—'

'I'm fine.'

She didn't look fine. In fact, Jack wasn't sure whether she'd just caught Nadia wiping away a tear with her sleeve. But before she could say anything, her mobile began to vibrate. Teddy's name appeared on the screen.

Jack answered, 'Hey.'

'Hi, I was wondering if you fancy a drink later? I've hooked up with a few climbers in the region. Thought it might help... with your case.'

'That's great. Yes, definitely. Where and what time?'

'Upstairs in the Welly. I told everyone eight.'

Jack glanced at her watch. She could grab some food on the way. Although, if you were desperate, you could always order in pizza at The Wellington. They never seemed to mind. 'See you then.'

Before leaving, Jack turned to Nadia. 'Fancy coming to meet a few climbing friends? We could grab some food on the way.'

Nadia glanced at her phone. 'I've got to get home. Sorry.'

Jack arrived at the pub a few minutes after eight and found that Teddy was already there with a few people she recognised. Suzy sat with her back to her, but turned and grinned when she spotted her friend in the mirrored wall. 'Let me get a round in. Jack, sit.'

Jack wondered what Teddy had said to Suzy – she hadn't been expecting a warm reception after their last meetup. She glanced around the room. She knew most people, but there were a couple of younger climbers she didn't recognise. Holding out her hand, she said to the first, 'I'm Jack Kent, and you are...?'

The young guy blushed and shook her hand. 'I know who

you are... wow. I'm Oliver and this is...' He pointed to the woman next to him. 'Eliza Summers.'

Eliza waved. She looked vaguely familiar, and then it clicked. 'The Olympic climber?' Jack waved back.

'Yep, that's me.' Eliza grinned.

Jack didn't know many of the sports climbers. But she knew Danny had trained Eliza when she was in the Midlands. She looked around the room. Danny wasn't there, so he had to be working or on baby duty, she surmised.

When the drinks arrived, Ted leant forward and said in a low voice. 'Jack's got this case she's working on and needs our help. The guy's a climber. That's right, isn't it?' Ted turned to her to elaborate.

Jack paused for a moment, taking a sip of her pint of Citra. For all she knew, the UC could be here amongst them. 'That's what we think. We've got a thief who's breaking into flats – from the balconies.'

Oliver laughed. 'You know what? I've looked at some flats and thought how easy that would be.'

The others nodded.

'Have you given up on the parkour idea then?' Suzy asked.

'Not entirely. He left a carabiner at one scene, but that could have been a red herring.'

Eliza pushed her hairband up off her forehead. 'Who loses a carabiner? You just lock it straight back on your belt.'

'I think it was left there deliberately.' Jack glanced at each climber in turn. They all looked confused but interested. So, she continued to describe a few more details from each scene. The overall view was that the guy was taking the piss. Then she got to the part about what he did with his haul: '...and then he leaves the money he gets on the doorstep of different charities in Brum.'

'What!' Oliver shrieked. 'No way.'

The others nodded in agreement until Paul, one of the older

climbers, said, stroking his beard. 'I'm beginning to like this guy.' He winked at Jack, which she ignored. Who did he think he was? She'd never met him before.

That was the problem. She could put out a photo of the UC in the press appealing for more information, but if she mentioned the fact that he wasn't just stealing the goods for his own gain, the public might actually decide to root for the guy, and then where would they be? She could always run it by the super in the morning and let him decide. It was her turn to go to the bar, so she turned to Suzy. 'Come and help me carry the drinks?'

As soon as they reached the bar, Jack turned to her friend. 'I'm glad you're here. I'm sorry about the other day.'

Suzy squeezed her arm in response. 'It's okay. All forgotten.'

But it wasn't forgotten. Not by Jack anyway.

The queue for the bar was still quite long. Eventually, Suzy turned back to her. 'I've been thinking. What's your climber trying to achieve? Recognition? Notoriety?'

It was a good point. If it was either of those things, then by going to the media, they'd be playing into his hands. 'Quite possibly both.'

'Umm...' Suzy waited until Jack had ordered the drinks, reminding her of a couple she'd forgotten. 'Or he might have a personal reason for what he's doing, I guess. Maybe he genuinely thinks he's doing good.'

Anything was possible. All this just reminded Jack she hadn't got any sort of real handle on him yet.

By the time she left The Wellington, the heavens had opened. Jack had decided after the first pint to leave her car tucked up in the police garage for the night. Of course, now she had to find a taxi without getting soaked. The others had left early to get the last train to wherever they called home. By 11 p.m., only Teddy and she were left. He offered to wait for a taxi with her, but she didn't need a minder.

She made a dash from one pub doorway to the next, lingering for a moment under the large canvas canopy of the Wetherspoons. A few rowdy revellers hovered in the doorway, waiting, just like her, for the rain to subside a little. One drunken youth chanced his arm. Rolling up to Jack, he slurred, 'Can I buy you a drink? One for the road.' It only took a look for him to stagger back to his mates, arms raised in surrender.

Eventually, Jack made it to New Street and flagged down a black cab. She sat back, realising how tired she felt. Her suit was sticking to her, but at least her backpack hadn't leaked and her laptop was safe. She hadn't realised that she'd dropped off to sleep until the taxi drew to a halt and the driver called loudly, 'We're here, love.'

As soon as she entered her flat, Jack stripped off her wet clothes and threw them in the general direction of the laundry basket; she'd pop them on a cold wash before heading off to work in the morning. Just as she tied the belt on her dressing gown, her door intercom buzzed. The picture on the intercom was grainy at the best of times but, coupled with the persistent rain, all she could see was the faint outline of a short woman. For the briefest of moments, she thought it was Hannah. Sighing, she muttered into the intercom, 'Hey, who is it?'

'It's me. Klaudie. Let us up, I'm soaked.'

Jack pushed the button to open the main door downstairs, then opened her front door and waited. Klaudie appeared moments later, gushing, 'Glad you're home now. I waited at the pub across the road until they chucked me out, so then I waited in my van. I half expected your neighbours to send me packing—'

Jack pushed her friend against the wall and kissed her long and deep, ignoring the dampness of Klaudie's jeans against the bare skin of her legs. Klaudie responded by holding Jack's face in her hands and exploring her mouth with her tongue, making Jack concerned for the briefest of moments that she tasted of stale beer. Klaudie's lip piercing gently rubbed against Jack's upper lip. It surprised Jack that she liked the sensation. The kissing stopped just long enough for them to share a look. Jack had never noticed how blonde Klaudie's eyelashes were until now. Taking her chin in her hands, Jack leant forward and kissed Klaudie's eyelids, her cheek, then she buried herself in her neck, licking and kissing, wrapping herself in Klaudie's moans, sensing her movements against the wall, her futile attempts to stay upright.

The perfume, the softness of her skin and her vulnerability engulfed Jack, forcing her to pull away. Overwhelmed, she wanted to cry and scream at the same time. Klaudie placed her hand on Jack's wrist, willing her to cross the space between them, to continue what she'd started. Instead, Jack scrunched her hands into fists, digging her nails into her palms. She looked the other way, not wishing to meet Klaudie's eyes, not wanting to see her disappointment. 'I can't, sorry... I'll get you some clean sheets for the spare room.'

Jack expected her friend to follow her, but Klaudie hadn't yet moved from the wall. Jack didn't turn back even when she eventually heard an audible sigh and sensed the movement behind her. As soon as they reached the spare room, Klaudie took off her T-shirt, not caring that she stood in front of Jack without a bra. Of course, Jack was tempted. Klaudie had an amazing body, a flat stomach, lightly sun-kissed skin, pert breasts and perfectly round darker nipples. But instead, she pointed to a drawer. 'There's a spare T-shirt in there if you need one.'

As Jack moved to leave the room, Klaudie said, 'I'm starving, mate. Got anything to eat?'

ELEVEN

1993

I hate PE. Hate getting changed in the classroom, stripping down to my pants and putting on the scratchy, navy-blue shorts. Mrs Beeton always shouted in PE. Some of the boys didn't listen when she asked them to stop running in the hall. She'd use words like 'safety first' and threaten to send them to change back into their uniform.

They should have told me in PE. The head teacher, Mrs Wainwright, should have called me to her room and told me there and then. Let me cry until I couldn't breathe. Given me tissues. Because that was when it happened. When I was in PE.

Instead, they'd waited until home time, two hours after the event. I knew something wasn't right when the social worker arrived in a taxi. It wasn't Thursday. It should have been Poppy at the school gates. The social worker just told me straight. 'Your mum died at 1:30 this afternoon. I'm very sorry.'

I thought they'd take me to Poppy's where I could hide in my room. But I was wrong. We did stop at Poppy's, but only to pick up my things. She waved but didn't say anything, not even goodbye. The social worker left the car to collect my small case filled with all my clothes and a carrier bag of my astronomy books. She wiped away the tears and snot that I'd left on her shoulder with a tissue as she walked.

Then the social worker got back in the taxi and we drove on. Past the tree where Joseph fell. Past the hospital where Mum died and past my school. Until we came to a town I didn't recognise. I clenched my fist until my palm started to bleed. Where was she taking me? *They should all leave me alone. I don't deserve this.*

TWELVE

Klaudie had left by the time Jack woke up. On the fridge door, held on by a Mont Blanc souvenir magnet, was a short note. It simply said: *Thanks for the dinner, bed and breakfast.*

Of course, in the light of the early morning, Jack regretted pushing Klaudie away. It wasn't as if she hadn't slept with Klaudie – and even one or two others – in the last year. She had. But those had been mindless encounters driven by the physical need to be close to someone – that need to cling to another body before falling off the edge of a cliff. Maybe she should see last night as progress, that she didn't want instant gratification but should now be looking more long-term? But in reality, it always came back to Hannah. There was no moving forward from that.

Jack opened the fridge door and grabbed the milk, then slammed it shut. She poured the milk into her coffee and stirred hard enough to almost crack the mug. Standing at the window in the kitchen, she watched the early morning joggers lap the park, wondering how they kept themselves sane and whether their demons kept them awake all night.

Her work phone buzzed to indicate a text from Nadia:

I'm not going to be in today. Unwell. N.

The protocol was that she should ring her line manager and, unless it was personal, give a more detailed reason for her absence. This only added to Jack's concerns for her colleague's welfare. She made a mental note to ring her when she got to the office.

It was during the taxi ride there that Jack changed her mind. Something was going on with Nadia. Just days ago, she'd been so involved in the Millings' case almost to the point of being too attentive. Maybe she was just ill with a virus or something, but Jack had a nagging fear that there was more to it. She picked up her car at the station and drove to Balsall Heath. Nadia lived near Cannon Hill Park a few doors away from her parents – she had been really excited last year that she'd found the house at such a good price. To her, being close to family was a bonus. Jack, of course, couldn't think of anything worse.

There was no sign of Nadia's car on the drive outside her house or further up the road at her parents'. Of course, she could be at the doctor's surgery, or the chemist. Biting her lip, Jack wondered if she was being the worst kind of boss by checking up on Nadia in this way, but that didn't stop her knocking on her door. No answer. She even peered through the patterned glass to see if she could see any movement within, but there was no sign of life.

Instead of driving off, she reached for her phone and dialled Marcus. He answered quickly. 'Hi, Jack. Everything okay? I'm in court in five minutes.'

'I'm just checking in on the Millings' case... all going smoothly?'

There was a slight pause. 'As far as I know. I thought DS Begum was leading on this?'

'Yeah. Sorry, I'm not checking up on her.' Although, of

course, she was. 'She's currently off sick, so I just wanted to be sure that there isn't anything that needs following up.'

'It'll be a while before this goes to court, Jack, so unless your officer's going to be absent long term—'

'No, I doubt that. Anyway, you need to go and present your case.'

'Sure. Keep me informed of any issues.' He rang off.

Jack took one last look at Nadia's house. There was nothing to suggest a problem. The blinds were open, and the front garden looked well-tended. Still, Jack felt uneasy. Something wasn't quite right.

Arriving at the station, all thoughts of her missing colleague vanished. Harry had arrived late, looking ashen. 'Sorry, boss. Just been called in to deal with an assault outside a pub in the city centre. Nasty beating – no rhyme or reason to it. I might need to rush off to the hospital, if he regains consciousness.'

That's all I need, another officer off the team, thought Jack. Then she shuddered, remembering that she'd been walking alone in town last night. She never thought of Birmingham as unsafe until random attacks like this happened.

Over the next two days, Jack received two more texts from Nadia along similar lines. She debated calling HR, but, instead, she logged the absences in the usual way. When she reached day seven, Nadia would have to send in a doctor's note or face disciplinary action. Jack hoped it wouldn't come to that. She replied to the latest text with:

> Call me please. I need to make sure you're ok.

She waited, but there was no response.

Jack was in the middle of reviewing some of the footage that

Georgia had sent over, including another grainy image of their climber, when her phone rang.

'Hi, it's me.' Shauna spoke so quietly that Jack had to press her mobile closer to her ear. 'I've got a suspicious death I think you should see.'

'Where?' Jack took out a pen from her inside jacket pocket ready to jot an address down in her notebook.

Shauna reeled off a flat number and the name of the block. 'Thing is, I've got some idiot from the Murder Squad laying claim, but I think you should be here. It could be down to your climber.'

Jack could hear a loud voice in the background. She tried to place it as she said, 'I'll be there as soon as I can. Make sure the body isn't taken to the morgue.'

Before setting off, Jack paused. She knew that she should have contacted her superintendent and at least attempted to get permission to access the crime scene. But she also knew that none of her male colleagues would do that. They'd just bound into the scene and, like a feral cat, piss all over the body to make their claim. At least she had the courtesy to get suited up and approach the officer in charge upon her arrival.

He happened to be demanding a timeframe from Shauna just at the moment Jack entered the apartment. 'And what does the body tell us about the time of death?' he boomed.

Jack knew what was coming next so stayed back, without interrupting, to enjoy it in all its glory.

Shauna put her ear to the dead woman's mouth. Then she sat back up. 'She couldn't tell me anything. Do *you* want to ask?'

Before her friend got a dressing down, Jack stepped forward, holding out her hand. 'DI Jack Kent. I'm not sure we've met.' The tall, red-headed detective seemed intent on dealing with, in his mind, the insolent pathologist, and ignored her.

Jack tried again, 'I believe this murder may be linked to a case I'm investigating. Can we discuss it outside?'

He looked from Shauna to Jack, clearly trying to decide who should get his attention. Eventually, he made the right decision and followed Jack to the hall.

After she had reintroduced herself as a detective, the man grinned. 'I know you. You're that mountaineer woman. DI O'Donohue.' He shook her hand this time with as much force as he could, crushing her fingers in the process.

Jack waited for a moment before speaking again. 'Have you considered that this might be a break-in? The thief might not have expected the victim to be home.'

DI Martin O'Donohue stroked his chin. 'The front door wasn't forced.'

'My guy enters through the balcony. Was the door leading to it locked?'

The detective had to admit that he hadn't tried it, being more focussed on the dead body.

Jack didn't admonish him. 'You see, I'm thinking it's entirely possible that the victim may have disturbed my burglar, leading to her death. Any signs of a struggle?'

'Well, I was hoping that the bloody pathologist could tell me that.'

Jack wondered for a moment how red in the face this man could get without having a heart attack. Now, of course, she could get all pally with him and agree that all pathologists are essentially stupid and should be hung out to dry. But she would never do that. 'If the perp's the same as mine, then I'm sure you'll agree I should have proper sight of the scene. It's what you'd expect in the circumstances.'

'Well... yes.' No doubt, he wanted to say no.

Jack moved back towards the living room before DI O'Donohue could stop her. The dead woman lay on her back, eyes fixed on the ceiling. Shauna turned her over so that Jack could see the deep gash on the back of her head, which had long since stopped bleeding leaving a smear of dry blood shrouding her long, blonde hair. 'Where was she found?'

DI O'Donohue came up behind and pointed to the marble fireplace. 'On her back, over there.'

There was a pool of congealed blood on the tiled floor in front of the fireplace. It appeared that she'd tripped, or possibly was pushed, and hit her head on the edge of the marble fire surround.

Jack turned to Shauna, almost expecting a wink. 'What's your view of what happened?'

Shauna stood and faced her friend. 'She hit the corner here,' she pointed to an edge of the fireplace that was smeared with blood, 'with a great deal of force, possibly staggered for a moment and then fell to the floor. It's a significant injury and – I won't know for definite until I've opened her up – but I reckon her skull fractured and caused a bleed on the brain. She'd have died very quickly.'

'She's not been hit with anything? Could she have been pushed?' Jack asked.

'In my view, she could have tripped, but there's nothing on the floor like a rug or an obstacle to suggest that. She also could have been pushed with some force. Of course, she's a slim, short woman and if she wasn't expecting it, she'd have been easy to push.'

Jack looked down at the corpse. Shauna was right; she was slightly built, below average height and probably middle-aged. She was only wearing silk pyjamas.

'Do we have a name?'

'We believe it's the homeowner's wife, Anastasia Marlova, a Russian surgeon. We found her passport.' DI O'Donohue passed it to Jack. She studied the photo, noting, not for the first time, that passport photos look more like the dead than the living. If she had to bet on it, then it was definitely her, but they'd need more than that for a positive ID.

'Have you found her phone?' Jack addressed this to the room and was met with no response from the SOCOs. She knelt down and peered under the few pieces of furniture. 'You might want to look under the chair.'

One of the technicians moved the chair back to discover the phone. After carefully bagging it, she placed it with the other evidence bags to be written up by the crime scene coordinator. Gesturing to the technician, Jack asked, 'Can I take a look?'

Keeping the phone in the bag, Jack used the woman's face to unlock it. She was interested in her recent calls and found one that had been received at 2.35 a.m. It was from someone with what she assumed was a Russian name, as it was written in Cyrillic, and lasted for just over three minutes. 'It looks like she was speaking to someone on the phone, maybe facing the fire-place, then perhaps she turned and saw the perp.'

'Surely she'd have been seen by the thief through the window before he entered the apartment?'

Jack couldn't deny that. If Anastasia was on the phone, then the screen would have illuminated her face. Perhaps the perp had already entered the apartment and was in the process of searching in another room when the call came in. It would have woken Anastasia, who might have left the bedroom which was to the right of the living room. There was a further bedroom to the left. 'Has anyone searched the second bedroom?' Jack pointed in the general direction.

The SOCO that found the phone stepped forward. 'Yes, it's an office.'

'Any signs of a break-in?'

The officer shrugged. 'Not that I could see. But I haven't done a full search. I just checked what room it was and looked for anything obvious.'

DI O'Donohue clenched a fist. He motioned for a couple of

his officers to do a full search of the office, then turned back to Jack. 'The person who called her last night needs to be interviewed.'

'I can do that.' Jack felt that now was the time to be forceful. 'If this does show more signs of a break-in, then I'm going to speak to my superintendent. I expect to be in charge of the case.'

She also wanted to find out more about Anastasia Marlova. Maybe there were clues as to why she was targeted in her or her husband's business dealings. It would help to know why she lived in Birmingham and Russia. Perhaps the person she spoke to last night would be able to help? She'd already taken over the case in her head.

DI O'Donohue stood his ground, but, before he could contradict Jack, his DS shouted from the office. 'You might want to come and see this.'

The drawers to the bureau at the side of the desk had been opened. Inside them were empty jewellery trays. The lock to the drawers in the desk had been forced, but it wasn't clear if anything had been taken from them. They still contained a handful of receipts for sales to businesses in the jewellery quarter.

'We've found business cards and headed stationery. Someone who lives here, maybe the husband, must be an importer/exporter of gold and silver jewellery.'

'Is the husband's passport here or his suitcases?' Jack asked.

The DS shook his head. 'Not found them. He could still be in Russia, but we'll need to check.' He stood up and moved to the desk. 'The headed notepaper suggests that Anastasia Marlova works as a doctor at the Grinweld Clinic in Edgbaston. It's a private hospital by the looks of it.'

Jack directed the rest of the search until Shauna appeared in the doorway. 'Is it okay if we take the body now?'

DI O'Donohue opened his mouth to speak, but before he

could give the order, Jack said, 'Yes, that's fine. I'll attend the post-mortem. Message me the time.'

Shauna grinned. 'Of course.'

Jack left the crime scene and called the number that she'd retrieved from Anastasia's phone from her car. A man picked up just at the point that Jack was mentally preparing a message for his answerphone. A male voice said, yawning, '*Privet.*'

Jack responded. 'This is DI Jack Kent from the police in Birmingham. Who am I speaking to?'

'Sergei Marlov. Is this about Ana, my wife?' Jack was relieved that he understood and spoke English.

'Yes. I'm afraid I've got some upsetting news.'

'I knew something was wrong.' Jack could hear the man's distress in his voice despite him trying hard to hide it. 'What's happened to her? She's not dead, is she?'

'I'm sorry, yes. She was found at your flat this morning. There was nothing anyone could do.'

Sergei began to sob. Jack waited for a moment, holding the phone away from her ear. It didn't matter how many times she had to tell someone that their loved one had been hurt or worse, it never got any easier. 'Can you tell me about the call you had with her last night?'

After a couple of long, deep breaths, Sergei composed himself enough to speak. 'She'd had a difficult shift. She's a surgeon. I've always told Ana she can ring me at any time. Night or day.'

'Go on.'

'It was a child that she'd just operated on. She died. It was expected, but even so... I'd told her that it wasn't her fault, maybe they got the new organ too late and then suddenly she said, "Who...?"'

'Just that one word?'

'Or... it could have been "you". I'm not sure.' Sergei took a deep breath.

'What happened next?'

'The line went dead. I tried ringing her back a few times. I thought of calling the police in the UK, but then I wondered if I might have misheard. I thought I was being paranoid – I told myself "She's fine, go to sleep, it will be okay".'

A few hours later, Jack waited in Campbell's office for his anger to subside. He'd ended this particular rant with, 'You need to learn to respect due process, Jack.'

'I do respect it, sir. And because I respect it, I can fundamentally see when it's superfluous.' She waited and saw the moment he pursed his lips. 'This is our case. I've no doubt that this woman was killed by our climber.'

Her phone began to buzz in her pocket like a wasp under a glass.

DSI Campbell sighed. 'I take your point, Jack, I really do. But now I've got to smooth things over with the Murder Squad. Perhaps you could take a secondary role in the investigation?'

The buzzing had stopped. 'No, sir – and this is with respect – this is *my* case, and you *know* it. You really should be fighting my corner on this one.'

Flapping his hand in her direction by way of dismissal, he muttered, 'I always do, Jack, I always do.'

Leaving the office, Jack turned the corner and came face-to-face with Councillor Mahmood, who she'd last seen at the mayor's inauguration. 'Ah Jack. How lovely to see you.' He held out his hand.

Jack shook it. She knew the councillor was a golfing buddy of the super which could explain why he was here. But he had also helped her out on occasion as the council representative on the police committee by putting in a good word for her when she needed time off to climb.

'I'm really shocked about this business with the mayor. We can't have the actions of some family members tainting others, though, now can we?' He smiled.

'I tell you what, you deal with the politics, and I'll deal with the crime. Now if you'll excuse me, I have to make a call.' Jack tried to dodge past him before he could say any more as she didn't want to offend him.

He touched her arm. 'Of course, it means nothing to me. But I do hate a scandal, don't you?'

Jack could only guess how the Jacobs' case was playing out in the corridors of the local council. 'I can't be held responsible for Birmingham gossip.'

'No, you're absolutely right. I shouldn't have brought it up. Now, is Campbell in? I was hoping to drag him out for a round.' Councillor Mahmood walked past her towards the super's office.

The call that she'd ignored was from Shauna. It was followed up by a text:

PM at 3.

Pulling up at the mortuary always made her feel slightly nauseous. It was funny that she never felt dizzy up a mountain, but being in an enclosed basement gave her vertigo, even without the stench of decaying bodies.

The body of Ana Marlova already lay naked on her front on the slab. Shauna smiled at Jack. 'I see you've got the morgue pallor on point again.'

'I don't even have to try.' Jack stepped back from the table under the pretence of giving her friend more space to work.

Shauna started the preamble for the post-mortem recording. 'We have the body of a well-nourished middle-aged female. Other than a wound of...' – she placed a tape measure above the gash on the victim's head and gestured for her assistant to record a close-up shot – '...approximately 3.9 centimetres in length at the back of the head, no other injuries are visible.'

With the help of her assistant, Shauna turned the body over. Then she lifted the hands and scrutinised the nails. They were still a perfectly painted pink, so pristine that Jack wondered if she'd come home and painted her nails after the child's surgery had gone badly. Perhaps this was her way of helping herself feel better?

'No evidence of defensive injuries,' Shauna continued.

Jack's mind drifted as Shauna cut open the body with a Y-cut, weighed the organs and described what the victim had eaten for an evening meal.

'You can come over here for a closer look if you like.'

Jack looked up to see Shauna waving a large dish of stomach contents in her direction. 'No thanks, mate. I'd rather not puke on your floor.'

The scalp was removed then. After the body was flipped for a second time, photographs were taken of the skull fracture. Shauna picked up a bone saw and cut through the skull. 'There's evidence of a significant brain bleed.'

'Is that what killed her?' Jack needed that certainty.

'Most definitely.'

'Anything else you can tell me? Time of death?'

Shauna shrugged. 'I'll need to record the body temperature readings I did earlier to be precise.'

'Ballpark?'

'Less than twenty hours ago. More than ten.'

'Yeah, that fits.'

Jack pulled her jacket tightly around her as she left the mortuary. Even the warmth of the May sun couldn't burn off the clinical coldness of a post-mortem. She always wondered how Shauna coped, but then it explained her dark humour and often outlandish behaviour.

It had to be him, surely.

Unless there was another thief with a similar MO, it had to be the Urban Climber. This was a turning point. He might even hand himself in. This might all be over.

THIRTEEN

When I reach my apartment, I double-lock the door, turn and slide to the floor with my back to it, expecting the devil to chase me down. I silently shriek and scream, biting down on my balled-up fist. Nausea rolls over me in waves until I expel the contents of my stomach onto the tiled floor.

Panting, I try to concentrate on a fine crack, following its journey up the wall to calm myself. That doesn't work. I hold my head tight in my hands, squeezing my temples with my fingers, trying to erase the flashing images within. But all I see is her turning to face me with that look of incredulity and shock. I replay it over and over in slow motion. Why didn't I just run?

That look. Did she know she was going to die? That one look, knowing that this was the end... that she'd never see her family again.

Pushing her came too easy. She just hit the fireplace and crumpled. No sound. No scream. Nothing. She just wasn't supposed to be there. It should all have been simple, like it was every time before. Climb up, enter the apartment, steal the jewels, climb down.

But then there was the blood... red, thick, almost pulsing as it flowed. And nothing to stem its tide. It mesmerised me. I've seen death, but there's never been blood before. Not like this.

I should have felt for a pulse, performed CPR, called for an ambulance... but I did none of these things.

Then it dawns on me. I'm no superhero, no masked avenger. I'm the villain. A murderer. I giggle. And try to smother it with my hand. But it escapes between my fingers until I am roaring with laughter.

FOURTEEN

Still no word from Nadia, not even any sign of a sick note. Georgia and Harry came into the office that morning, both eager to be involved in a potential murder investigation. Georgia had organised childcare with her mother despite there being no promise of overtime. It made Nadia's disappearance even more bizarre. Jack decided that she'd visit her at home later that evening and, if she still got no response, then she'd have to report her as AWOL.

Jack had received word late yesterday that the Marlova case was hers. She didn't have time to get excited or even nervous. Instead, she'd spent the night listing the tasks ahead. Planning for at least a team of ten, she was disappointed and angry to learn that only eight officers had been assigned. Jack eventually dispatched emails at five in the morning assigning each individual their tasks.

Three hours later, she called the team to order. 'Morning everyone. For those who don't know me, my name is DI Jack Kent. Anastasia Marlova, known as Ana, a Russian national, was found dead early at her home yesterday morning. From the evidence gathered so far, it appears that there was another person or persons unknown in her flat at the time of the murder. Ana Marlova died of a bleed on the brain caused by a fall against a marble fireplace. We're awaiting the full pathology report.' Jack paused and scanned the room, pleased to see that everyone was paying attention. 'We've also discovered evidence of a break-in. It's possible that the person who broke into other flats in the area is responsible for this murder. I hope you've all read the case notes related to those.' Several officers nodded. 'You should all have your assignments. Questions?'

Instead of a flurry of hands, this was met by the low hum of movement and discussion of a team at work. Jack took a breath and hoped that no one had spotted the slight tremor in her legs as she'd delivered her speech.

Georgia approached her first. 'Boss, I've spoken to Sergeant Travis and he can give us a team of six for the door-to-door this morning. Do you want me to lead on that? I can review the footage from the local area after.'

Jack smiled. 'Great idea. But don't worry about the CCTV. I'll assign it to someone else and you can help them when you get back.'

Within an hour, the numbers in the room dwindled to four, leaving Jack the opportunity to concentrate on her work. She couldn't rule out that this was personal. They needed to know more about the victim, which was why she'd contacted Europol. She opened the report that they'd sent.

Anastasia Marlova was a fifty-six-year-old Russian citizen. She lived in Moscow with her husband, Sergei Marlov. Her two daughters, Polina and Sofia, both worked in the jewellery business like their father; Polina in the import and export of fine jewellery and Sofia as a designer. Sergei's business was red-flagged. Jack opened the attached report. It listed several concerns relating to money laundering, but no convictions. The Investigative Committee of Russia (SKR) had linked him to the Mafia. None of this came as a surprise to Jack. There were plenty of Russians in Birmingham who'd have such a record, but that didn't mean they were actively involved in anything illegal or were high-ranking Russian mafia members. It had more to do with the SKR having its fingers in many pies and flagging everyone to justify their surveillance.

An Internet search for Marlov revealed that he was something of a philanthropist. In the UK, he'd supported several charities that helped Eastern European migrants, including the Roma. This was surprising. In Russia, just as across Europe, the Roma were considered second-class citizens. Most Russians would seek to distance themselves from them. Jack made a note to look for more evidence of a link.

She reached for her mobile to call Sergei, then checked the time. Sergei and his daughters would arrive in the UK in the next hour, so there was no point ringing him while in flight. 'Harry, are you free?'

Harry looked up from his laptop. 'Sure, boss.'

'We're going to the airport to pick up the Marlovs.'

Birmingham Airport was busy as usual with several arrivals within the same hour. Jack mentally calculated how long she expected the Marlov family to be, considering they had to collect their baggage and get through security. Despite this, Jack and Harry had to wait for three-quarters of an hour longer in the arrivals lounge than they'd expected. Jack spent her time on her phone reading through the digital reports that were trickling through. The door-to-door had so far not yielded anything of importance, but they hadn't yet finished the block.

She glanced up and spotted two young women and an older man huddled together, entering the lounge from customs. One of the women pushed the luggage trolley piled high with three extra-large suitcases, while the other led the man with linked arms. All three looked exhausted, but particularly the women, their eyes the kind of red raw that make-up couldn't hide.

Jack approached them. 'Sergei Marlov?' Jack held out her hand. As the man nodded, Jack introduced herself. 'I'm so sorry for your loss. We're here to take you to your hotel.' West Midlands Police had suggested a bed and breakfast, but the Marlovs had preferred to book somewhere for themselves. Jack didn't blame them.

'Can I see her?' Sergei asked in a firm voice. This was a man clearly used to getting his own way.

One of his daughters tried to protest. 'Papa, no. Are you sure you want to?'

'Polina, I must do it to identify her.' He tapped her affectionately on the arm and turned to Jack. 'That's what you said, yes?'

'We can arrange that as soon as you wish.' It would only take a quick phone call to Shauna and the coroner to set up.

'Then I'd like to go now.'

Polina leant into her father, sobbing. Her sister hadn't spoken a word and seemed detached from the family group by both distance and emotion.

Fortunately, the Range Rover could accommodate all the passengers and their luggage. Polina and her father spoke in Russian throughout the journey to the mortuary. Sofia just stared out of the window at the various houses and shops on the A45, causing Jack to wonder what was holding her attention. Perhaps even more peculiar was that none of them sat glued to their mobiles. Maybe this wasn't a thing in Russia? It made Jack consider emigrating.

At the mortuary, Sergei insisted on not only being the one to identify his wife but also that he didn't need the support of either daughter. This made Polina howl more, whereas Sofia retreated further into her shell. Both women were of a similar age, in their mid-twenties, and yet they were almost polar opposites, particularly in the way they were handling their mother's death.

Jack escorted Sergei into the family viewing room. The mortuary staff had covered his wife with a white shroud up to her neck. Another shroud covered her forehead and what was left of her blonde hair so all that was visible was her face. Of course, Jack had seen the post-mortem and knew that beneath the sheets were the rough stitches made by a technician to hold the body together.

Sergei leant forward and kissed the corpse of his wife on the lips. Placing his hand on the top of her head, he murmured something in Russian. Then he turned to Jack. 'Yes, this is she. This is Ana.'

'Thank you.' Jack said, then added. 'Do you want some more time?'

Sergei shook his head and turned towards the door.

In the short time they had been in the viewing room, Polina had composed herself. She now wore the largest pair of sunglasses that Jack had ever seen, no doubt to cover her tear-stained face.

Sofia stepped forward. 'Can I see her?'

'Of course, and Polina, if you want to.' This just caused the young woman to cry again, which Jack took as a no. She led Sofia into the room. She immediately ran to her mother and lay across her body, suddenly sobbing. Jack gave her a few moments and then moved towards her placing a hand on her back. 'I'm so sorry for your loss,' she muttered.

By the time Jack returned to the hall, everyone seemed keen to leave. On the journey to the hotel, they said very little. Jack knew families were complicated – she only had to look at her own – but Sofia's reaction to her mother's death seemed slightly strange. While in her father's presence, she barely seemed to acknowledge what had happened, but as soon as she was away from him, she broke down. At some point, Jack would need to speak to her on her own. Maybe there was more to Sergei than even British intelligence knew? There was something about the way he carried himself as though he was used to being in charge and expected everyone to acknowledge that. Or maybe the different responses of his daughters were simply because he was closer to Polina than Sofia, and Sofia was much closer to her mother.

Back at the office, Jack took Georgia and Harry to one side. 'Have either of you heard from Nadia?' Neither replied. Georgia started playing with her lanyard, twisting and untwisting it. Harry just looked blank. Jack tried to make light of her question. 'I thought I might pop by... make sure that she doesn't need anything.'

Georgia met her eyes then. Jack stared at her, willing her to speak, but she just looked away.

Jack said, 'Harry, can you check on the Marlovs? Make sure they're comfortable. I'd like to interview them tomorrow, individually if possible. Maybe the hotel has a meeting room of some description we could use.'

'Sure, boss.' He stood and returned to his workspace, leaving Jack alone with Georgia.

'Have you seen or heard from Nadia? I'm worried, or I wouldn't ask.'

Georgia shook her head.

Jack persevered. 'But there's something you're not saying.'

Georgia spluttered as though she'd been holding her breath. 'It's nothing. She spoke to me a couple of days ago. There's a family issue that's causing her stress. I'm sure she'll be back tomorrow.'

It just didn't ring true. What family issue would be serious enough to keep you away from your job for more than a week?

That made up Jack's mind. Before the day was through, she needed to visit Nadia's place again.

On the journey to Balsall Heath, Jack tried to concentrate on the case. They'd need to hold a case review in the morning, but, so far, no major leads had turned up. She couldn't even say for certain that the climber had entered Anastasia's apartment. The forensic report hadn't shown conclusively that a murder had been committed, only that the victim died after a fall onto the fireplace. Unless they found evidence to the contrary, they could be looking at an accidental death, which would down-grade the case even further.

There were no lights on at Nadia's house despite it being late in the evening. Jack still knocked on the door in the vain hope that she might be home. Her parents' home, by contrast, showed a light in every window. After getting no response at Nadia's, Jack knocked on the parents' door. It was opened almost immediately by a slender woman adjusting her colourful headscarf. Jack recognised her as Nadia's mother, Mona.

Mona smiled. 'Jack, is that you? It's been so long. Come in, come in,' she said, giving no sign that there was anything to hide or that she wasn't welcome.

Jack entered the house and was ushered into the scrupu-lously tidy front room.

Mona gestured. 'Please, sit. I'll make us some tea.'

Before Jack could protest, she'd disappeared into the kitchen. A loud conversation in Bengali then ensued. Jack stood, keen to check its origin, but, at that moment, Mona returned with a plate of samosas. 'Please, eat. I know you get little chance at work. Nadia's always starving when she gets home. She always comes to us for food. I don't know why she bought her own house.'

'It's Nadia—' Jack began, but before she could say anything more, Mona scurried back to the kitchen.

The distant conversation resumed. As the volume increased, Jack realised Mona was speaking to a man, so it couldn't possibly be Nadia. Fearing that they would see her as disrespectful, Jack waited for Mona to return. She picked up a plate and helped herself to a couple of the samosas. They were hot and spicy, fresh from the oven. Soon, Mona returned with tea, closely followed by a young man who waited in the doorway to the lounge. Jack recognised him as Nadia's younger brother, Abdul. Mona ushered him away, waving her arms in his direction like she was swatting a fly.

As Mona poured the tea, Jack considered how she'd start the conversation. Something was clearly not right. 'I'm worried about Nadia. She hasn't been at work for over a week.'

Mona sat back in the chair and sighed. 'She's fine. You mustn't worry.'

'We need a doctor's note if she's sick.' Jack scrutinised Mona's response. She just played with the hem of her kameez, not meeting Jack's gaze.

After a few moments, Mona smiled, dropping the hem of her tunic. 'The doctor was too busy on Friday. She couldn't get an appointment. You'll get it tomorrow.'

'Where is she, Mona?'

'She's staying with my sister for a few days, so she can be looked after.' Mona wouldn't meet her gaze. 'I can't. I work, you know.'

Jack knew Mona worked at the pharmacy in the local Boots. 'If she's in trouble, I need to know. I can't help if you keep me in the dark.'

Just at that moment, Abdul returned to the doorway. 'Nadia's fine. Stop harassing my mum. You should leave.' His face was screwed up in rage.

'I'm here to help, Abdul, not to harass.' Not willing to

engage with the petulant youth, she turned back to Mona. 'I'm sure you can understand why I'm concerned.'

Mona's eyes flitted to her son. She looked afraid. But of what? Abdul? Jack herself?

'I think it's time you left.' Abdul made it clear again that she'd outstayed her welcome. Without a word in response, Jack stared him down.

Mona, on the other hand, pleaded with her son, 'Abdul. This isn't right. Jack is Nadia's friend, not just her boss.'

'If she was a friend, then she'd know when to leave her and her family alone,' he sneered.

Jack didn't flinch, keeping her gaze fixed on Abdul. She was going to be the last to blink.

Abdul snorted and left the room, surprising Jack that he'd given up so quickly. Mona appeared more comfortable when she turned back to her. 'My husband's working this evening, so Abdul thinks he's the man of the house. Children, huh?'

'It's fine. I understand, but I do need to know what's going on.'

Mona nodded. 'Believe me, Nadia's okay. But it's best that she's not in Birmingham at the minute. Too much is...' She seemed to struggle with the words. 'This case she's involved in—'

'The burglary?'

Mona furrowed her brow.

'Or the rape?'

She nodded then.

'I need to speak to Nadia if she's being threatened in any way.'

'Not threatened. She's fine. But it's all too much for her.' Mona stood, making it clear that it was time to leave. 'You must understand. She just can't deal with this right now.'

'At least let me speak to her.'

Ushering Jack towards the door, Mona said, 'You'll get your note by tomorrow. I promise.'

The next morning, Jack and Georgia arrived at the Grand Hotel. It was posh enough to have a valet service, but that didn't impress Jack. The interior, though, was something else. The resplendent facade gave way to opulent ceilings as they entered the lobby. It could only be described as the height of decadence. Jack surmised that regular accidents must occur in the ground floor reception area as guests glued their sights on the view above their heads.

Harry had managed to book a suite on the upper floor for no charge. They headed up there in the elevator. Jack chose the panoramic elevator that steadily rose up the outside of the building, affording its passengers a view across the city, and relished the calm, slow journey to the upper floors. Georgia faced the other way towards the elevator doors, concentrating on the flashing red numbers as they rose from floor to floor.

'I hadn't realised you didn't like heights,' Jack said, still with her back to Georgia.

'How can you even look?' Georgia closed her eyes.

Jack laughed. 'This is nothing.'

The door pinged and a disembodied voice informed them that they'd arrived at their floor. Jack followed Georgia to the Empress Suite. She'd arranged to meet Sergei first at 9 a.m. and he was already there, lounging on one of the two sofas in the room. There were also tea and coffee-making facilities and a plate of Danish pastries, none of which had been touched.

After going through the preliminary details and questions, Jack moved on to the evening of Ana's death.

'I know we spoke on the phone about the call that Ana made to you, but can you describe it to me again?' Jack gently asked. Georgia sat next to her with her pen poised to take notes.

Before he spoke, Sergei removed a tissue from his pocket and dabbed his eyes with it. Jack wondered if this was for her benefit. 'Yes, of course. It must have been about two in the morning, and she'd not long got home from completing surgery on a young girl. The girl died, unfortunately, and it upset her. Children always do. I always said to her that she's not alone, any problems or worries, then she must ring me...'

'Did you answer her call straight away?' Jack didn't want to rush Sergei but wanted to keep him on topic.

'Yes, after a few rings.'

'And did you get the impression that she was alone when she rang?'

Sergei paused, pulling at the tissue with his fingers. 'Yes, of course. Why on earth wouldn't she be? Are you suggesting she was having an affair?'

'Sorry. No, of course not. I just wondered if she was with anyone. Did she have friends that she met at the flat?'

'She was in Birmingham to work. You have to understand my wife is a top transplant surgeon. She has no time for friends.'

Jack smiled and nodded. 'I understand. What did you say to her?'

'I just talked for a minute. Let her tell me about the poor little girl and her family. We were just too late.'

'Too late for what?'

'She needed a kidney transplant. My wife was too late in finding a donor, the girl was too weak.'

'Why did you say *we* were too late?' What did it have to do with him?

'I meant she was too late. The doctors...' He tapped his head with his fingertips. 'I am sorry. I am grieving.'

'Could you tell where your wife was at this time? Was she in bed?'

Sergei didn't respond. This was clearly a more difficult question and required him to think carefully. 'I'm not sure, but I heard the bed creak when we first started talking and maybe a door... I don't know.'

'Then what happened?'

'She just said, "Who?" and that was it.' Wiping his face with a fresh tissue, he continued. 'That was the last thing she said to me.'

'Did she end the call then?'

'Not straight away.'

'Could you hear anything else in the background, maybe?'

Sergei shook his head. 'Nothing.'

Georgia put down her pen. 'Sergei, were you chatting in Russian on the phone?'

'Yes.' He looked confused.

'And when Ana said the word "who", was that in English or Russian?'

'English... I'm sure of it.'

Jack paused. It could have been important, as were the words that she spoke. She didn't ask what the person was doing there; she asked who they were. Or at least that's what could be assumed from the single word she said. So, in all likelihood, she didn't recognise the person in front of her. The only other possibility was that she was going to say, 'Who sent you?' Could she have thought the person in front of her was sent there to kill her? And, if so, who had ordered him to do that? Was it Sergei?

Jack leant forward in her chair. 'Tell me more about your wife.'

Sergei spoke as though he was reading from a script. 'She was kind, a loving mother to our children, and she loved her work. This is why she travelled to ensure Russian children had access to transplants across the world.'

'And what about you, Sergei? What is it you do?'

'I'm just in the jewellery business. I import and export the finest Russian jewellery.'

'And your girls are carrying on that tradition.'

Sergei grinned. 'I am proud of them both. I told Ana just give me boys, but my girls have carried on the family business.'

'You're proud of Sofia too?'

'I'm sorry?'

'Sofia's not a jeweller. She's a designer, is that right?'

Sergei looked away, not meeting Jack's glare. 'Of course I am proud of her too. Her work... is exquisite.'

'There's something I must ask.' Jack began knowing this question was as important in real-life as it appeared to be in films. 'Is there anyone you can think of that might have wanted to harm your wife, Sergei?'

'No!' Sergei shrieked. 'No one.'

Jack paused for a moment in case he had second thoughts, then moved on to his and his wife's charitable work. Sergei gushed at this point about what a caring entrepreneur his wife was.

'And we know that you support Roma charities here. Was that the same in Russia?' Jack asked, not expecting a positive response. Openly supporting the Roma would be disastrous for him there.

Sergei scowled. 'The Roma?'

'Yes, we know you donate quite large amounts to them and are quite open about it here.'

'I set up a foundation. They decide where the money goes.'

This caused Georgia to interject. 'And does that concern you?'

'That my money goes to gypsies? No, I'm sure they're needy.' Sergei brushed the remnants of the tissue off his trousers, then stared at Jack, who held his gaze.

A few other questions followed before Jack thanked Sergei Marlov for his time, though they had learnt little from him. He appeared used to being asked questions, making Jack wonder if he'd been interviewed by the police before.

The next interview with Polina wasn't due to start for

another twenty minutes, so Jack poured herself a coffee and helped herself to a cinnamon whirl. Georgia did the same, preferring an almond croissant.

Between mouthfuls, Georgia asked, 'Do you think he's legit? They're clearly a wealthy family. They've taken the largest suite in the hotel. It's incredible. I had a look on the website.'

Jack shrugged. 'I think that's worth following up. We need to know more about him and his wife. Why would she come here to practise, for example? Why don't you ring Europol later and see if you can talk to a real person?'

Not long after, Polina marched in. 'What have you said to my father? He's so angry.'

'Sit down, Polina.' Jack spoke with authority and Polina complied. 'Just a few questions.'

Jack planned to speak to her about the business, but it took her a few goes to get any coherent answers. Polina only wanted to babble on about how her family was being mistreated because they were Russian. She didn't seem to understand that they were there to find her mother's killer.

'Please stay on track if you can. Why was your mother in Birmingham?' Jack asked.

'You know why. She's a surgeon and she works here sometimes.'

'And your father? Why does he come to Birmingham?'

'Selling. He knows some wonderful jewellers in the city. He often comes to sell to them. They pay a good price and love our products.'

'Which are?'

'Mostly chains in fine silver and gold.'

'That they couldn't source here?'

'You don't know much about the business, do you?'

Jack wasn't sure if she simply meant that she wasn't a jeweller or if she was referring to her lack of adornment, apart from a few earring studs. 'No, so why not tell me more? How's the business doing?'

'Pretty good, thank you.'

'No financial concerns?'

Polina snapped. 'Does it look like it?'

Not on the surface, but who knew what swam underneath? This particular daughter wasn't much help. If there were family skeletons, then she was unlikely to offer them up. Sofia was the daughter that Jack most wanted to speak to, especially if she was right in thinking the woman had distanced herself from her domineering father.

Whilst waiting for Sofia to appear, Jack checked her emails. No sign of a doctor's note, but she wasn't expecting one. Whatever was going on with Nadia would not be solved that quickly. Jack's visit to Nadia's parents had only thrown up more questions.

Sofia arrived at the meeting room ten minutes late. She slouched in and flopped down on the chair. She reminded Jack of a hormonal teenager, not the twenty-something woman that she was. Luckily, she answered the preliminary questions at an audible level and with clarity.

Jack moved on to the salient questions. 'Describe what you do for a living?'

Sofia looked blank. 'You know what I do. I'm a jewellery designer.'

'And?'

'I design and make pieces made from highest-grade Russian silver. Prices start at one million roubles, so probably outside your price range.' Sofia played with the toggle on the black sweatshirt she was wearing. Even if Jack had that kind of money to spend, jewellery wouldn't be her first choice. But then, a million roubles were worth about £10,000 – not a fortune for someone of Sofia's wealth and, in actual fact, only a fraction of what Jack had to raise every year to fund her climbing.

'Does your father sell your pieces?' Jack wondered if any had been stolen in the break-in. From what she'd seen of Sofia's designs, they were unique and eclectic.

'My father is a philistine. He hates everything I produce. He said my designs lack taste and he wouldn't be seen dead trying to sell them. Not that I care what he thinks.'

The irony wasn't lost on Jack. 'Tell me about your mother.'

'He makes her do it.'

Jack sat up. 'Do what?'

'Work here. She's an excellent surgeon, but he tells her what to do, where to work...'

Sofia twisted the thin chain around her neck. Jack noticed that the charm it carried was similar to the designs on Sofia's website. After staring at the floor for a few seconds, Sofia said, 'She'd never admit it, of course. It's why I left home – so I don't have to watch him do it.'

'Do what, Sofia?'

Jack hoped Sofia's individual creations weren't important to her, as she could see this one falling to the floor at any moment.

As though sensing that, Sofia let go of the chain. 'The usual. Screwing other women, using violence to get his own way.' She paused for a moment. Up to now, she'd remained calm and monotone. She took a deep breath. 'Everyone thinks he's a good man who cares. In public, he'll shake your hand – but in private, he'll stab you in the back.'

Jack could sense there was more. If she wanted Sofia to blow the whistle on her father, then she needed to tread carefully. 'Can you give me an example?'

Sofia started kicking the leg of the chair. 'I want to go now.'

Georgia looked up. 'We can't keep you here, but we do need to know more about your father, good and bad.'

'It would help us a great deal to form an accurate picture of your parent's relationship. So far, all we've got is from your father and sister,' Jack continued, hoping Sofia would open up.

Instead, she giggled. It began as a low rumble, then grew louder and more hysterical. 'You're crazy if you believe he's trustworthy.' Then she stood, kicking the chair out of the way. 'You're all crazy.'

Jack watched as Sofia stormed out of the room, then looked at Georgia, who just raised her eyebrows. They now had two diametrically opposed views of Sergei and Ana Marlov and their marriage. Jack knew which one she preferred to believe.

FIFTEEN

I didn't sleep last night. I drifted from hysteria to excitement and back again. A cesspit of emotions. Every time I closed my eyes, I saw the red blood that oozed, pulsed and flowed. It consumed my entire vision. Then the smell... it was overwhelming, making me vomit. The putrefaction and death stench were as strong as though the body lay in my room, rotting in front of my eyes, mocking me.

There's no going back. This is the dark side.

I haven't bothered to contact anyone to say that I'll be absent. No one will notice. I'm desperate to discover more about the woman, the frail little bird, whose body haunts me and remind myself why I chose that flat. Who did I kill?

Opening my laptop, I type her name — Anastasia Marlova. I've already read the newspaper articles relating to her death that described her as a doctor, a caring surgeon, and her husband, Sergei as an entrepreneur, a hero of the local Russian community. My stomach lurches at each glorious description. Few people are the innocents they appear.

What does this make me? If I hadn't pushed her, she'd still be alive. Then I stop, switch screens and click on a folder, one of many that I store on this dark Cloud provider. The laptop in their apartment gave up so much information in the weeks before I killed the wife. This is the true story of Sergei Marlov: he made money buying and selling gold and silver jewellery – but that's only half the story. It doesn't explain the huge balance in his accounts or the payments to various individuals that had nothing to do with the jewellery business. He was a crook, lowlife scum with a taste for violent porn. I need to remind myself of this. But it wasn't him that I killed. I killed a caregiver, a person that prolongs life, a paediatric surgeon.

She must have known her husband is evil. She let him keep on behaving that way – what does that make her? Sucking in my cheeks, I realise I don't actually care. So what does that make me?

1995

One Friday afternoon, I hid in the school library. I didn't want to play hockey on the muddy field. The other kids loved to have the opportunity to whack my ankles with their sticks. I'd even heard two boys boast about the number of times they'd smashed me. It was just a game for them. It was getting harder and harder not to show emotion... not to break. If I did, I knew there would be no going back. I imagined shooting them all on a rainy day when they were all congregated in the Sports Hall.

A boy in one of the other Year 8 tutor groups was hunched over a computer, another fugitive from outdoor games. I snuck further behind a bookcase so I could just see his screen. He could type so fast that it was hard to keep up as he swept from one screen to the next. He eventually opened a spreadsheet headed, 'Trip Money, Year 8 Residential'. Within seconds, the boy had changed one column and closed the page. He was just about to switch off the screen when I sneezed. It came out of nowhere with no warning, probably brought on by breathing in the dust of long-neglected book covers.

'Who's there?' The boy turned in a panic.

I could have run, but curiosity got the better of me. I left the security of the shelves and stepped out in front of him. Maybe he could be another Joseph? But, no... he looked too intelligent for that. He might have his uses, though. An idea began to form in my mind.

SIXTEEN

Georgia cut the call with Europol and whooped. 'Boss, you're gonna want to hear this.'

The office fell silent. All eyes on Georgia, Jack urged, 'Go on. What have you got?'

'I managed to get hold of a Sergeant Pasternak. He wrote one of the reports mentioning Marlov's business.' She paused, grinning. 'He's not the innocent he appears, and nor is his wife.'

'Isn't his wife a doctor?' PC Brown asked.

'And that's the whole point –' Georgia was clearly enjoying the attention. '– organ trafficking.'

Bloody hell, thought Jack, pushing all the many questions this created to the back of her mind so that she could concentrate on what else Georgia had discovered about this local hero.

'Sergei finds people desperate for cash and offers them money for their organs. Kidneys, part of a liver... and then his lovely wife harvests them. Then they sell the organs to those who are in desperate need. The jewellery business is just a cover for finding victims and clients and to get them through customs.'

'I don't understand.' Jayden asked what others were thinking. 'Why don't they just do this in Russia? Why Birmingham?'

'Not sure, but Europol have their eyes on a private clinic here that offers transplants for a huge fee. Questions have been asked as to where the donors have come from—'

Jack interjected, 'This could be the reason Sergei is supporting the Roma community – it could be hush money. What about his wife? She must have been aware that these were trafficked organs. So... either she was complicit, or being forced to transplant organs? I wonder which it is?'

Georgia shrugged. 'I'll look deeper into it. Is this a motive?'

Jack wondered what they were really dealing with. This could have nothing to do with the Urban Climber. This could be a whole other ball game. There could be many people out there with a grudge against the Marlovs. Someone whose family member had died, or who was extremely ill after the harvesting, or a client for whom they hadn't managed to find an organ might easily want him dead. It would have been all too easy to disguise what happened to Ana as a burglary...

She decided she needed to speak to Sergei again and confront him about the organ trafficking. But they'd need to get that approved first and the National Crime Agency would want to be involved. She slammed down her pen on the table. Why did it always have to be so complicated?

DSI Campbell took off his glasses and rubbed the bridge of his nose. 'I think I'm getting a migraine.'

'Sorry, boss. I thought you'd want the heads up before I call Sergei in.'

'I'll have a chat with the chief and get back to you later this afternoon. We don't want to go in guns blazing and ruin an ongoing investigation.'

Anthony Campbell looked as though he had something else

to say. Jack fidgeted in her chair. 'Jack, you, er... seem to be missing a member of your team.'

'Nadia?' Jack bit her cheek. 'I'm dealing with it. There's a family issue which I'm sure will be sorted soon.'

'I've had HR on the phone. You haven't completed the correct forms.'

'Oh. Well, I've had other things on my plate.' Jack nodded her head towards the rest of her team in the adjacent office.

'Just sort it. And I'll see if I can get you the go-ahead for an interview with Sergei Marlov.'

At lunchtime, Jack positioned herself in the queue at Boots pharmacy with a packet of Tampax and a box of paracetamol in her hand. She could see Mona at the till ahead considering how she could get out of serving Jack. The grey-haired woman between them asked a question that needed the pharmacist, leaving Mona facing Jack. She held out her hand for the Tampax and pills and rang them up on the till. 'That will be £3.10.'

Jack held up her debit card and tapped it on the card reader. 'What time's your break?'

Mona sighed. 'In about half an hour.'

'Do you know the Costa round the corner? I'll meet you there.' Jack turned to leave, not giving Mona the time to back out.

It was more like forty minutes later when Mona showed up. Jack stood when she approached her table. 'Do you want anything?'

Mona took off her raincoat and placed it on the back of a chair. 'A cappuccino would be lovely, thank you.'

Jack watched her from the queue. She sat scratching at her arm. Dark shadows shrouded her eyes, making her appear older than she'd looked in her home environment. Jack collected the drink at the end of the counter and sat down opposite Mona.

'I thought it might be easier for you to talk without the rest of the family around,' Jack said.

Mona adjusted the front of the plain hijab she wore for work, covering the worry lines on her forehead. 'I've told you, Nadia's fine.'

'So why isn't she at work? And I didn't get a doctor's note. You wouldn't want her to be disciplined, would you?'

Mona played with her mug. 'You don't understand.'

'If you won't tell me what's going on, then you're right – I won't understand.'

Mona sniffed. 'You can't make me say it.'

'No one else is here. Abdul and your husband... no one will know you told me.'

Jack could see the tears form in Mona's eyes before they fell. Mona tried to rub them away with the back of her hand, but Jack knew that secrets just festered until they boiled over.

'Mona, please. You need to tell me what's going on here.'

'She was raped. Nadia was raped.' It was said in almost a whisper.

Jack wasn't sure whether she had misheard. 'Who? When?'

'Years ago. It happened when she was walking to school. She was only fifteen. Every morning, she took a shortcut across the park. There were always lots of kids around going the same way. But on this day, she was running late. I'd asked her to drop Abdul off at his primary school. Someone grabbed her and hurt her so, so badly.' Mona picked up a napkin and blew her nose on it.

Jack didn't know what to say. It explained why Nadia had such empathy for Sara and why she had needed time out. Eventually, she asked, 'Did they catch the bastard?'

Mona sat back and covered her face with her hands. She looked ashamed. 'We never reported it. She came to my work in a state. I just took her home. My husband called the imam. He said we mustn't talk about it. It would bring shame to the whole family. So we never have.'

'Mona—'

'I know it's wrong. But we thought it would be better for Nadia. She wouldn't ever have to talk about it. But the nightmares... the crying... she never wanted to leave the house.'

'Will she talk to me? I can get her help from Occupational Health if she wants it.'

Mona nodded. 'I'll ask her. You know, it was funny. She must have been about seventeen when she just came out with it – "I'll join the police. I'll put this right."'

Jack took Mona's hands in her own. 'Thank you for telling me. I know that must have been hard.'

'There's more.' Jack must have looked confused. 'Nadia's been warned. There was a note pushed through the door over a week ago. It said, "When you give evidence at the trial against Jacobs, make sure he's found innocent or you'll be sorry." It wasn't signed. The thing is... we're a close-knit community and I know it might affect our family, their businesses, whatever, but I don't even care about that. But I'm scared they'll hurt her. I can't let anyone hurt my daughter. You understand?'

'Do you still have the note?'

Mona shook her head. 'I threw it away. Put it straight in the dustbin. I didn't want it in the house.'

'And Abdul? The way he behaved the other day. What does he know?'

Mona sighed. 'He wants to sort it out. He wants Nadia to stop working and thinks he can find out who threatened her.' She glanced at her watch. 'I have to go. But I'm worried, Jack. Abdul's always been a bit, you know, impulsive. If he finds out who sent the note, I don't know what he'll do.'

'I can warn him off.'

Mona shook her head and stood. 'It's okay. I'll tell Nadia that she must call you.'

There was a message on her desk when she got back to the office. DI Amelia Barton from the National Crime Agency had called to say they could interview Sergei Marlov. They wanted a recording of the interview but were happy for them to go ahead without a minder. Jack booked an interview room and discussed with Georgia the questions that she intended to ask.

'This whole thing seems to have taken an odd turn.' Jack wasn't sure what they were now dealing with. She sat back in her chair. 'What do you think? Could Ana's death have been to do with the organ trafficking instead of our climber?'

'I can't get my head around it, to be honest, boss.' Georgia sucked her pen. 'Does she bring harvested organs from Russia to the UK?'

'My thoughts are that we're dealing with two separate setups. So, you've got a British side and a Russian side. You've got a clinic here that harvests and undertakes the transplants for UK clients and a clinic in Russia that does the same. The clinic in Russia is probably run by Ana Marlova too.'

'But do they traffic from the UK to Russia?'

A sudden thought came to her, and Jack picked up her phone and found the number for a doctor she'd once dated, Emily Fisher. Surprisingly, Emily answered on the second ring, something she'd rarely done when they were together.

'Hi, Emily. It's Jack.'

There was a pause. It sounded like Emily was moving to another place so that she could speak more openly. 'Jack, this is unexpected.'

Jack blushed, worried that Emily had got the wrong idea. 'I'm sorry to disturb you, but I've got a medical question.'

She listened for any hint of disappointment. Emily was

gorgeous and kind, but they'd never really bonded. They both had busy schedules and hadn't made a massive effort to get their relationship to work. It wasn't meant to be.

'Go on.'

'Organ transplant. Could you ship an organ from, say, Russia to the UK and it still be viable?'

'What are you caught up in this time? Um... yeah, it's possible, depending on the organ. You couldn't ship a heart, but a kidney can last for over two days. At a push, a liver can last a day. But you'd have a hard job explaining it at customs.'

It was possible then. That's all she needed to know. Jack continued the call for a minute out of politeness, then hung up and told Georgia what she'd learnt.

It was time to pick up Sergei Marlov.

They didn't phone ahead. It was better to risk him not being at the hotel than give him any warning that they were on to him. The receptionist at The Grand looked particularly bored when they walked in, until she spotted them and looked up with a wide smile. 'Can I help you?'

Jack flashed her warrant card, which didn't change the young girl's demeanour. 'The Marlovs. Are they in their suite?'

The receptionist looked down at her computer. 'I think they checked out this morning.' She tapped some keys. 'Yes, at six o'clock. They said they had an early flight.'

'Bollocks.' Jack admonished herself, then reached for her phone.

It was then that she spotted Sofia Marlova pulling her suitcase towards the revolving doors. 'Wait!' She ran up to her.

'I'm not going back.' Sofia stood in front of Jack, eyes darting.

'Back where?' Jack asked.

'To Russia. I'm staying here. He's not treating me the way he did Mama.'

'Who, your father?'

A young man grabbed Sofia by the arm and led her towards the door. 'Leave her alone. She's just lost her mother,' he snapped.

Sofia turned back to Jack. 'This is Sean, my boyfriend. I'm fine.'

Jack watched them go, having managed to get Sofia to tell her where she would be staying. She could wait until she was on her own without the over-protective boyfriend.

By the time they got back to her car, she'd learnt that there had been a flight at 8:20 that morning and that Sergei and Polina Marlov were on it. Jack instructed Georgia to break the bad news to the NCA and Europol. They might not be arresting them today, but they still had Sofia. Jack wasn't letting this case go without a fight.

Jack turned to Georgia. 'What we need now is the SOCO evidence. Let's hope we find something that can either link this to our climber or rule him out. Otherwise, this just got even more complicated.'

SEVENTEEN

Eyes wide open. All that she could see was iridescent white. She blinked and the cold, white mass drifted closer to her eyeball. An oppressive weight pressed down on her body... an ice tomb, compacted, solid, crushing every bone. Breathing in filled her mouth with wet snow, asphyxiating. Paralysed with fear, she attempted to claw with outstretched fingers, praying for a gap, but she could barely move her hands, barely even a fingertip. No space to shovel the snow and ice away from her mouth, no chance to breathe or to survive. Each attempt brought her closer to death. The ice sat like a devil on her chest, smothering her.

On the last breath, Jack woke with a jolt. This wasn't the first time that she'd experienced sleep paralysis since Annapurna. Each time, she hoped it would be the last. She tried to convince herself that this wouldn't happen again and that she didn't need professional help, that she was getting better. But she wasn't. If anything, these episodes were becoming more frequent.

There was far too much to do to worry about it, emphasised by the number of emails that had come in during the last few hours. She groaned and headed for the kitchen. Coffee first, then she'd consider what needed to be tackled and in what order.

By 8 a.m., Jack had completed the day's task list and emailed it to all parties. She yawned as she read through the last batch of emails in her inbox. Kicking herself, she spotted one from SOCO that she'd missed. Why on earth didn't they flag their emails as urgent? Jack typically got over 100 emails a day and had little time to keep up with them.

She opened it. They'd found a medallion on the edge of the balcony, snagged on one of the pot plants. A photograph was attached. Jack clicked on the file. It took a moment to download. As the picture became clearer, Jack immediately recognised it. She had one of her own that she kept in her climbing jacket pocket, a medallion of Saint Bernard, the patron saint of climbers – not a huge, fluffy dog carrying a casket around its neck, as most people imagined, though if you were stuck on the Alps, you might prefer the latter.

All climbers had their own superstitions and beliefs. The puja ceremonies, prayer flags, and altars on the Himalayas only added to the mysticism. Many climbers developed habits and rituals to keep them safe. Jack never wore a St Bernard medallion around her neck, as she preferred dog tags. If she died on the mountain and was dug up years later, she wanted her rescuer to know who she was. The Sherpas had etched a metal plaque for Hannah at Annapurna, later replaced by a formal memorial laid by Hannah's parents. Jack couldn't describe what the first one looked like as shock clouded her senses. All she remembered was the flapping of the brightly coloured prayer flags and how inappropriate they seemed. She didn't attend the second memorial event despite Hannah's parents inviting her and even offering to pay her airfare. She never wanted to set foot on that mountain again. The image of the goddess with outstretched arms haunted her night and day, and she couldn't get over the feeling that she'd let them down by not protecting their daughter.

The medallion told her one important thing. The likelihood was that the climber had been at the flat some time that night. Jack felt relieved. The last thing she wanted was for the investigation to shoot off in another direction. The NCA could take over the organ trafficking angle, leaving them to concentrate on the break-ins and the suspicious death. Now they just had to find the climber.

The traffic into town that morning barely moved. Even with the congestion charges, commuters still entered the city every day. If Jack had a choice, she would drive to one of the local train stations and get the train in. Unfortunately, she knew that during any given day she might need her car, so there was little choice but to continue with the stop-start procession. To make it worse, it began to pelt down with rain. Jack rarely listened to music in the car. At home late at night, she might play a few of her dad's old records. She still had his turntable and an extensive selection of jazz and blues. It was her guilty pleasure. She turned on her car radio now, pre-tuned to Jazz FM, just in time to hear the end of a Billie Holiday classic. Immediately, she felt calmer.

It was 9:30 by the time Jack arrived at the station. She muttered, 'Traffic was a nightmare...' to no one in particular.

Nadia glanced up from her laptop. 'There was an accident on the Hagley Road, apparently.'

Jack started, then smiled, pleased to see her colleague back in action. She didn't comment, though, as she didn't want to embarrass her. Nadia would speak to her in her own time. Instead, she said, 'I guess you've all seen the SOCO email. The medallion is a climbing one, so we're back to that angle. We need to find the Urban Climber. Today, I want you to go back through video footage from all the burglaries and charity drops. This guy knows these flats, and he's picking certain victims.

How does he know they're not in or not supposed to be home? How does he know they're wealthy? I want some credible leads by the end of the day.'

With the suspicious death, it was even more vital that they catch the climber, and the climbing angle was their key clue. Jack needed to speak to more climbers. Someone must know something. Her team was busy with various tasks. All of them were glued either to their phone or their computer. She sent Nadia an email welcoming her back to work and asking if she wanted to go for a coffee later. Then she left them all to it and found a quiet spot away from the now cramped office.

On the fire escape stairs to the roof, Jack reached for her phone and dialled Danny's number. When he answered, she simply said, 'Have you got any free slots for today?'

'I'm here now, cleaning up from last night. In half an hour?'

Her bag of gear sat waiting in the back of the Range Rover – might as well kill two birds with one stone. The drive to Danny's took minutes. The rain had stopped now, leaving very few puddles despite its earlier intensity.

Danny must have spotted her arrival on the CCTV. He stood in the doorway to the climbing centre, leaning on a broom. 'Just got to finish cleaning up reception. Why don't you get changed? I thought you might fancy the high wall today.'

Jack could chat and climb with Danny belaying. She wasn't bunking off work. Plenty of questions swam through her brain that he could help to answer.

She was soon changed and completing her warm-up in the gym. Her arms and shoulders were stiffer than usual, so she took her time stretching these muscles. By the time she was ready to tackle the high wall, Danny had set the ropes. He stood at the bottom, ready to attach the rope to her harness. She studied the wall first. There were a couple of tricky sections. She spotted that he'd included a chimney. As he'd had little time to prepare for her arrival, Jack wondered who'd asked for this route. It reminded her of some place she couldn't quite recall. Her muscle memory might bring back the course as she climbed.

Powdering her hands from the bag of chalk on her belt, she took hold of her first handhold and began to climb. After the first few simple moves, she balanced on her toes and a hand and glanced down at Danny. He looked deep in thought, staring at the wall rather than at her. 'Hey, Grandad. You with us?'

He gave the rope a short tug in reply. Jack reached for the next hold. It was just out of reach, so she curled her toes around one foothold and pushed off with the other, giving her an extra few centimetres. Then she moved further up the wall. These holds were pretty solid, so she took a moment to powder up again. She shouted down to Danny. 'Missed you at the pub the other night.'

His response came quickly. 'Yeah, sorry 'bout that. Gemma needed a break.'

'Things okay?'

Danny released more rope. 'She's just suffering a bit. Lack of sleep and she's always a bit down for the first year after she's given birth.'

Jack moved further up the wall. 'Sorry, mate. I didn't know.' She should have known this. Being able to observe what was really going on with people was part of her job. How had she missed Gemma's depression? But parenting wasn't anything that she'd ever imagined doing herself.

She was soon at the chimney section. Like every climber, she loved the variety of climbing positions. She leant into the crack in the wall. Keeping a steady momentum going, she moved her feet up the other side of the wall and pushed her bottom and back up the right side. This was just a short section until she reached a handhold on either side of the gap and cut across it with her feet. With more speed, she crossed the gap to the other wall and continued the climb up there. So far, there'd been no drama.

Finding a good place to pause, she glanced back down at Danny. She was quite far up now. She could complete the route or abseil back down. At least she'd cleared her head and completed a good practice run. Perhaps now was the time to bring the session to a close? She signalled to Danny and began the abseil to the floor. As soon as she reached it, she unclipped.

'Thanks, I needed that.'

'Not at work today?' asked Danny.

'I thought I'd grab a quick session before I ask you a few questions.' She nodded at him. 'So, in a way, this is work.'

Danny tied off the belay rope. 'Oh, you still think I can help with your climber? I've racked my brains and I can't think of anyone.'

Jack took off her harness and laid it down on the ground. There were a couple of benches in the middle of the room. She sat on the nearest, ignoring its squeak. They always reminded her of school gyms. She'd spent a lot of time in those, trying to avoid the stares of the other teenage girls in her year. It was the only place she excelled. In every other subject, she was average or even mediocre.

Danny sat down next to her, jiggling his leg. He wasn't used to sitting still. *It must drive Gemma mad,* thought Jack. 'We found a medallion at the last scene.'

'A climbing one?'

'Yeah.'

'I'm surprised you're that bothered about finding him. What's he doing? Stealing a few bits of jewellery? It's not likely the rich bastards he's stealing from are going to miss it.'

Jack hid her surprise at his outburst. 'One of them died.'

Danny looked blank. 'What do you mean?'

'At the last break-in. We found a body. It looked like she'd been pushed and hit her head.'

'An accident?'

Jack shrugged. 'So you see, we've got to catch this guy. The stakes have risen considerably.'

'Have you got a photo of the medal?'

'Yeah, on my phone. Hold on, I'll fetch it.'

It only took a moment to retrieve it from her locker. She returned to the hall and sat back down, then scrolled until she found the photo that SOCO had emailed. She showed it to Danny, who enlarged it.

He stared at it for a moment and said, 'I've only seen this particular type for sale in mountain shops in the Alps. They sell most of them in Catholic shops next to the St Christopher medals. The religious ones have the saint embellished more prominently. But this one's quite specific to climbers.'

Jack inspected it and could now see the outline of Mont Blanc in the background. 'I never had you down as an authority on medals. So – he's climbed in the Alps. Doesn't exactly reduce the pool of possible climbers.'

'You reckon he's local?'

'To Brum?'

Danny nodded. 'Yeah. Or at least do you reckon he lives around here?'

Jack put her phone away and glanced at the wall she'd just climbed. 'I think he lives here now at least, and possibly works in the local area.'

'I get quite a lot of local climbers contact me to book sessions. I turn most of them away. They don't tend to ask twice.'

Jack smiled. Fortunately, she'd never had to ask Danny if she could climb here. That was a given. They were practically brother and sister. But more importantly, she was the class of climber that the centre catered for. Danny didn't let just anyone through the doors, unlike Suzy and practically every other climbing facility manager.

Danny stood up then. 'Mind you, I might have to open for everyone if this bloody council keeps putting the rates up.'

Jack looked up at him. 'So, if you were a climber who has, let's say, climbed in the Alps, where would you go to train in Brum?'

'Who's to say they'd use an indoor centre? I always suggest Boulders. Chris runs a tight ship. He's always safety first.'

Jack tried to place him and then remembered that Chris was the guy who had behaved like a sexist idiot the one and only time she'd been to that venue. That was for a photo shoot for one of her sponsors. But Danny seemed to rate him – maybe he hadn't been mansplaining when he told her how to use the equipment; maybe he was just conscientious?

Boulders was a short, ten-minute drive from Danny's climbing school. Jack decided that she might as well pay them a visit before returning to the police station. Before starting her car, she checked her phone. Nadia had messaged to say that she would like to meet up. It made sense to do that somewhere relatively private. Jack knew a great Turkish café a few minutes' walk from their office. It was usually reasonably quiet and had booths to sit in. It also had a small Bedouin tented garden that the owner might well open up to them if she asked. She suggested they meet there for lunch.

The drive to Boulders proved to be quite therapeutic. Traffic was light, giving Jack the chance to think. One area that they hadn't covered in enough detail was how their perp knew about the jewellery and money. He also seemed to have an idea where these things were kept in each flat. They'd checked out if the targeted flats had common cleaners or caretakers, but they were all different. The cleaning companies covered some flats, but not all. They didn't employ individual cleaners across all the flats and there was little crossover of caretakers or even management companies. Up until now, they'd only cross-checked names. Maybe it would be a good idea to look more closely at the individuals. It would take time to interview them all but might throw up some extra information about the break-ins too.

Then there was the jewellery angle. Jack had little time or interest in studying Birmingham's industrial history, but she knew that, after the market for munitions dried up, jewellery-making became its number one industry. The Jewellery Quarter still stood proud, bringing together makers and sellers of all kinds. They'd spoken to the dealers and fences – maybe they needed to talk to other traders and makers? The Urban Climber could be one of them, possibly meeting his victims through that line of work... a jeweller *and* a climber? The combination seemed odd to Jack. Climbing was so physical, whereas jewellery making relied on fine motor skills and creativity.

Jack reached Boulders but didn't bother taking her gym bag and harness, leaving them in the back. The receptionist sat perched on a high stool, reading a book. Her long, brown hair was plaited and her choice of mountain wear accentuated her slender physique. Jack hoped she wasn't staring.

'Hi, I'm DI Jack Kent. Is Chris about?'

'DI? So, you're police, yeah?' Her accent was pure New Zealander.

'That's correct. Tell him not to worry. I'm not here to arrest him.'

The New Zealander grinned and whispered, 'I wish you would.' Then she led Jack to Chris's office.

Chris Mayfield was an ex-army officer. If Jack hadn't already known that, then the photos on his office wall would have made it obvious. Both in desert uniform and formal dress, Chris looked commanding and had an air of understated menace. As she entered his workspace, he held out his hand.

Jack waved it away. 'It's nothing formal, Chris. I just need your help.'

He motioned her to sit. With the desk between them, Jack sat opposite him on the only available chair. Chris still kept his head shaved military style, but now wore thin, frameless glasses. He still had that air of absolute authority. 'Always happy to help law enforcement, Jack,' he said, arms folded across his chest.

'We're looking for a local climber who's been carrying out a few robberies in the area.'

Chris held up his hand. 'I wondered when you'd get to me. I've heard the rumours.'

Of course, she could have spoken to him before, but then he never had struck her as being the helpful type. She'd also wanted to make sure that this guy was an active climber before speaking to others. Up until now, she'd only spoken to those in her inner circle. Maybe this had been a mistake. She told Chris what she knew.

He sat and listened. 'I take it you don't think this guy is a youngster?'

'We can't rule anything out at this point, but I don't think he's in his teens. These are quite organised crimes. They're not the opportunist, chaotic crimes that a young person would undertake. But that's only my opinion.'

Chris nodded and rose. He turned to a set of filing cabinets. 'We have a membership system here. We get everyone to fill in their contact details. I'm assuming data protection isn't an issue in this case?'

Strictly speaking, it was. Jack had a choice. Chris was willing to hand over the personal details of his customers. She could get a court order but wasn't certain that she had enough grounds to meet the strict criteria for it to be granted. 'Perhaps we should stick to anyone that you're concerned about.' All the CCTV footage that they had appeared to show a man, but she didn't want to restrict the pool of possible suspects just yet.

Chris scratched his head. 'Why don't I take a look and pick out any I think might be worth talking to? It probably won't surprise you that, apart from those who have only climbed once or twice, I know my customers quite well.'

'That doesn't surprise me at all.' Jack squirmed a little in her seat, wondering what a climber would need to do to impress the former soldier. 'I know you run a tight ship and I'm grateful for your cooperation.'

'This will take me a little time. Why don't you pop back later? I've got a school group coming at two. I'm sure they'd love to meet a real-life mountaineer.'

Jack stood. 'I can't promise it will be then.' Then she shook Chris's hand and found his handshake to be a lot gentler than she'd expected. Perhaps she'd misjudged him, after all.

EIGHTEEN

No one's come to interview me. No one's knocked on my door or sought me out at work. As the hours progress and days pass, I can breathe. The more I calm down, the more I can think.

The moments leading up to my panicking and killing the Russian woman had been a blur, but I can see her clearly now. The look of shock as she saw me standing there in front of her! I know her husband was no saint. I choose my victims carefully, and he had done more than most. I may not have expected her home at the time, but the flurry of messages following her death only make me feel stronger. It was the right thing to do.

My attention turns to the clinic that was so desperate to contact her that they left twenty messages in a day. They either haven't read the papers or haven't realised that the 'woman found dead in a Birmingham flat' is their surgeon and the wife of the organ trafficker. Apparently, they have an impatient new buyer, saying Marlov needs to deliver the package soon or it'll be too late. It's certainly too late for Marlov and his wife. I've even started to feel sorry for her as I've read the cruel words that were sent in the days leading up to her death. The vile threats of violence.

Then there's DI Jack Kent. That bit of all of this is coming along nicely. I guessed she'd be the lead officer for the investigation and so she is. I'm sure she'll investigate the whole family and understand why I targeted them. Maybe even applaud me a little. A climber with a conscience, that's DI Jack Kent. I've read the newspaper interviews where she blames the rich for turning Everest into a rubbish dump. Maybe I should help her out a little with her case and explain why I did it? I reach for a pen and paper. A single comment on social media just wasn't direct enough. I'll write her a letter and include a link to the messages from The Grinweld Clinic. She can thank me later.

1995

On the day of the school residential to Plas Y Brenneth Outdoor Education Centre, I left the children's home at the normal time wearing my school uniform. I had Dominic, the hacker, to thank for my place on the trip. We both had our secrets. Little did anyone know that I'd hidden my backpack in one of the neighbouring gardens to collect on the way, or that Dominic had brought along some spare boots and a sleeping bag for me. By the evening, the staff would just think that I'd done a runner. I wouldn't be the first, nor the last. It was a weekly occurrence, after all. They'd just contact my social worker and the police, then think nothing of it. I'd be back in a few days with my tail between my legs. It might even give me a bit more kudos with the other kids, especially the boys. They might even talk to me instead of leaving the room when I enter. Actually, scrub that. I'd hate them to speak.

I'd never been on a coach before. I sat next to Dominic for the first half hour as we headed through areas of the West Midlands that were new to me. Then Dominic started puking, so they moved him to the front of the coach near the teachers. He left a lingering stench in his wake.

It wasn't long till we reached the countryside. I'd never seen so many shades of green. And animals – sheep, herds of cows, even the odd horse or two. My nose was almost pressed to the window as I soaked up the sights. Maybe someday, this is where I'd live. Other kids had family holidays. I had social services. But one day I'd redress the balance. I could wait.

The other kids got noisier and noisier. The girls sang pop songs, and the boys screamed, 'Shut the hell up!'

Eventually, Miss Troughton, the Deputy Head, bellowed at them to be quiet and to my horror, moved Jason Marten to sit next to me. He scowled as he slumped into the seat. But then we had our first view of the mountains. Jason nudged me. 'You ever climbed, crater-face? You're gonna love it. If you don't fall and break ya damn neck.'

I just smiled. When it came down to it, I knew I wouldn't be the one breaking their neck.

NINETEEN

Jack arrived at Mount Ararat restaurant before Nadia. She convinced the owner, Emir, to let them have exclusive use of the garden. Above her, multicoloured rays of light reflected from the lanterns that were carefully tied to a pergola. In the winter, Emir added many layers of patterned fabric to the lanterns to create a false ceiling for the garden but, in the warmer months, these were removed to prevent the space from being too hot and oppressive. Jack knew that shisha pipes were smoked here, and Emir had faced fines for indoor smoking until he'd pointed out that it was actually exterior to the restaurant.

A few minutes later, Nadia arrived, shortly followed by the meze and bread that Jack had pre-ordered. Emir waited for them to choose their drinks and then swiftly left the women to talk.

'Thanks, boss. This looks yummy.' Nadia sat next to Jack on a low bench covered in plump, maroon cushions.

'My pleasure.' Jack couldn't resist pulling off a large piece of bread and dipping it into the homemade hummus.

Neither spoke for a few moments as they filled their plates and tucked into the feast. Emir returned with a jug of water and an English and Turkish coffee. After placing them on the table, he grinned. 'Anything else? Or shall I leave you gorgeous ladies to it?'

Both Jack and Nadia grimaced a bit at that, but Emir didn't seem to notice. Maybe he took their lack of response to mean that they had all they needed, and he left them to it.

'My mum—' Nadia began.

Jack held up her hand. 'Before you say anything, it wasn't her fault she told me. I used my best negotiation techniques learnt at Hendon.'

'You never went to Hendon, ma'am.'

This was true. Jack went to Ryton Police College, just as Nadia had. 'You know what I mean. She was a tough nut to crack, though.'

Nadia shook her head. 'I bet she wasn't.' Then she paused. 'I'm glad she told you.'

Jack finished munching on a filled vine leaf. 'I understand why you couldn't at the time. But I'm more than happy to listen now.'

Nadia looked down at her fingers and sighed. 'It's not like I'll ever forget it.'

Jack waited for her to continue without responding.

'It broke me. I don't even remember the girl I was before, but I remember that day like it was yesterday. I don't understand what happened... I'd walked that route a thousand times. It was always full of people going to work, school, jogging, riding bicycles.' Nadia stopped for a moment and took a deep breath. 'But for once, it was empty. No one heard my screams when he dragged me along by my hair.' Choking on a sob, she stopped.

Jack took her hand and held it in her own.

'I didn't wear a hijab back then. My hair was long and thick.' Nadia bowed her head. 'He pulled it from its roots and held my arm twisted up my back to stop me from getting away. He whispered in my ear, "You're going to die today.'"

Squeezing Nadia's hand tighter, Jack turned her head away so her friend couldn't see her tears. It was so different to hear this from a friend rather than a stranger as part of her work.

'A few metres away, on the edge of the park, were some closely planted bushes. He practically lifted me off my feet and threw me into these. They scratched my face and hands, but that was nothing compared to the pain that followed. When we were hidden, he pushed my face into the dirt and held it there. I choked on it, knowing there was far worse to come.'

'You don't have to...' Jack said. Nadia looked up at Jack, her deep brown eyes seeking out hers. Jack grabbed a napkin to hide her own tears. 'I'm sorry. Ignore me... go on.'

Nadia continued. 'He sat on my legs so I couldn't move. Then he undid his jeans... I heard the pop of the button and the zip. I knew what was coming. I didn't scream. I didn't speak. I shut my eyes and prayed that I'd die.'

Nadia began to sob then, and Jack held her, both knowing what happened next. They were sisters united in the horror of it.

It was minutes before either woman moved, spoke, or ate anything. Eventually, Nadia pulled away and wiped her face. 'I'll just...' She pointed in the direction of the toilets.

Jack nodded. The feast before her had lost its appeal, but she managed some more of the bread and hummus, which now tasted of sand and cardboard.

When Nadia returned, Jack waited for her to choose to speak. For a while, they both just ate and sipped water.

Eventually, Nadia sat back. 'I'm so glad I've told you all this. I've bottled it up for so long. Not just because of my family, but my position too. Who wants a detective who's still scared about something that happened years ago? You know what it's like. We have to be stronger, more resilient than any of the lads.'

She continued. 'I needed some time to get my head back together. Sara's rape got to me. It brought back a lot of memories; some I didn't even know I had. But now I'm back at work, I just want to find the bastard who threatened my family. Maybe he even knows who raped me. Will you help me, boss?'

Jack dropped the knife that she was using to load up a cracker with cheese. 'Absolutely.'

Jack walked back to the office with Nadia. As they passed the Council House with its pompous columns, Jack wondered what lay beneath. Who would gain from threatening Nadia? She would testify at Steven Jacobs' trial about the case – maybe the mayor and his cronies believed they could turn her or ruin her testimony, making it questionable? That's where the answer lay, Jack was sure of it.

Jack stopped walking and turned to Nadia. 'Your mum said she told your imam about the rape. Is he still around?'

Shaking her head, Nadia said, 'No, he died about two years ago. His eldest son is the imam now, but we don't attend that mosque anymore.'

'Which mosque was it?'

Nadia rattled off a name that Jack didn't know. She mentally filed it for later.

They carried on in silence for a few minutes. The shoppers and sightseers strolled past them clutching their bags, no one paying any attention to the two women returning to work deep in thought.

Eventually, Jack broke the silence. 'You can talk to Marcus, you know. He'll happily walk you through the questions they'll ask you at trial. It could be weeks before the arraignment.'

'I might do that.' Nadia nodded. 'I hear you know him well. That's the rumour anyway.'

'I can imagine. What are they saying? That I've seduced

him, no doubt – the PCs think I'll sleep with anyone, don't they?'

'Pretty much.'

'Really?' Jack sighed. 'Well, in this case, there's some truth to it. We've been friends for a while. We had a brief fling when he was a junior barrister and I was a PC. It was more friends with unclear boundaries than anything serious.'

'I guessed as much. He's rather hot, though.' Nadia smiled.

Jack grinned back at her. 'He's married now. And I hear that his wife is lovely. And I have some limits, despite what the lads at the station think.'

Nadia didn't meet Jack's gaze, just kept walking. They just had to cross the ring road, so they walked towards the underpass. This was one of the areas of central Birmingham that Jack particularly disliked. The underpasses had been cleaned up in recent years, but her police radar always pinged when she entered poorly lit places with few people around. It wasn't her safety she was concerned about but others, especially young single women or the elderly, or even teenagers with their phones glued to their hands and their attention on their screens. Any could be a victim of theft or worse. Despite the fresh lick of paint, some of the lights weren't working, creating areas of dark shadow. The council should be on top of that, she thought. Jack made a mental note to send them a sharp email when she got to the office.

Nadia walked with her head down, Jack noticed, hurrying to the other side of the underpass as if she, too, could feel the tension and danger. Waiting until they reached daylight, Jack said, 'You can talk to me anytime if you need to. And I *will* help you, if I can, to find out who's threatening you.'

'Thanks. I'd appreciate that. At least it might stop my brother from getting into trouble – if I can convince him that it's being taken seriously, that is.'

'Of course. I thought I'd start by visiting the mosque. Do you think they'd speak to me?'

Nadia stared at her, looking her up and down as though passing judgement on her suitability. 'Obviously, if you're going to the mosque, you'll need to cover your hair. Do you have a scarf?'

Jack mostly wore face buffs to keep warm as they were better to climb in. Then she remembered the scarf that her sister had given her for Christmas. It was straight out of her boutique and far too feminine for Jack, but she could cover her hair with it at a push. 'Sure, I've got something.'

'Trousers are fine, and a jacket that covers the tops of your arms. I know I don't have to mention that you'll need to be polite and respectful. That's a given. What are you going to ask them?'

Jack shrugged. 'I'll think of something.'

It was difficult. She wouldn't betray Nadia and tell the new imam about the rape. That was unthinkable. But she would need to let him know that Nadia had been threatened over something only his father had been aware of. To do that and stay respectful might be difficult.

During the rest of the afternoon, reports flooded in from each of the officers working the Urban Climber case. As each officer came in to fill up the enclosed space, it became hotter and more oppressive. By four o'clock, Jack was tempted to see if the superintendent was using his office. She would even have considered breaking and entering to get away from the sweltering, overfilled workspace. Instead, she undid the cuffs on her blouse and folded up the sleeves, then reached for her water bottle from the mesh pocket in her backpack.

It was coming up to five when Jack remembered that she needed to pick up the list from Chris at Boulders. She motioned to Nadia, who immediately left her laptop and came and sat on the stool next to her. 'Yes, boss?'

'Do me a favour. Pop over to Boulders and pick up a list from the owner, Chris. I said I'd do it this after and forgot. I don't want to get talking to him.' Jack ran her hand through her hair, suddenly realising how tired she was. 'I really need to get a handle on all the information coming in.'

'Sure.' Nadia didn't need to be asked twice, which made a pleasant change, but then Jack couldn't know what toll the rape was taking on her. Would she be able to keep things together if the same happened to her?

There was no point in visiting the imam until after evening prayers. Jack left Nadia to follow up with a basic background check on the names that Chris provided. She'd make a basic profile for each one: name, age, contact details, where they worked, that kind of thing. Then they'd look for any links with the scenes of crime or victims. Jack would look at their climbing history later tonight. Fortunately, Chris had provided extra details with each name. In fact, he'd been surprisingly thorough.

The last worshipper left the mosque, leaving a man, who Jack assumed was the imam, to lock up. It was quite a nondescript building not much larger than the terraced house it was attached to. A sign in Arabic above the front door was the only sign of its use. Jack had expected something more elaborate with maybe a dome and a minaret.

She watched the young man cross the road, open the unlocked door to a house and go in. A light came on in one of the rooms upstairs. Maybe the imam was changing out of his white thobe. Jack waited for a further ten minutes until the light was switched off. Adjusting the scarf that covered her hair, she approached the house and rapped hard on the door. It was opened by a teenage girl wearing a colourful headscarf, a long T-shirt and jeans.

Jack asked, 'Is the imam home?'

The girl turned and shrieked, 'Baba, it's for you.'

Close up, the imam looked older than Jack's first impression, but still younger than she would have expected for a religious leader. He now wore a black shirt over a pair of jogging pants and a tired pair of trainers. His beard and hair were neatly trimmed, emphasising his heavy eyebrows which were raised in confusion. 'Yes?' he said without inviting her in.

Jack showed him her ID. 'I'm Detective Inspector Jack Kent, I work with Nadia Begum. Can I have a word with you in private, please?'

He didn't move. Instead, he folded his arms. Not looking at Jack directly, he stared across to the mosque as though she was invisible.

Jack wasn't put off by this show of hierarchy. 'It's important.'

He spoke quietly, barely above a whisper. 'I know many Nadia Begums.'

It was perhaps one of the most common names in this area of Birmingham, she had to give him that. '*Detective Sergeant* Nadia Begum,' she clarified.

Smiling, he unfolded his arms and ushered her into the house. 'You should have said. Of course I know Nadia. You must call me Basheer.'

Jack was surprised not to be led into the lounge. Instead, he headed to the kitchen at the back of the house. On the table sat a steaming bowl of chana dal and a plate of chapattis. 'Will you join me?' he asked, motioning Jack to sit at the table. He reached for another bowl and filled it with dal from a saucepan left simmering on the stove. 'My wife and children ate earlier, so it would be nice to have some company.'

Jack hadn't realised that she was hungry until he placed the bowl in front of her. She waited until Basheer had started to eat in case there was a custom to follow, but it seemed that all that was expected of her was to eat and enjoy the meal.

It wasn't long before they'd both cleaned their plates. Wiping up the last of the spicy sauce with the bread, Jack said, 'Thank you.'

Basheer took the bowls and placed them next to the sink. Then he turned to face her. 'One of my neighbours spotted you in the street and let me know you were here.' He waved his arms around the kitchen. 'I wanted you to feel welcome.'

Jack nodded. 'And you have.' Even with the initial show of bravado.

'Good. So now you can tell me why you're actually here.'

Before she could answer, the kitchen door swung open and a young lad crashed into the kitchen at full pelt. The boy grabbed Basheer's trousers in his fist, clawing at them. The imam laughed. 'Is it time for bed, little one?' He reached down and lifted the boy up, bouncing him in his arms.

A barefooted woman in a pale blue shalwar entered the kitchen. 'I told him you were busy, but he insisted.'

Basheer passed the boy to the woman, who Jack assumed was his wife. 'Thanks for the food,' Jack said.

The woman turned to her, and Jack was immediately struck by her warm smile. 'Oh, I didn't cook it. That was Basheer. He always has a pot of food on in case anyone wishes to speak to him after prayers.' Leaving the kitchen and closing the door behind her, she said, 'I'll leave you to it.'

Basheer sat back down.

Jack felt obliged to get to the point of her visit. 'There aren't many women like Nadia on the force and, as you might imagine, it's not always easy for her.'

Nodding, Basheer said, 'There aren't many Muslim men either, but I can see how it would be more difficult for a woman.'

'The problem is twofold, both within the police and the wider community. In particular, racism from other officers and the general public. Being a woman only makes that worse. And Nadia's an excellent officer with great potential.'

'I can see that.' Basheer laid his hands flat on the table.

'Nadia and her family used to worship at your father's mosque.'

He nodded. 'They left for a shinier new one, like many others before them. I don't hold that against them.'

'When your father was alive, did he ever speak to you about Nadia and her family?'

Basheer raised his eyes to the ceiling and rubbed his thumb between the thumb and finger of his other hand. He didn't answer for a few minutes, then said, 'I can't recall anything specific.'

'Are you sure?'

'My father wasn't one for gossip, DI Kent. He was very much like one of your priests. Whatever was said to him was kept in confidence, as it is with me.'

One of your priests. Jack wasn't in the least bit religious. She did sometimes pay homage to the gods and goddesses of the mountains, but that was more to do with superstition than faith. It couldn't do any harm to keep them onside.

She trusted her gut instincts more, and they were telling her that Basheer's father had spoken to someone about Nadia's rape. It probably wasn't Basheer who was threatening her. It was more likely someone connected to the mayor. She might as well be direct. 'Did your father have any political allegiances?'

Throughout the visit, Basheer had maintained his composure. Whether he was coming across as having the upper hand or being more relaxed and friendly, he was in charge. For the first time that evening, he looked uncomfortable. He began to tap the table with his fingers and shuffled in his seat. 'It's a difficult balance.'

'What is?'

'There are Muslim politicians of all colours and some that
will join whichever party will get them elected. We don't have
any particular allegiance in my family. We try to keep everyone
onside.'

'That must be impossible, not difficult. I'm assuming that, at
election time, they all come looking not only for your vote but
also those of the worshippers at the mosque.'

Birmingham had always had its fair share of voting corruption allegations and even cases of fraud. The pressures from
certain politicians must be immense – but who would Basheer's
father have spoken to, and why? That's what Jack needed to
tease out of him.

Silence engulfed the room, which now felt stuffy and
airless. Jack couldn't tell Basheer that Nadia had been raped
and she believed his father had told someone. So, what could
she ask that might help her find out who that person was?

In the end, she didn't have to come up with a better question. Basheer said, staring at his hands, 'I know what you're
asking. Did my father pass on information about members of
the mosque to others who could gain from it? I'm ashamed to
say that I think he did.'

Jack raised her eyebrows. 'What makes you say that?'

He sighed. 'It was why so many left the mosque before he
became ill. They'd had visits from prospective councillors basically saying that they expected their vote or that they'd make
public some of their family secrets. They even gave them election posters supporting their particular candidate to put in their
windows.'

And these secrets were no doubt shared with whoever in
the party would benefit from them. Once they were elected,
these councillors would make changes to planning decisions
and decide where the budget was to be spent. At some point,
Basheer's father had passed on the details of Nadia's rape. It

was easy then for someone like the mayor to use that information at a future date.

Besides, Nadia had told her that she had many cousins in Birmingham. If the secret was spread, it wouldn't just shame her immediate family; it would have repercussions within the wider family too. Including her uncle, who was a local solicitor and had many community connections. And her Aunt Saira who owned a fabric stall on the market.

Basheer wasn't finished. 'It's taken me years to win back the trust of the community. I may only have a small mosque, but everyone knows I won't speak to anyone about anybody's private business. I hope you're not going to reopen this can of worms.'

'Who did your father speak to about what happened to Nadia specifically?' Jack glared at him. 'If you can tell me that, then I'll leave you in peace. I just need to find the person threatening her.'

Standing, Basheer went to a set of drawers next to the sink. He opened it and took out a pen and pad of paper. He wrote a name on it and passed it to Jack. She glanced at the name, which wasn't much of a surprise, and put the paper in her pocket.

TWENTY

I keep records of everyone I follow. I file them away on my computer and label them red, amber or green. I considered grading them like mountains, but that became a complex mess of letters and numbers. Most people are amber. There are a few greens. These are extraordinary, rare and unusual in the mad and broken times we find ourselves in.

Laura is a green. She always has a kind word to say to everyone, even though she's suffering. No one would know it by looking at her, but every day's a challenge for Laura. Each step that she takes is painful. I've seen the medication in her bathroom cabinet and the pillboxes she prepares for the day. The dosage of each tablet is astronomically high. It's a wonder that she has the strength to work, yet she does. Every weekday morning at 8.20 a.m., she leaves her apartment and heads to the bank where she is the assistant manager.

Pierre is an amber. Sometimes, he's sociable and sometimes, he isn't. He enjoys a beer and a takeaway. Most nights, he watches Netflix or plays on his PS4 before going to bed and wanking in front of a video on Porn Hub. On Friday nights, he goes out with his mates and pretends that he fancies girls. He's neither good nor bad, kind nor mean. He sits somewhere in between like the majority of people.

Darius is a red. He makes money from other people's addictions and grief. In his front room, he cuts coke with flour and any other crap he can get away with. His troops deal at the local park in front of the young kids playing on the swings. Women are his playthings and dispensable, to be given away as a reward to his army of dealers or forced to be a decoy to bring rival gang leaders to be murked.

I've finally decided.

Darius is going to be my next target.

1995

I hadn't thought about what we'd do when we got to the Outdoor Education Centre. My thoughts had only got as far as escaping from the home and getting here. As soon as we arrived there, I felt this immense sense of excitement and relief. I'd never left the city before, let alone seen the mountains. They hugged the place, dwarfing it with their beauty and size. They were a perfect collage of competing materials and textures. It immediately drew me to them, and I barely listened to my teacher's instructions about preparing beds, rules and routines.

Dominic stared at me as though I was stupid. 'You've got to come down out of the clouds. You can't make a show of yourself.'

Make a show of myself? I've spent years on the periphery. Unnoticed.

I put my head down and followed the others into the main house. It was just like the children's home, only larger and colder. What felt like hours later, we were let out of our dorm and allowed to hang around on the front lawn until teatime.

All I wanted to do was head up one of the mountains. I tried to sneak away from the lads playing football, but Dominic grabbed my arm. 'Where are you off to?'

I was starting to get annoyed at his telling me what to do, but I just gestured towards the path leading to the back of the house.

'No chance, mate. There's plenty of time to explore tomorrow.'

I decided to wait. Tomorrow couldn't come quickly enough.

TWENTY-ONE

Just another inch. Then another. Jack knew if she ignored the pain in her ungloved hands and kept digging through the compacted snow and ice, she could reach Hannah alive. A faint fading hope... seconds became minutes, time that Hannah didn't have. Jack dug through the snow, throwing it aside like a dog searching for its bone.

Another inch and her fingertips touched skin. She dug faster in the same area until she freed an arm. Squeezing the hand, it was soft and pliable, yet deadly cold. She lifted it to her cheek for a brief second. Frantically, then, she dug until, with a strength that she hadn't realised she still possessed, she wrenched her lover from her snow tomb. Falling backwards onto the snow, Jack held her friend's lifeless body, wrapping her in her arms, blanketing her in her warmth. Only two hours before, they'd lain just the same, swaddled together, asleep in their tent. Holding her close, Hannah's familiar scent of coconut oil comforted Jack as she pulled back her hood and stroked her hair.

Hannah wasn't breathing. Howling in pain, Jack turned her on her back, wrenched open her mouth and forced her frozen fingers inside to clear the snow that blocked her airway. Then she covered Hannah's lips with her own with a life-saving kiss. She blew into Hannah's lungs again and again, then pumped her chest in the vain hope that this would restart her heart. After four turns, she felt for a pulse. It fluttered faintly under her fingertips. Placing her cheek above Hannah's lips, she felt a whisper of breath on her tear-stained cheek.

Before Jack could embrace her, Hannah disappeared. Of course, she wasn't alive. She'd watched her die repeatedly on a never-ending loop. Over and over again, she'd heard the thunderous roar of the avalanche that swept the woman she loved off the mountain. Dreams would only taunt her with new endings to the tragedy, like the sad musings of a director never satisfied with the conclusion to their film. Hannah was dead. There'd been no point in even looking for her body as the avalanche had dragged her deep into an ancient crevasse at the mountain's heart. Annapurna had claimed and imprisoned another victim within its core, entombed, never to be discovered. Jack needed to accept this. Crying, screaming and torturing herself with happy endings was pointless and weak. She didn't deserve to be a mountaineer; she certainly wasn't behaving like one.

Jack had fallen asleep on the sofa. She groaned as she stretched. It had been far too long since she'd had time to hit the gym. If she didn't raise her fitness level soon, then her days as a mountaineer would certainly be over and a new era as a couch potato would begin. The paperwork sent over by Chris at Boulders lay strewn across her coffee table. Most of the climbers he'd suggested were young men. Few were known to Jack. Chris had made some notes on their skill levels. Most were intermediate. They had some skill and regularly returned to the centre, but they didn't have any real mountaineering experience. Jack's gut told her that the Urban Climber wasn't just a casual user of a climbing wall. He would have climbed actual mountains and felt the sharpness and undulations of real rock rather than just the smoothness of a hard, plastic handhold. However, she would discount no one on a hunch so would assign officers to check all the men out. She put a few aside, the climbers she would interview herself.

There were no women in the pile. Jack wondered if this was because of sexism or if Chris didn't have any women clients above beginner level. She picked up her mobile and called him. He answered on the third ring. 'Hi, Jack. Did you get the names?'

Jack picked up a pen. 'Yeah. Thanks.'

'I was expecting you to pop by to get them, to be honest. And so were a group of kids.' Chris didn't hide the annoyance in his voice.

'Sorry about that. But listen, you've only sent me men's names. Why is that?'

There was a pause. 'I thought you were looking for Robin Hood, not Maid Marion.'

'We haven't completely ruled out that a woman might be responsible. Is there anyone who attends the centre that would fit the bill?'

Another pause. 'Maybe one or two. Why don't you head over this time, and I'll see what I can dig out?'

Jack sighed. She didn't have time to play games. What was his issue? She couldn't decide whether he was flirting or wanted to exercise control over her in some way.

Chris continued, 'In fact, why don't you pop over after work when the centre's shut and we can go through the names together? That's if your other half doesn't mind.'

So that was it. 'I don't have an "other half", as you put it. Maybe I *will* pop by later.' She put on her most seductive voice and decided that she'd send one of the male police constables instead.

Even a clear drive to the office free of traffic hold-ups and red lights didn't improve Jack's mood. Neither did making a few calls to set up her work for the rest of the day. It just reminded her how much she needed to do, and they were no closer to finding a suspect. By the time she'd drunk her second cup of coffee, she'd managed to snap off the heads of two colleagues, one because he hadn't updated his case notes from the day before and the other because he didn't make his report succinct enough to skim read. The person delivering the post would have been next in line if the handwritten letter on the top of the pile hadn't distracted her.

'To Jack Kent, world-class mountaineer,' was emblazoned across the front of the envelope. *Someone's taking the piss*, she thought, but just in case they weren't, Jack took a pair of gloves from the office supply and put them on. She cut across the top of the envelope with a pair of scissors and took the letter out with a pair of tweezers.

Nadia spotted what she was doing. 'Everything okay, boss?'

The letter was signed, 'Your friend, Robin.'

'Come and see for yourself.' Jack laid the letter out on the desk for them both to read.

Dear Jack,
I hope this letter finds you well. I do so admire you both as a climber and as a police detective.
With that in mind, I want to help you out a little. I really didn't mean to hurt Anastasia Marlov. I wasn't expecting her to be there. But then, the more I've learnt about the Marlovs, the more I think that they deserved to suffer.
If you sign into—

What followed was a link to a website. It wasn't in the usual format. Jack jotted it down and called the technical team to check it out. The last thing Jack wanted to do was download some kind of virus to the police network. She then sealed the letter and envelope inside a plastic wallet ready for it to go to forensics. They might, if they were lucky, get some information from it. Or they might even, from those few sentences, capture a profile. It was amazing what psychologists could find out about a person from their use of grammar or tone.

'This is weird, boss – look at the name on the envelope. Do you think these robberies are all about you?' Nadia looked concerned.

'Don't be ridiculous. It's all about him wanting attention. But we'll have to see what he's passed on to us. My guess is it's nothing we don't know already.' Secretly, Jack couldn't help also wondering if it was personal. A crazy fan or stalker was all she needed. She knew at least one climber who had experienced that. His stalker was only caught when she turned up at his house and threatened to kill his wife with a knife.

It was likely to take a while for the tech team to get back to her about the website, so Jack concentrated on the list of climbers that Chris had sent over. She turned back to Nadia. 'Do you fancy coming on a road trip?'

'Where to?' Nadia closed her laptop, obviously keen.

Jack smiled. Nadia's mood since returning had improved substantially. Her leadership skills shone through when she was on form. Harry and Georgia should look up to her.

'I've got a few addresses for local climbers to check out from that list that you got from Boulders.' Jack paused. 'Which reminds me... PC Brown, get your arse over here a minute.'

He scuttled over, as keen as Nadia, it seemed, to do anything other than the work he'd been assigned. 'I need you to go to Boulders Climbing Club. Tell the owner, Chris Mayfield, that I sent you and pick up a list of names and addresses of women climbers that he has for us.'

'Sure thing.' He smiled, making Jack wonder if he was so pleased to be leaving the station that he'd probably take the long way to get there. Chris, of course, would fume that she'd sent another of her officers, especially a male one, but she was nobody's lap dog, and she was completely disinterested in him in that department. She didn't keep her sexuality a secret, but, for some, being 'bi' meant being attracted to everyone, which was far from the case. If anything, she was even more choosy than her straight and lesbian friends.

Jack hadn't told Nadia about her visit to the imam. She didn't intend to share anything about who she believed had threatened her, or at least been an accomplice to the act, until she'd confronted them with it. She hoped that might be soon, but she wanted to be sure that she had her information straight first. The best person to help her with that was a local newspaper hack. As soon as they'd finished interviewing the climbers, Jack intended to call her and arrange a meetup for later.

They arrived at the first house on the list and were greeted at the grubby front door by a harassed mother with a child bawling at her hip.

'Is John home?' Nadia asked.

'If he was, he could give me a break.' The woman sighed and shifted the child to the other hip. 'Can I help you with summat?'

Nadia flashed her badge. 'We just need to ask him a few questions.'

The woman screwed up her face in obvious confusion. 'He's done nothing wrong.'

Jack wasn't sure if this was a statement or a question, but it seemed unlikely that he had. For one, if this was the Urban

Climber's house, then why hadn't he kept the money to spend on his family?

'Your husband climbs?' Jack asked. It was as much a statement as a question.

'Look, d'you want to come in, then I can put this 'un down?' The baby did seem to be wriggling its way out of her arms.

'Sure. If it's no trouble.' Nadia took a step forward.

The woman led them into the kitchen and placed the baby in a highchair. Then she grabbed a plate of toast soldiers and placed them in front of the child, who immediately gummed one.

'When's your husband likely to return?' Jack searched for a chair, but each was covered with piles of recently washed baby clothes.

'He's not my husband. We've just lived together since...' She gestured at the baby.

'Sorry, I shouldn't have assumed.'

'It's okay.' The woman stared at Jack. 'Do I know you from somewhere?' Jack shrugged. 'You're that policewoman that climbs. John showed me your photo in the paper. Said you were amazing.' The baby tipped the plate of toast onto the floor. 'Oh, for goodness' sake.'

'I'm really sorry if we're in the way. Will John be home soon?' Jack asked.

It was the woman's turn to shrug. 'Depends when he finishes his deliveries.'

'Who does he work for?' Nadia asked.

'He just does Hermes' deliveries. Doesn't pay much. I've told him we haven't got money for extras like his climbing, but he still sneaks out.'

'Is he ever out late?' Nadia continued.

'What, climbing? Or with his dopey mates? Never past ten, to be honest. This one keeps us up every night, so we're both knackered.' As if to labour the point, she yawned, covering her mouth with a hand.

It was becoming increasingly obvious that they could cross this guy off the list. There was no point wasting more of their time. Jack handed the woman her card. 'Can you ask him to ring me when he gets home? We just need to check his whereabouts for a few nights. It's just routine.'

When they returned to the car, both Jack and Nadia sighed. Nadia said, 'I never want kids. Did you notice how ripe it was getting in there? I know what she'll be doing right now. What a little stinker.'

'I reckon he's not our man. Shall we move on to the next one?' Entering the next address into the sat nav, Jack started the car.

There was no one home at the next address. Heading to the third one on the list, Jack looked across at Nadia, who seemed to be in her own world staring out of the window at the duplicated streets and row-upon-row of carbon copy terraced houses.

'I think I'm becoming my mother,' Jack said, keeping her eyes on the road.

'Sorry, boss?'

'Making ridiculous judgements about people, I mean. Take the family we just visited. I've already decided he's not the one we're looking for.'

'I agree – I don't think he is either.'

'What are we basing that on?'

'Can't speak for you, but I'd say he goes climbing to escape his chaotic homelife. What reason would he have to be our Urban Climber?'

'What reason would anyone have to do what he's done?'

'We probably won't know that until we catch him. And even then, we might never know the real reason, just something concocted up by his defence team.' Nadia smiled. 'Anyway, the girlfriend said John was home every night, so he's not climbing up the side of flats at midnight.'

'She could've been lying.'

'Come off it. She didn't seem the type to be loyal. Sounded sick of him, if anything. We should be coming up to the next address.'

Another row of terraced houses. One stood out with its lurid pink pebble-dash.

Nadia tapped the dashboard. 'This is the place.'

Of course, they were going through the motions. Eliminating possible suspects was part of the day-to-day investigation, but if they didn't find a lead soon, they'd be in trouble. Jack knew this but wasn't expecting to find much here.

The man who answered their knock didn't fit the bill of their climber either. Jack held up her warrant card. 'I'm looking for Alastair Smith.'

'That's me. You'd better come in.'

Alastair wheeled himself backwards to give them some space. He ushered them both into the lounge, then followed them in, the hallway being too narrow for him to turn.

Jack and Nadia sat on the small, two-seater settee, their legs touching. Alastair wheeled his chair in front of them, then sat with his hands in his lap, expectant.

'We were told you're a regular climber at Boulders?' Jack said, barely meeting his eyes. Under her breath, she cursed Chris. Had he sent her on a wild goose chase?

'I am... was.'

'What happened?' Nadia looked up from her notebook.

'I got bored, so I took up a new hobby.'

'I...' Nadia began.

Then he laughed, eyes sparkling. 'You can stop trying to be PC and going round the houses. I had an accident. Three months ago, on The Tsunami. All my own fault. I should have checked my equipment. One of the quickdraws snapped.' He held up his hands. 'Jack'll tell you, it's a lovely spot to climb at Cheddar Gorge, but like anywhere, it doesn't suffer fools.'

'Sorry to hear that. What's the prognosis?' Jack asked. She wasn't surprised that Alastair knew who she was. Out of all the names on Chris's list, he stood out as a proficient, experienced climber. Most pro or enthusiastic climbers would recognise her even out of context. Of course, it was a surprise that he was on the list after his accident. Maybe Chris wasn't aware it had happened? It made Jack wonder just how organised the instructor really was.

'Why don't you come to the point of your visit?' he asked, still smiling.

'We're looking for a particular climber who's been carrying out burglaries in the centre of Birmingham.'

'And you've decided that climber isn't me.'

'Not unless you're trying to get some extra benefit payments.' Jack bit her tongue. 'Sorry, I know there are many disabled climbers who use adaptations to climb – but climbing up the side of a block of flats would be more... well, difficult.'

Alastair didn't answer for a moment. Instead, he appeared to be weighing Jack up. His lips pursed, he finally continued. 'I should, if I'm lucky, be out of the chair by the end of the year. The damage isn't permanent. But whether I'll ever climb again is another matter.'

'I guess you know other climbers in the city, though?'

'And you don't?'

It was a good question. Yes, Jack knew other climbers. But they were of a different class, and Alastair knew that. 'Can you think of anyone who—'

'Who'd steal from flats? Yeah, I've got plenty of dodgy mates. But then you probably know people too. Those you met on the way up your dazzling climb of success.'

Nadia's leg twitched beside her.

What was this guy's problem? 'You're right, it was a stupid question. I'm sorry we're wasting your time.' Jack stood to leave.

Alastair was blocking her path to the door, but he didn't move.

'Sit down, Jack.' Alastair's smile was one of amusement, with no hidden menace. 'I'm playing with you. I haven't got much to do at the moment, as you can imagine. Tell me more about these robberies. Maybe I can help.'

If he wasn't a climber, Jack would have pulled him up on his over-familiarity. But she'd got used to fellow climbers speaking to her like they were her best friends. It was a close-knit world at the best of times. Jack described, in sketchy detail, one of the robberies. Alastair asked a few pertinent and intelligent questions. After a few minutes, he scratched his chin. 'There is someone.'

'Go on.' Nadia raised her pen.

'A bit of a geek. A people-watcher, not a joiner-in. Spotted him a few times at Boulders. He always climbs the intermediate routes, but he's better than that. Flies up the wall every time like he's on steroids. Never says much either.'

'What is it about him that stuck in your mind?' Jack asked.

'He tries to disappear.'

'Sorry?'

Alastair rubbed the top of his leg. 'Blend in, I mean. Like he doesn't want to be noticed. He speaks to people. Asks for help when he needs a belay but never talks about himself or stuff like that. I remember he said he could help one of the staff with an issue that they had with their laptop, but apart from that, I couldn't tell you anything more about him.'

It wasn't much to go on, but, then, they currently had nothing. 'What's his name?'

'Phil. Or Stew, something like that. Maybe.'

Jack couldn't remember anyone called Philip or Stewart from Chris's list. But if he'd only been climbing intermediate routes, then she may have given his folder to one of the others on her team. 'Anything else?'

Alastair shook his head.

'Thanks. You've been a great help.' Jack closed her notebook, ready to leave.

'I'm sorry about earlier. I didn't mean to be rude. There are some real wankers in the climbing world.'

Jack didn't disagree with him.

There was one last visit Jack wanted to make that day. Alone this time. It had taken a while, but Sofia Marlova had finally decided to meet with her.

It wasn't Sofia that answered the door when she knocked, it was her sullen faced boyfriend, Sean. 'Come in.'

Jack followed him into a large, functional kitchen, dominated by a wooden table, which appeared to serve as a workbench for Sofia's jewellery making. Sofia sat cross-legged on a dining chair. She was wearing just a long white shirt. Her boyfriend motioned Jack to sit and then left the two of them alone.

Sofia rolled up the sleeves of her shirt before speaking. 'I've made a decision. Your phone calls were not for nothing.'

Jack nodded. 'I'm glad. Your mum deserved better.' Whenever she had a spare moment, Jack had rung Sofia. Not only to check on her. Losing a parent was never easy, particularly in a violent way. But also to try and convince her to tell the National Crime Agency what she knew about her father's business.

'I spoke to that police officer, DI Barton. She says that as soon as my father returns to the UK, they will arrest him.' Sofia looked down at the floor, composing herself.

'Thank you for doing this, I appreciate how hard this must have been.' Jack made a move towards Sofia to comfort her.

She shook her head. 'I'm fine. It was the right thing to do. My sister will hate me. So be it.'

Families are overrated, thought Jack.

Back at the station, Jack scoured the list of climbers that Boulders had sent over. There was a Philip but no Stewart on the list. PC Brown had interviewed him. Jack checked his log. Either he hadn't interviewed Philip Dyson, or he hadn't completed his notes yet. She found PC Brown huddled over his laptop. He looked up as she approached. 'Boss?'

'You interviewed Philip Dyson yet?' Jack sat down on the other side of the long table set aside for the newer members of the team.

'Yeah. This after. Just writing up my notes.'

'And. What did you think?'

PC Brown shrugged. 'Seems an okay guy.'

'You weren't there to find a football buddy.'

'No.' He had the cheek to grin. 'He's a computer technician. His front room's full of computer parts. On the nights that the robberies took place, he said he was either fixing computers or online and could give us a log of times. Climbing's just a hobby for him to get him out of the house.'

Jack considered whether she needed to do a follow-up visit. Just because someone seemed nice didn't rule them out of a murder investigation. 'Get him to send you his log. I want to see it before we rule him out.'

'Will do.' Jayden tapped his pen on the table. 'Boss, there's something else. The guy who runs Boulders, what d'you think of him?'

Jack paused. Sexist pig came to mind. 'Why do you ask?'

'I know he's ex-military and all that. But he's a climber and he was clearly angry that you hadn't turned up to get the list. In fact, he never shut up about you while I was there.'

Could there be more to this? 'Let's not rule him out either. Send him a list of dates too. Let's find out where he was when the flats were being burgled.' Jack smiled, knowing he wouldn't like that.

Then she turned back to her laptop to catch up on her emails. The IT tech had sent a report with the document referred to as 'Robin' attached. It contained the details of emails between Marlov and a private clinic.

Jack picked out some salient points.

The product should be available by Friday. I suggest that you prepare for midday as it won't stay viable for long.'

It took little to decipher what Marlov was touting to them, even if they weren't explicit. The report stated that the link was to a messaging service on the dark web that would have been difficult to hack into and decipher. Jack wondered how the climber had got hold of them, but she wasn't investigating Marlov's criminal dealings. She forwarded the report to DI Barton at the National Crime Agency. Now Sofia had agreed to give evidence, Sergei Marlov was dead meat. Any jury would surely convict, that is if he ever returned to the UK so they could arrest him.

Her attention then moved to her meeting with Catherine Summers. The reporter had texted her to suggest that they meet at a pub close to Jack's flat. Now all Jack had to decide was how much she wanted to share about the corruption of local politicians.

The King's Head had a back bar that was usually quiet, bordering on deserted. Jack had taken the opportunity to freshen up and complete some paperwork at home before heading to the pub. She hadn't eaten, so she ordered a plate of the pub's more than edible pie and mash before sitting down at a table. Catherine arrived minutes later and called over, 'You eating?' before approaching the bar.

'Yeah, and I've already got a drink.' Jack raised her pint of Guinness.

After ordering, Catherine weaved her way between the tables carrying two pints. She placed another Guinness in front of Jack.

Jack groaned. 'I didn't mean...'

'It'll put hairs on your chest.' Catherine winked.

The reporter had been a friend of Jack's for many years, often turning up at The Fox on a weekday evening or Saturday afternoon. She played a mean game of pool and could drink anyone under the table, even the mouthy young lesbians who were vying to be the most seen and heard. But, of course, where a story was concerned, her work came first and foremost, and she wouldn't think twice about selling your soul to the tabloid devil.

'This is completely off the record for now,' Jack said. Even Catherine understood this and would be bound by those words.

'But if there's a story I can use...?' Catherine raised her glass to her lips.

'We can discuss how you could do that without it getting back to me, but this might be something you'll have to hold back on for a while at least.' Jack bit her lip. This was risky. The relationship between cops and reporters had long since dissolved partly because there were so few investigative reporters left, and partly because officers had ended up in prison for leaking information about live cases to the press.

'Sounds fair. Go on.'

Jack took a deep breath. 'You know about voting corruption in the Midlands, Birmingham, in particular.'

'Like the banana republic scandal in 2004?'

'Yeah. I mean, everyone knows about that. This could have

been around the same time.' Jack tried to place the year of Nadia's rape. 'It could even have come after.'

'And is it still going on?'

Catherine had a good point. The information that the imam had passed on was certainly being used to attack Nadia, but could it still be used to garner votes? 'Possibly. I guess that's for you to discover.'

'So, vote rigging circa 2004.'

Jack told Catherine what Basheer had told him about his father. Before Catherine had a chance to comment, their food arrived. Jack tucked straight in, not realising how hungry she was, but then, she hadn't eaten since breakfast.

Catherine had time to digest Jack's story, as well as most of her meal, by the time she spoke again. 'You've got evidence that this information is still being acted upon?'

'You can't use this as it links to an investigation, but, yes, the opposition party leader on Birmingham Council received the information directly from the imam and it's been used to threaten one of my officers.' There, she'd said it and now had to trust that Catherine wouldn't go public about the threats until after the trial. 'What I need to know is: who else knows, and is this part of a wider conspiracy?'

'If Councillor Mahmood's involved, then Jacobs will be. Thick as thieves, those two.' Catherine rubbed her hands together. 'Chances are if they've got the dirt on others, then they'll continue to use it as long as they can. There are so many dodgy deals going on, you wouldn't get your breath. Half the bloody council are landlords and the other half have business interests that regularly benefit from their decisions. Getting elected is just a small part of this.'

'What I want is for them all to be brought to book with nothing getting out about my officer.'

'If she's done something wrong—'

Jack sighed. 'She hasn't. What they have on her is personal.'

Catherine didn't look convinced. 'She was raped as a teenager and, understandably, doesn't want that made public.'

Of course, Catherine might easily put two and two together to make four, but Jack knew she had integrity and would keep Nadia out of it. In fact, it would probably make her more adamant to discover the truth, and as soon as she got all she could on Mahmood and the mayor, Jack was going to throw them to the wolves.

TWENTY-TWO

Darius lays asleep in front of me, his foot soldiers long gone for the night. He'll never know how stupid that was. Of course, the sleeping pills he takes each night are a bonus.

I listen to him snore and smile as I reach for a pillow. This is going to be too easy. He doesn't even struggle as I hold it down, smothering him. At the last moment, I sense him fighting for his breath and he tries to push me away, but I kneel on his arms. Suddenly, I realise that I'm going to miss his dying moments, so I toss the pillow to one side and put my hands around his neck. His face turns puce and his nose starts to bleed. He soon stops struggling. I count the seconds in my head. A minute should do it, just to be sure. As his body slackens, I grin. A spreading rush of excitement forces me to squeeze harder. I'm doing this for all the victims. I am a hero.

1995

On the first morning of the trip, I woke up smiling, not quite believing that I was still there. I'd expected a social worker to turn up by now to drag me back to the home with my tail between my legs. Maybe they didn't care that I'd done a runner, or maybe they were too stupid to guess that I'd come on the trip. Either way, I was looking forward to seeing what the day would bring.

After breakfast, they lined us up in front of the instructors. They called out the names of the pupils in their group. One instructor was much taller and broader than the rest. He looked just like a bear, with furry arms, a beard and curly brown hair, but the best part about him was his smile. He called out Dominic's name. I crossed my fingers behind my back in the hope that he'd call mine.

Two more names and he'd now got eight pupils, the same as the other groups. My heart sank. Then he said, 'And I'm the lucky guy who gets the extra one.' I didn't think I'd heard right at first until he said my name. I bounded up to him. Dominic grinned and put his hand on my shoulder. I don't think I'd ever been happier than I was that morning.

The day just got better. We were all taken to a large cabin that contained the climbing equipment. Inside were rows of harnesses, brightly coloured ropes and metal clips. The instructor called us over one at a time to fit us out in a harness, apart from David. They sent him back to the dorm to change out of his shorts. He'd missed the instruction that we needed to wear long trousers. My jogging bottoms were a bit thin and worn at the knees, but the instructor looked me up and down and said, 'That's the ticket.'

I couldn't help rubbing my hands on the webbing of the harness and turning the screws on what I found out later was a screwgate carabiner. I stood to one side, hopping from toe-to-toe, impatient for the others to get harnessed up. Eventually, I felt a tap on my shoulder.

'Go on, lad. You can lead the way up the mountain.'

TWENTY-THREE

Days passed before the second body was discovered. If it hadn't been for one tenant in the block noticing the odd smell coming from Flat 206, then it could have been much longer.

Jack stood next to Shauna as she examined the large body of Darius Moore. Fighting back the urge to retch, Jack asked, 'How can you stand the smell?'

'This is nothing. My favourite is charred remains.' Shauna winked. 'And I can still eat a bacon sandwich even then.'

Darius was well-known locally as a dealer. A real Mr Teflon, he was able to summon up an alibi for any crime as fast as Harry Potter could cast a spell. His chosen profession must have made his mother weep, Jack thought. He had a university education; his dad was a banker and his mother a teacher.

'There's fingertip bruising around his neck and on the arms where he was held down. Blood has dried from a possible nose-bleed and there are signs of petechial bleeding from asphyxia-tion.' Shauna examined his throat. 'Possible hyoid fracture, but I won't know for definite until I x-ray the body.'

'Someone strangled him then?' Jack stepped back to allow Shauna to examine his fingernails.

'That would be my guess.'

'And when did it happen? In days, I mean. I don't expect you to tell me in minutes until after the post-mortem.' Jack winked at her friend.

'Ha bloody ha.' Shauna continued to probe and poke the body. 'There are no signs of rigour, but there's bloating around the abdomen.' She pulled up his top lip and blood-stained foam bubbled from his mouth. 'Classic signs of putrefaction. My guess is he was killed three nights ago, but that's a guess until I've taken more precise scientific readings.'

Jack nodded. They would check his phone for last calls, which should also be a good indicator.

It was pure luck that Jack had been called in to investigate. The sergeant on duty knew about the robbery cases in the flats but had first tried to get hold of DI O'Donohue. He hadn't answered his phone, so then he called Jack, something he admitted over the phone without prompting. She was now expecting O'Donohue to turn up demanding the case, just as she had with the Marlova case. There was no reason to assume the killer was her climber... but then again, it was highly unlikely to be a gang hit. Birmingham gangs liked to air their laundry in public. Hits were usually outdoors and involved guns or knives rather than manual strangulation. The only issue was that nothing had been taken. This wasn't a robbery gone bad.

As Shauna completed her initial examination, Nadia entered the bedroom. 'You need to see this, boss.'

Nadia led Jack to the balcony, where a red carabiner was hanging from one of the struts. Just like the carabiner that had been left on an apartment roof, there was no reason for it to be there. It must be the climber, and he was teasing them again with what could only be described as a calling card. Either that or he wanted to lay claim to the murder. This was his way of rubbing their noses in it.

. . .

After the preliminary forensics were completed and the body of
Darius Moore was taken to the morgue, Jack took the elevator
down to the ground floor, striding past a cleaner bent over a
mop. Out of the corner of her eye, she sensed a quick movement
outside in the forecourt to the flats. She shivered; a sense of
unease spread through her body. Her criminal radar spiked, and
she burst through the doors. Picking up speed, she expected to
see someone retreating to the right and glimpsed a person
darting between the blocks of flats opposite. Jack broke into a
run and reached the alley seconds later. The figure in front of
her took off to the right. The chase was on.

Jack lengthened her stride and turned the corner to see a
young, fair-haired lad ahead, gaining on her. He jumped over
the low wall that ran the length of the back of the flats. Crossing
the road without looking, cars screeched to a halt to avoid
hitting him. Jack drew closer, holding out her hand in front of
the cars before they inched forward. They'd reached a row of
shops with the lad now just metres away. He caught his arm on
an old woman's bag as he ran, pulling her round so that she fell
just in front of Jack. Fortunately, other shoppers ran to her aid.
Jack couldn't stop now with her prey so close.

The lad darted down a side road and then into an alley at
the side of a row of terraced houses. Jack could almost touch
him now and could hear his panting as he tired. Regular
sessions in the gym meant she could keep on running for as long
as it took to catch him. A high metal gate blocked the end of the
alley. The lad careened into it and tried to place his foot in a
position to climb up and over the obstacle, but Jack got hold of
his collar and pulled him to the ground.

Only then could she see how young the boy was. He
couldn't be more than twelve. 'Why did you run?' Jack asked.

'You're the five-o, ain't ya?' the boy spluttered, still out of
breath as he stood and backed away from Jack.

'And?'

'Just saying. Not like I've done nothing and ya can't say I have!' He pushed his blond hair away from his eyes and rubbed his nose.

'Did you know Darius?'

The lad looked ready to run again. 'Who?'

'Darius Moore. You might as well come clean because I'm taking you in if you don't.'

He seemed to weigh up his options as he shuffled his feet. 'Might know him. Why?'

'We found his body in his flat this morning.'

The blood drained from his face. 'Shit.'

'Yeah, exactly. So, what do you know?'

'I don't know nothing. I'm just a mate and I watch out for him...'

'How long have you been watching?'

'I do nights.' He bit his lip. He'd said too much, and he knew it.

'And did you see anything? He could've been dead since Tuesday.'

The boy shook his head. 'Nah, I'd have called him, warned him like. Shit, I didn't see a thing.'

'Surely you must have thought it weird that he hasn't been around?' He'd been lying dead in his flat for days. So much for his foot soldiers paying attention.

'Darius told me to wait until he went out. I watch the flat and ring him if I see 'owt odd. But I didn't see a thing. No one's been round... checking on him, like.' He chewed his lip. 'I'm in some real shit. That's how it is.'

'But... it's been days.'

'Shit.' The kid was shaking now. 'I knew summat wasn't right. I tried to tell 'em. But no one disturbs Darius.'

'You didn't think of checking on him?'

'I knocked on his door. I told the others, but they were all, like, he's got some woman, or he's off somewhere.'

His boss had been murdered in his sleep. If the rest of the gang knew this, then the lad was dead meat. In their eyes, someone would have to pay, and the bottom rungs in a gang always got off worse. She began to feel sorry for him.

'And you saw nothing?' Jack took a step back, making it clear that he was free to run if he wanted. 'You wouldn't be grassing to the police. You'd be helping us find Darius's killer. This wasn't gang-related. I'm pretty sure of that.'

The lad now looked confused, screwing up his eyes as though avoiding the sun, and she didn't blame him.

Jack continued. 'Why don't you give us a statement? You're a witness and you're not in trouble. I don't give a shit what else you've done.'

'I can't—'

'You can. And we can do it in such a way that no one will ever know.' Jack leant in and touched the boy's shoulder. He flinched but didn't move away. 'Trust me.'

Something she said must have resonated with him. Ten minutes later, she pulled up at the station with the boy she now knew was Freddie Bowers in the passenger seat of her Range Rover.

Jack found, with the help of the desk sergeant, a suitable interview room. They needed an appropriate adult present before she could ask him a question, so she'd tasked the sergeant with locating a social worker. In the meantime, she found him a can of Coke and a dry-crusted cheese sandwich. Freddie seemed happy enough, so she left him to it.

Earlier, she'd sent Nadia on a hunt for CCTV footage covering the streets near the crime scene. Jack found her in the team's office dishing the footage out to anyone that they had spare. Jack called her over. 'We've got a lad downstairs who might have seen something on the night of the murder. I need you to help me interview him.'

'That's great.'

Jack nodded. 'He's only thirteen, so we're getting a social worker in. You need to help me get him to open up. He's street-smart. Probably been in gangs since he could walk.'

'I can do that.' Nadia smiled. It was good to see her coming back to her old self. The last couple of days, she'd seemed more engaged in the case and had taken a lead in organising the tasks for the team, giving Jack more time to work on strategy.

Freddie looked his age sitting next to the middle-aged social worker. He sucked the side of his thumb as Nadia took his general details – name, address, sex, race, and date of birth.

The social worker kept patting him like she might a pet Labrador, and then flicking her shoulder-length, auburn hair back and smiling at Jack. Her long, flowery skirt reminded Jack of the sort of tat that her sister would wear. She shook her head to erase that thought and concentrated on the first question to Freddie, who now sat up straight and stared at her.

'Where were you on Tuesday night, Freddie? That would be the 4th of June.'

Freddie shrugged. 'Don't 'member.'

'Are you sure? It was only three nights ago.'

Nadia butted in. 'Come on, Freddie. It was the night that Aston Villa announced their new manager.'

He grinned. 'What time we talking?'

'Why don't you just tell us what you did from say... 6 p.m.?' Jack sat back in her chair and waited for his response.

'I'm not going to get into trouble for anything...?' Freddie glanced from Jack to the social worker, who patted his knee again.

'Depends if you killed Darius. But anything less than that, I think we can overlook.' Jack grinned.

Freddie laughed. 'As if.' His left leg now started jigging up and down. 'I had a delivery to make before I got to the flats. So, wouldn't have got there until about nine.'

'Was there someone else watching until then?' Jack didn't bother to ask about the delivery, as it was pretty obvious what he meant.

'Darius was out until nine. I got a text to say that I needed to do a shift. He normally stays out later unless he's got someone staying over.'

'And did he have someone staying over?'

'I saw his car drive up into the underground car park and he was alone.'

'How long did you stay watching the flat?'

'Maybe till about seven next day? I had to go home and get changed for school.'

Jack almost didn't believe him, but he didn't blink as she stared at him. It was as though staying out all night and then spending the day at school was the most natural thing in the world. It was no wonder he was wired if he hadn't slept properly for days. It was a good thing the social worker didn't pick up on this admission, or they might well be looking at suspending the interview until he'd got some sleep. 'Did you notice who went in and out of the flats?'

'Yeah. Just the usuals.'

'The usuals?'

'I've been doing this a while, so I know who lives there. There wasn't anyone new, like.'

'No one had any visitors?'

He shook his head. 'I'd know.'

Jack didn't doubt that. 'And you didn't spot anyone in Darius's flat or on the balcony?' He lived on the third floor, so it would be difficult to spot anyone unless they came to the window. But the climber did step onto the balcony to place the carabiner. Whether he climbed up there wasn't yet clear. Jack could almost hear the ticking of the clock on the wall as she waited for him to answer.

'I didn't see no one.'

It must strain his neck looking up. The chances were that he couldn't train his eyes on the balcony all the time and it would have taken the climber just seconds to place the calling card.

Jack sighed.

Nadia asked, 'Did you see anything else? Anything unusual? As you say, you know the building.'

Freddie's knee bounced more quickly. 'Yeah. There was someone on the roof. I saw a torch. I guessed it was the caretaker.'

'The caretaker?' Nadia tapped a pen on the table. 'What sort of time was this?'

Freddie shrugged. 'About one, maybe two. The torch wasn't on long.'

'Thanks, Freddie. You've been a great help.' Nadia could transcribe the interview and get Freddie to sign it. Jack wanted to speak to the caretaker as soon as she could to either rule him in or out of being the roof stalker.

Before she got the chance to check with the property management company for Darius's building, PC Brown called her over. 'You've had a call from a John Sanders following up from a home visit.'

John Sanders was the guy with a young child and a harried partner who hadn't been home when she and Nadia stopped by. Jack decided to ring him first so she could tick him off her list. She held her phone to her ear as she asked PC Brown to ring the management company for the contact details of the caretaker.

John answered. It only took a couple of seconds for him to confirm his whereabouts on the nights of the burglaries and the murder. Then Jack asked him about the other visitors to the climbing school.

Pausing for a moment, he said, 'I get on with most people. They're a nice bunch there.'

'Most?'

'There's one guy I went climbing with one weekend. He seemed great when I first met him, really quiet, and not arrogant like some climbers are. But after we went climbing, he was a little full-on. Kept ringing me, asking me if I'd go climbing again – but I've got a baby and the missus'd kill me if I went away every weekend... In the end, I had to tell him to stop calling.'

'And after that?'

'He still kept ringing. Took me a few goes. Now he ignores me. Well, he ignores everyone. I feel quite sorry for him, to be honest. He was obviously looking for a friend.'

Jack asked for his details.

'I just knew him as Phil.' Jack wrote down his name and underlined it. Phil would definitely need a visit now.

She put down her phone. PC Brown was standing in front of her, waving a piece of paper. 'The caretaker's details.'

'Jayden, can you fix up a visit to Philip Dyson this evening? I want to see him myself after I've paid a visit to the caretaker.' He turned to go. 'Oh, and remind everyone that we've got a briefing at nine sharp tomorrow.'

From a distance, Jack thought she'd met this caretaker before at one of the flats that had been burgled. She checked his name, Adrian Semple. It wasn't a name she'd previously heard. As he strolled up to her in the reception area of the block where Darius was murdered, she realised her mistake. He may have been the same height and build as Pete, but that was where the similarity ended. This guy must have been at least ten years younger. His skin was smooth and clean-shaven with an abundance of curly, brown hair. 'Hi, I'm Ade,' he said, holding out his hand.

Jack shook it. 'Is there somewhere private we can talk?'

'They only provide me with a broom cupboard here. There's a café across the street.'

The café looked little more than a truck stop, with a menu to match. The only difference was the pricing. It was double what you'd expect to pay on an industrial estate. Maybe this was the new thing – truckers' chic?

Jack was tempted to buy an all-day breakfast since she hadn't eaten for hours but interviewing with egg yolk dripping from your chin wasn't a good look. Instead, she ordered an Americano and a round of toast.

Adrian looked expectant as she sat down. She wondered if he was hoping for some gossip about the dead crime lord in 206. He sipped his cappuccino and waited for her to speak.

'How long have you been working here?'

The caretaker smiled, showing deep laughter lines. Jack had thought he was in his late twenties but now made him out to be slightly older than that. 'Five years. I work a few other flats in the same management company.'

'Actually, I'd like you to provide a list of locations where you've been over the last week and for some other dates that I'll provide after we've spoken, if that's okay.'

'No problem.' He winked. 'Always happy to help the police. In fact, I always wanted to be a police officer, but I wasn't that good at school.'

'Good.' Jack moved him quickly on. 'Tell me about Tuesday evening.'

'Is that when...? I think I was at home that night.' He reached for his drink.

'Can anyone corroborate that?'

He slammed the cup down on the table; some of the brown

liquid slurped over the rim. 'Wait... You don't think...?' Then he laughed.

'I should tell you we have a witness to you being at the building.'

Bowing his head, he finally said, 'Tuesday... Oh yeah, a resident reported a leaky pipe, so I was in the building, but not for long, only needed a washer.'

'Did you go to the roof?' The waitress arrived with her toast and plonked down the plate next to her coffee cup. Jack ignored her.

'No, why would I?'

'Is the roof kept locked?'

'No. Actually, it isn't, and I keep telling them – my boss, that is – that's crazy. I know people use it for parties, Darius for one. And it's dangerous. But will they listen?' Adrian's voice rose as he spoke, and his fists curled tighter around his cup. 'Sorry, but it's my job to keep the flats safe and secure.' He smiled and let go of the cup.

Jack wasn't sure if this was for show. 'And did you see anyone on Tuesday who isn't a resident? Or anyone using the roof?'

'Nope. No one. As I said, I was there twenty minutes tops. And I didn't see a soul.'

A text came through from PC Brown as Jack finished her toast.

> Philip Dyson will meet you at his flat in half an hour.

Jack stared at Ade. He didn't flinch. 'I'll send you the dates and times that I need to know your movements for. If you can return them by the end of play tomorrow, that would be helpful.'

He nodded, stood and left the café, leaving Jack just enough time to drive to Philip Dyson's flat.

. . .

It was an uneventful drive over to Small Heath. The rush-hour traffic had dissipated. The lack of rain and rising humidity meant that the pub gardens were full and locals were enjoying an evening meal and a pint, reminding Jack that it was the weekend – another missed opportunity to take off to a climb with just a tent, a sleeping bag and her gear. She reached a row of shops and was immediately hit by the stench of overflowing rubbish. The council never seemed to bother emptying the large wheelie bins that stood overflowing in these alleys. Her sat nav told her she'd arrived. Philip must live in one of the flats above the shops.

After missing the plain brown door twice, Jack finally worked out that this was the entrance to flat 439B. It wasn't marked by a number, but was the only door on the street between two sari shops at 439 and 441. She turned the steel handle to find the door unlocked. An unlit passageway led to concrete stairs. At the top of these were two white PVC doors, one marked 439A and the other 439B. Jack knocked on Philip's door and waited for an answer.

The door was opened by a slender man in his twenties wearing thin-rimmed glasses. He ushered Jack into the living room at the back of the flat. To sit down on the sofa, Jack had to push aside various computer parts. Every surface, including the dining table, was similarly covered. Philip grabbed one of the dining chairs, seemingly unaware of the wires that slipped from it to the floor, and sat down on it opposite Jack.

He then half stood. 'My manners... can I get you a drink?'

Jack shook her head, surmising he rarely got visitors.

He sat back down and cupped his hands in front of his face, blushing. 'At some point, could I... could I, please, get your autograph? I can't tell you what an honour this is.'

Jack was used to being recognised by climbers and occasionally on school visits a few of the kids had asked her to sign her name on a grubby bit of paper, but this was the first time she'd been asked for an autograph when interviewing someone for a case. She should have been flattered, but instead she felt mildly annoyed. 'Before I go... yes, okay.'

He dropped his hands. 'Thank you.'

'To get back to why I'm here—'

'Oh, I know why you're here. That nice policeman told me. You're looking for a climber and you want to know where I was on a few dates and times... I'm honoured, by the way. I'd hardly call myself a climber. Not like you, I mean.'

'It might help if you've got a diary, then we can get the dates ticked off?' The room was beginning to feel claustrophobic.

'Of course.' Philip stood and went to the table. Next to a pile of laptops was a precarious mountain of paperwork. He began to shuffle through it. 'It's here somewhere. You'd think I'd have an electronic version considering my job, but I prefer a pen and paper for organising my thoughts.' Eventually, he turned up a black notebook and waved it in the air. 'Here it is.'

Jack took her laptop out of her backpack. She'd just sent the caretaker the list of dates by email from the car, and asked Jayden to do the same for all of the caretakers they had spoken to, so the page was still open. As she read out a date, she jotted down Philip's answer straight into his file.

For all the dates, he had a meeting with a client that evening for his business, but, of course, that didn't account for late at night when the robberies took place, and all the meetings were reasonably local. He had to admit that, since he lived alone, no one could provide him with an alibi for the middle of the night. 'Surely you don't think I'm a burglar, Jack?' he said after date number four was ticked off.

Jack didn't answer – though his familiarity irritated her – and just moved to the two most important dates. The first was the day that Anastasia Marlova was killed. She rattled that off.

Philip consulted his diary. 'I wasn't doing anything that day or night.'

'Would anyone have seen you? A delivery driver? Maybe someone from the shops downstairs?'

'You know how it is, Jack, when you live alone.'

Jack's chest constricted and her heart beat faster. 'What do you mean?'

'Sorry.' He blushed. 'I just assumed, as you don't have a partner...'

She must have looked as annoyed as she felt as he turned deathly pale. 'I mean Wikipedia doesn't mention a partner... so I thought.'

'This interview isn't about me. So, can we get back to where you were on that evening?'

'I just meant that I didn't see anyone and had no visitors, so no alibi.'

The same turned out to be true for the Tuesday of Darius Moore's death. Jack could have taken him in, but on what grounds? That he was a single man who climbed, had no alibi, and people found a little odd? She asked a couple of follow-up questions and stood to leave.

'Wait.' He stood in front of her, arms straight out, almost touching her chest. Jack took an automatic step backwards. 'My autograph.'

He rummaged through the paperwork on the table again until he found a pen and a slightly crumpled black-and-white photo of Jack and Hannah taken just before the ascent of Annapurna.

Jack could feel her hands start to shake. She took a deep breath to steady herself. Of all the photos! Taking the pen from Philip's hand, she hastily signed her name in the cloudless Nepalese sky above her head.

Philip took the photo from her, raising it to his lips as though he was about to kiss it.

Jack left the flat as quickly as she could. Her car was parked opposite the flat in front of an Indian restaurant. The strong spicy smell of curry caused her to salivate. A takeaway would help with the long night she had before her preparing for the morning's briefing.

Entering the restaurant, Jack noticed it was full of Southern Asian customers, which was always a good sign of authentic, tasty food. She approached the counter to check that they did takeaways. The man who greeted her smiled and nodded.

Jack ordered a chicken bhuna, saag aloo and a garlic naan. Whatever she didn't eat tonight would be a feast for later. While she waited for her order, she chatted with the waiter at the desk. After talking about his hometown of Islamabad, which Jack had visited twice when climbing K2, Jack asked him about his neighbour, Philip Dyson. The restaurant was open most nights until late and they'd have a prime view of his coming and goings.

The waiter rapidly spoke in hushed tones, requiring Jack to move forward close to the counter. 'I know him. Strange guy. Comes and goes with bags of stuff, all times of the day and night.'

Jack tried to pin him down a little. 'What sort of times? After midnight?'

He shrugged. 'Maybe. Very late – sometimes.'

'And his bags. What size?'

'Large. Big enough for a body.' He grinned.

Now Jack was pretty sure he was joking, but it was certainly worth looking more closely at Philip Dyson.

TWENTY-FOUR

I'm getting tired of reading the newspaper cover to cover, waiting for a mention of the drug dealer's death. When they find his body, I expect to see an article on how he won't be missed by anyone apart from his mother: 'He had a good side, you know. He loved his nan and did her shopping every Saturday'. I even consider dropping a little note to Jack to tell her where to find him.

But then I spot the police entourage pull up at the entrance to the apartments: the red-headed pathologist with more inks than a merchant sailor; a few PC plods; the hijab-wearing sergeant; and then, of course, Jack. I whisper, 'This bastard's for you.'

It isn't long before I spot someone on the balcony. They bend down to examine the carabiner I left attached to the railing. Before removing it and putting it into an evidence bag, they go to fetch Jack. I wish I could see the look on her face. Was she pleased or perplexed? For a moment, I want to stand up and wave. 'Hey, it's me! I'm over here.'

1995

The lesson on how to climb went on forever. I tried to listen, but I couldn't keep my eyes off the rocky face of the mountain we were about to ascend. It was beautiful. My heart raced and my palms began to sweat. I just knew I could do this. I'd climbed out of windows and up onto roofs without a rope and harness. It couldn't be any harder than that.

The instructor bellowed out my name. He wanted me to go first. The rope was knotted and attached to my carabiner, and he showed me where the first handholds were, then I was on my own. I took a deep breath. The rope was pulled tight, so the harness rubbed into the skin on my thighs. As I reached up for the next handhold and moved my feet from one thin shelf to another, I soon forgot the rope and harness, loving the feel of the cold, sharp rock face against my fingertips. I reached the first bolt pretty quickly, and the instructor shouted up instructions to abseil back down.

I watched the other kids get no further than halfway up before their hands slipped from a poorly chosen hold. They were carefully lowered back down to the ground and given a second go. Part of me wanted to tear them from the boulder to let me go again. Perhaps the leader spotted my impatience because he took me to one side while Dominic was attached to the rope. 'We'll try a harder grade for you tomorrow, lad. Looks like you're a natural.'

A natural. I'd never been good at anything, according to all those that claimed to care for me, but all the climbing of trees and up the sides of houses had paid off it seemed. Perhaps I'd found my superpower. Dominic got past the halfway mark, and I joined in with the others in the group, chanting his name.

TWENTY-FIVE

The next morning, Jack started the briefing promptly by sharing what they knew about the death of Darius Moore.

'...And Shauna Scott will be undertaking the post-mortem this afternoon.' Jack paused as DSI Campbell walked into the briefing room with a guy in a suit. She recognised him as Detective Inspector O'Donohue. What was he doing at her briefing? They both sat down at the back, saying nothing.

Jack called on Nadia to give a report on what they'd found in the CCTV footage for the apartment and surrounding streets.

Nadia stood next to her boss and introduced the next slide. 'As you can see, we've concentrated on four main cameras: one in the reception area of the block, one in the car park and two on the road leading to the flats.'

She pulled up a couple of recordings of interest. 'These are the only individuals we haven't identified as residents. The caretaker was really helpful as he knew most of the occupants by sight.' She clicked on a recording from the flat's foyer. A short, middle-aged woman carrying a sports holdall approached the elevators then entered the one on the right. 'This was at

9.45 p.m. on the evening that we believe Darius was killed. She doesn't leave until approximately 8 a.m. the next morning. She may be a friend or girlfriend of one of the residents. We haven't completed the door-to-door yet.'

Nadia clicked on the next video. This featured a young black male wearing a tracksuit and trainers. He, too, walked through the foyer to the elevators. 'This guy arrived at the flats at 7.30 p.m. the same night and left at approximately 8 p.m. It's a short timeframe and, again, he could have been visiting someone. He could have even visited Darius.'

PC Brown raised his hand. 'I thought the lad we interviewed said he hadn't seen anyone leave?'

'Which makes me think the woman might be a regular visitor or girlfriend of one of the tenants, and the guy was one of their crew and he didn't want to give him up,' Nadia said.

She then asked if they had any further questions. The room stayed silent. Jack glanced at O'Donohue at the back of the room. He was listening to Nadia and rubbing his chin. It niggled Jack, rousing her suspicions that they were looking to add him to her team. She wouldn't mind more help but needed feet on the ground, not another senior officer, who would just get in the way.

Nadia finished her section, so Jack took over to allocate duties for the day, each team having more than enough to fill their hours. 'Oh, and PC Brown, I'd like you to speak to DS Maton on the Gangs Team. I want you to find out as much as you can about anyone with a beef against Moore. Best to rule that out too. Don't forget to show him the CCTV footage of the unidentified guy at the flats and, if we don't get an ID, then the middle-aged woman too.' She glanced around the room, spotting the odd grin from her colleagues. 'Anything else?'

A few shook their heads and one or two stood to leave, impeding DSI Campbell as he moved forward. He didn't wait until he reached the front. Instead, he said, 'Jack. I need you for a moment in my office.'

Jack didn't rush to turn off the monitor and collect her bag. Whatever he wanted could wait a few minutes.

Nadia raised her eyebrows as she put on her jacket. 'Everything okay, boss?'

'Looks like I'm about to find out.'

'I'm going back to the flats to lead the door-to-door, but ring me, yeah?'

Obviously, everyone thought this was it: she was for the chop on this one or demoted to second-in-command on the case.

Jack sighed and made her way to Campbell's office. Minutes later, she took a deep breath and knocked sharply on the door. Hearing the 'Come in,' Jack entered and was surprised to discover DSI Campbell was alone.

'Sit down, Jack.'

He hadn't looked up at her at all yet. She sat perched on the edge of the chair.

'I'm afraid we've had a complaint,' Campbell said, shuffling the papers on the desk in front of him.

'What about, sir?' *A complaint?* These weren't unusual, but they were unusual for Jack. She wondered for a moment if it was from Chris at Boulders for snubbing him.

'It's from Imam Basheer Khan. He says you entered his home by force and threatened him and his family.'

'What the hell?'

'I take it you know him then?'

Jack could barely think. *This was madness.* 'Yeah. I visited him the other day, but he invited me in. We even ate dinner together.'

'I'll need to see your notes. I take it this was about the Urban Climber case.'

Her mouth went dry. 'No... it wasn't about that case. It was something personal.' It wasn't up to her to tell her boss about what had happened to Nadia.

DSI Campbell looked confused, and she didn't blame him, but she wasn't prepared to betray any confidences either. 'I'll need a report on my desk by tomorrow morning.' He coughed. 'And I should warn you that DI Martin O'Donohue is waiting in the wings, so to speak, to take over the Urban Climber case if I don't get a satisfactory answer as to why you were at the imam's address.'

Leaving the office, Jack did the one thing she shouldn't: she drove straight round to Basheer Khan's home.

He answered on the second knock. Opening the door, Basheer grimaced. 'DI Kent. I, er—'

'I think we need to talk.'

Basheer looked up and down the street. 'Okay, come in.'

He led her into the front room. There was no sign of the rest of the family. Jack assumed the kids were at school and his wife at work or the shops. 'Please sit. Can I get you something? Tea... coffee?'

'I just need to check you're not going to accuse me of forcing my way in.'

He looked at the floor, eyes focussed on the Turkish kilim rug, clearly not wanting to meet Jack's gaze. *And you should be ashamed*, Jack thought. Eventually, he mumbled, 'I'm sorry. I had no choice.'

'You had no choice but to lie?'

Basheer's fingers glanced at the tips of his ears as though he was about to pray. 'I had a letter from the council.'

'About me?'

'Not exactly.' Basheer sat down on the chair opposite Jack.

He looked at her then. Gone was the cheerful cleric with an empathetic smile; he looked scared. For a moment, Jack wondered if he thought she was about to attack him, but then she realised it wasn't her he was scared of. 'What did the letter say?'

'That I didn't have planning permission for the mosque and that they were going to tear it down. There's going to be a hearing about it in a couple of weeks.'

'Is that true, about the planning permission?'

'Of course not.' He grabbed the cloth on his trousers and squeezed it. 'I spoke to my solicitor – he knows people and the council, and he told me if I put in a complaint about you, they'd withdraw the letter.'

'What?'

'Everyone's in it together, Jack. You have to understand that this community is a law unto itself.'

'Who's your solicitor?'

'I've felt ill. I've been physically sick since I wrote the complaint. *Astaghfirullah.*' Sitting forward, he held his head in his hands.

'Basheer, I need you to withdraw your complaint. This is about me, not you. Whoever is behind this knows you've put a complaint in. They don't have to find out that you've since withdrawn it.' Of course, she couldn't promise that. Who knew how far the corruption had now spread?

'They'll have seen you come here, just as they saw you the first time. If I withdraw it, they'll know... and what will they do then? *Astaghfirullah, astaghfirullah, astaghfirullah.* I'm as bad as my father,' he sobbed, shoulders heaving as he uttered the Islamic phrase asking for forgiveness.

'Listen, I'll leave straight away. But please consider withdrawing the complaint. We can protect you.' Jack hesitated. 'This is corruption, and they shouldn't win. They mustn't win. You know that.'

· · ·

Jack knew she'd done as much as she could to try to convince Basheer to withdraw the complaint. Her day couldn't get much worse, yet she still had the post-mortem to get through. With a deep breath, she entered the morgue and was greeted by an upbeat Shauna.

'Hey, mate. Glad you could make it.' Shauna looked up and paused. 'You okay? You look like someone's run over your cat.'

Jack replied, 'They might as well have. Looks like it could be my last day on the case.'

'What the...?' Shauna stopped short of swearing, an accomplishment in itself. 'That's just crazy. You're far and away the best person for this.'

'I'll tell you about it all later.' Jack sighed. 'Let's just get the PM out of the way.'

It wasn't long before Shauna was cutting through Darius's midline. Prior to the post-mortem, she'd taken samples of his bodily fluids and blood, as she explained for the videotape. 'The temperature of the body and the comparative temperature in the room where he was found suggest that life was extinct in the last few hours of Tuesday, 4th June.' She turned to Jack as she finished the cut. 'I can't be any more precise than that.'

Shauna began to remove the internal organs, weighing each in turn. Then she emptied the stomach contents into a bowl. 'Do you want to come and look?'

Jack took a step closer, knowing that the contents might give them an even better idea of the time of death. Swimming in the gastric stew was what looked like fusilli pasta shapes, and there was still a strong whiff of garlic.

Shauna leant further into the bowl. 'Can you smell that?' She put the bowl down on the counter next to the body. 'A garlic smell could be a sign of arsenic poisoning. We'll have to wait for the toxicology results on the stomach contents.'

'...Seems unlikely, don't you think?'

Shauna smiled. 'Look at the size of him. I'd want to subdue

him.' She then concentrated on the bones in his neck. Beckoning Jack closer, she pointed out the hyoid bone. 'There you go. Obvious fracture. He was almost definitely strangled.'

Jack returned to the station after promising Shauna that she'd meet her for a drink later at The Fox – that's if she had the time in the middle of the investigation. She needn't have worried since pretty much as soon as she walked through the door of the building, she was summoned to DSI Campbell's office.

This time she stormed in without knocking and wasn't surprised to see DI O'Donohue with his feet firmly under the table. He'd probably been chatting about golf with the DSI before she'd entered.

'Jack. Sit down,' DSI Campbell boomed. Martin had the temerity to blush. 'I haven't received your report.'

'I've been at the PM for Darius Moore, so I haven't written it yet.' Might as well be partially honest, Jack thought, though she'd decided not to bother. There was no way she was going to discuss Nadia's rape with her boss.

'The thing is,' he leant forward on his desk, 'the powers that be have decided that this needs fully investigating. It's culturally sensitive. So, I've got no choice Jack – you must understand – but to suspend you until we get to the bottom of this.'

The room fell silent as if the centre of the hurricane was passing overhead. Jack stood, breathing deeply through her nose. 'Well, I'll leave you boys to it, shall I? Thanks for taking the time to wait to hear my side of the story and believing that this was something that I'd never do.'

'Jack, you know how difficult these things can be—'

'Do you really think I'd act like that? Who the hell said I did? And you'd take their word without investigating first?' Jack folded her arms to stop herself from waving her fists at her boss.

'We will, of course, carry out an investigation. A thorough

one. But in the meantime, we have to suspend you. That's how it is.'

'How long for? What do you think I'm going to do while I wait?' She knew what she'd like to do but kept it to herself.

'I don't know. It depends... but we'll be as quick as we can.'

His unease and lack of confidence only made her feel more shafted.

'I'll need your...' DSI Campbell began. But Jack had already left the room, slamming the door behind her.

She didn't leave the building. Instead, she sought the shelter of the women's toilets. Standing at the sink, hands flat on the marbled counter, Jack began to sob, biting her lip to prevent any sound. This was her first big case. Her first murder. And it had been ripped from her.

Jack was on her second pint before she even mentioned her bombshell to Shauna, who had spent the first fifteen minutes of their get-together rubbing her back. They sat in the garden area, where Jack usually felt most comfortable, but the low awning that covered the space now felt oppressive.

She took another sip of her Guinness, then turned to Shauna. 'I've been suspended.'

'What the actual fuck!' She pulled Jack closer to her. 'Why? That's just crazy.'

Jack pulled away, took a deep breath and told Shauna what had happened with the imam. She didn't mention Nadia, just that she'd been to interview him and he'd later accused her of racism and harassment.

'You? Threaten an imam? That's just bollocks. Anyone with an ounce of a brain—'

'But that's the problem. There are plenty on the force with an ounce of a brain who'll believe it. Jack Kent, the mountaineer dyke now gets her comeuppance.'

'You're not a dyke.'

'I'm not sure that's the point.'

Shauna grinned. 'I'm just saying. You're not a lesbian. They could call *me* a dyke, but then I'd have them for homophobia.'

'After you'd stopped whacking them round the head.'

'What are you going to do?'

Jack took another sip of her pint. A few seconds later, she said, 'Not much I can do. I just hope the imam comes clean about what actually happened.'

'It's not right. I just don't get it. Why would he say those things? He's a man of the cloth.' Shauna downed her pint. 'How about a whisky next?'

Jack nodded, and Shauna headed to the bar. She hadn't noticed that Fran was in the bar until she sat down opposite. 'You okay, mate?'

'No,' was all Jack could manage before she began to sob again.

TWENTY-SIX

Something's happened to Jack. Last night, I saw her in tears. What could drive such a fine, strong athlete to break down like that?

I tried to eavesdrop on her conversation with those weirdos she calls friends. But all I could hear was the odd word... *imam... threaten... case removed.* I needed to know more but couldn't think of a way to make that happen. There was only so long that I could pretend to the gay couple I sat with that my Grindr date had stood me up. And I didn't want to turn in Jack's direction as there was a chance that she'd look up and recognise me.

Perhaps I should follow her again today, but each time I do, I risk being noticed. I have plenty to do, researching my next victim. This will be the best yet. Jack will think all her birthdays and Christmases have come at once. There's no doubt that he deserves it, no doubt in my mind at all.

1995

The next morning, one of my teachers hauled me out of the dining room. I stood in front of him in the hallway.

'You're not supposed to be here, according to your social worker... I'm sorry, lad, but we've got no choice. You've got to go back home.'

I bit my tongue to stop the tears. I couldn't let him know just how much the thought of 'going home' hurt. All I wanted to do was climb. All I wanted to do was something that I excelled at. Something for me. But, of course, it was just a silly dream. Looked-after kids didn't get to be rock climbers. Their path was already laid from children's home to hostel to prison. Do not pass go, do not collect £200.

Melodie Selasi, my latest social worker, arrived at the centre two hours later. I sat on the front porch next to my suitcase watching the instructors run round in a frenzy. Apparently, Jason's harness had broken and he'd had a nasty fall. *How sad.*

Melodie climbed the steep steps up to the porch and stood in front of me, wheezing. She took a slow, deep breath.

'Come on, lad. Time to go home.' She leant down to pick up my case, but I grabbed the handle before she could. The last thing I wanted was to be responsible for her keeling over.

Under my breath, I muttered, 'Sorry.'

'Don't worry. You're alright. No harm done. But I can't speak for your key worker at the home. She sounded pretty angry.'

'She always does.'

Melodie tutted. Climbing down the steps to the car park must have been easier than up, as she no longer wheezed and had stopped wiping her brow with the sleeve of her heavily patterned blouse. After putting my case in the boot and making sure I'd strapped myself into the passenger seat, Melodie squeezed herself into the driver's seat of the Mini. 'You boys'll be the death of me.' Then she grinned and patted my knee. 'But at least I got a day out in the country.'

As we passed the mountains leading to the motorway, I almost pressed my nose up against the window. Even if I had to run away a thousand times, I knew I'd be back. I'd found my true home. I no longer wanted to be a superhero. I wanted to be a climber, and no one was going to stop me.

TWENTY-SEVEN

Sometimes, you have to face your demons, look them straight in the eye and fight them head-on. This is how Jack came to be driving to the Peak District on the day after her suspension, to Raven Tor, her nemesis.

She hadn't climbed here since she was a young teenager and had vowed never to set foot on the crag again. But as she'd slept most of the day and was still shaky after her night at the pub, it called her name. There was nothing she could do about her suspension. But there were other, more persistent demons to slay.

On 10th November 2004, her father had driven here to attempt what turned out to be his last climb. As she drove through the peaks, she wondered what he'd thought about on his journey. What emotions played through his head? Was he calm, excited... angry? Did he see the crag as a challenge? It wasn't even a mountain, just a limestone cliff, a tricky but inter-esting climb that fell in and out of favour with her peers. Many fallen climbers had their names etched in far more renowned and famous locations. There were no base camps here, not even a tourist information sign.

Ironically, Jack had decided, as she threw together her gear, that she'd attempt a route up Mecca. Considering what had happened to her with the imam, it just seemed to fit. On site, she'd decide whether to reach the extension section of either Hajj or Kaabah. Both had their appeal.

But it was her father's death that ultimately drew her here, not the climb. For the first time in fifteen years, she needed to come to terms with that. She needed to conquer the crag and its unforgiving rock.

Several signs were displayed in the lay-by. **No parking overnight.** That's exactly what she planned to do. It was late in the evening and the shadows were lengthening. She planned to start early the next morning after sleeping in the back of her car. There were other cars parked here too. Maybe a couple of climbers were camping nearby, but company was the last thing she wanted tonight.

Later, sitting in the boot of her Range Rover, she watched the sun as it descended behind a hill, leaving a pink-grey hue in its wake. She completed her equipment check and switched on a camping lamp she'd attached to the interior of the car. Reaching for a map, she lay back on her sleeping bag and memorised the route for the morning.

At first light, she hiked up to the rock face carrying her gear on her back. She gazed up at the gentle giant, placed her backpack on the ground and reached for her rope. The bird-like crag with its foreboding, sharp beak rose before her. It was easy to see how the crag earned its name.

The overhang at the base of Raven Tor required all a climber's bouldering skills, but she soon managed to pull herself up to the cliff face at the bottom of the Mecca route. She might have been better starting on an easier path to warm up her muscles, but she wanted to be a hundred percent focussed on

the climb. Anything too easy and stray thoughts about her
suspension or the Urban Climber case could easily permeate.

Raven Tor pulled the climber into a deep embrace. Many of
the holds required fingertip crimp precision with the body
grazing the cliff face. Being short meant that Jack couldn't over-
reach for a new hold. Instead, she had to seek the tiniest crack or
shelf closer to her. Pressing deep into the rock, she could take its
pulse and decide whether it would hold her weight as she
shifted position.

Tapping in her first anchor, she wondered if her father had
climbed solo without ropes that day. It seemed even more
unlikely, crazy even, as she clipped on her rope. He was so
conscious of his family, taking only the most sensible of decisions on any mountain, cliff or crag that he climbed, weighing
up risk and working out the odds of returning to the warm
embrace of his home and family. A slip would mean that he'd
want to swing free and feel the tug as the rope caught. Jack
sought a crack above her with the fingers of her right hand,
squeezing the tips into its edge. Then she lifted a knee, ensuring
the rope wasn't caught around it. Seeking a firm foothold, she
continued the climb, following the route up to the crux.

She hesitated, her fingers turning numb, introducing her
right hand to the chalk before passing the rope up to an
advanced anchor. The stretch between holds was almost too far
and, where the rock bulged, she couldn't lunge across.
Clutching on with her right hand, she sought a closer hold, even
if it was a mere scar on the surface; she needed some stability to
move her foot. With some scrabbling, she found a positive hold
and dragged her leg up and over the bulge, giving her sufficient
grip to propel forward over the crux. Then just a kneebar to
complete, a hold born out of necessity and practised by her
peers. She could breathe now for a minute. The minerals in the
limestone glinted in the warm, early summer sun, but she had
little time to admire the rock's beauty.

The Urban Climber would have felt the breath of a mountain on his face. He would know that feeling of exhilaration at completing a tricky route. He would understand how precarious life is. And yet he'd chosen to kill, to end the life of another.

Jack shook her head to dislodge the negativity. This was no way to think when she had so much further to climb. Hajj lay ahead, and she needed to focus on each handhold and foothold. She'd decided on the Hajj despite it being more of a bouldery route than the Kaabah route. It had been completed by fewer climbers before her, but she needed a challenge today.

Hajj was a crimpy climb, which required full stretches between holds. Each time she placed her feet, she needed to stand fully to push herself to the next handhold. She could no longer hear the road below her. Even the birdsong grew faint as she focussed on each movement, a voice in her head urging her on, helping her to make the most confident choices.

One more grasp at the coarsest ridge. A miss. The weight of her body on one set of fingertips tore at her already broken skin. Another attempt and success. Pausing, Jack assessed the damage to her hand. The bloodied scratches just added to the myriad of scars on her serially abused and calloused fingers. Grimacing, she carried on climbing.

She was prepared for as many attempts as it took, and it surprised her that her upper body strength and handholds remained firm as she climbed higher. The last bolt appeared before she expected it and, in some ways, she wished it had taken her more attempts to conquer. Only when she reached the top did she smile. Instead of the usual euphoria and shrieks of delight, a slight shiver rose through her body and she felt at peace. It had almost felt like her father had climbed every step beside her – not to protect her, just to make sure she had the strength to reach the top.

. . .

Instead of packing up and driving home, Jack stayed another night. She set up camp just beneath the crag's overhang and heated a can of stew on her camping stove. Even though she knew she had to return and fight at some point, tonight she just wanted to be close to her father, to hear his belly laugh and imagine the scratchiness of his beard on her face as he pulled her into a hug after completing a complex route.

It was a warm night, so Jack laid out her mattress on the ground without bothering with a tent. She lay in her sleeping bag and looked up at the stars. Despite all the effort of climbing both routes, she wasn't particularly tired. Her phone was in her backpack as she didn't want to be distracted by it, but it was within arm's reach just in case of emergencies. Earlier in the day, a couple of young lads had attempted some of the easier routes on the Tor, but tonight she was alone. She reached for her phone just to check that the world hadn't ended in her absence.

There was a smattering of missed calls. Shauna and Nadia were more persistent than most. Jack sent them a short and sweet message to let them know she was alive and well. Another call was from a sponsor to ask if she'd do a photoshoot for a camera advert. Jack doubted that she'd have the right look for that at the moment – unless they were going for the moody, depressive vibe. The last call was from Danny and was followed by a text:

Call me. It's important.

She debated with herself for a few minutes as to whether it was more important than her inner peace right now. In the end, her curiosity got the better of her and she called him. He answered on the second ring. 'Where the hell are you?'

'Hi, Danny. I'm fine, thanks. How are you?'

There was a slight pause. Maybe he was assessing what

tone to take – concerned parent or pissed-off friend. 'I heard what happened and then Dad rang—'

'Seriously, I'm fine.'

'Jack, he saw your car... he said you were heading for the Tor.'

She'd forgotten how close Uncle David lived to the crag. He also knew that she'd vowed never to climb it again. Now she understood Danny's concern. 'I climbed the Hajj – first time.'

Jack heard Danny breathe out forcefully. 'What the hell, Jack! You could have been hurt and no one would know.'

'There are always others around on Raven Tor. I'm sure someone would have helped if I needed it.'

'Are you staying there tomorrow? I can cancel my appointments and join you.' He paused for a second and when she didn't respond, said, 'Or I can ask Dad to join you, if you want.'

Uncle David hated the Tor as much as she did. And she'd no idea what she was going to do tomorrow. During the call, she'd felt her dad leave her side. Maybe he knew as much as she did that it was time to head back to reality. 'I'll be back in Brum tomorrow. Why don't I stop by and have a warm-down session with you? If you've got a slot.'

'I'll make one.'

Jack lay back on the mattress, pulled up the sleeping bag to her chin and shut her eyes. 'Night, Danny.'

It was just before midday when Jack pulled up at Danny's climbing school. She knocked on the red wooden door under the aged sign of a climber hauling his rope. Danny opened the door and immediately pulled her into a hug. He knew how momentous the previous day's climb had been. No words needed to be said.

Danny led Jack to the picnic table in the main climbing hall where they'd often drunk coffee and put the world to rights. He sat down on the bench and Jack sat opposite him. He reached into a cooler bag and brought out a package wrapped in foil. 'Gem's made us her speciality baguettes.'

He handed one to Jack, who was already salivating at the thought. Jack took a huge bite out of the sandwich, ignoring the trail of mayonnaise that dripped down her chin. Danny laid out some tubs of salad and coleslaw. After another bite, Jack asked, 'How is Gemma doing? Oh, and please thank her for me.'

Danny nodded as he spoke. 'Actually, she's getting better. We both are. Molly's finally sleeping through the night and the doctor's sorted out Gem's meds. They're saying now that if we have another, they'll start her on medication straight away.'

'Have another?' Jack stifled a laugh. Happy as she was that Gemma's postnatal depression was being taken seriously, she couldn't imagine that Danny would even contemplate another child. Surely three was enough for anyone?

'I know. God forbid.' Danny grinned.

They ate in silence for a while. Jack scraped up the last of the coleslaw and put down her fork. 'I've been making plans.'

Danny looked up at her with a glint in his eye. 'Which mountain?'

'Can't decide between Kangchenjunga or Nanga Parbat.'

'Both good choices and you've not climbed either.' Danny shook his head. 'Who are you hoping to climb with?'

Jack reached for his hands, cupping them with her own. 'You?'

Danny's laugh, as he pulled away his hands, told a million stories. 'If only.'

'You're the best climber I know and the one person I'd want by my side. I'm thinking next May. That gives us nearly a year—'

'Gemma would—'

'Yes, I know. And she'll hate me even more. But think of it. When was the last time you climbed an 8000-metre?' Jack wasn't sure whether she was wearing him down at all, but if she didn't at least try...

'You know when. It was eight years ago. But times are different.' He raised his hands, taking in the climbing centre. 'There's this place, for a start.'

'Your dad could run it for a few months. In fact, I'm sure he'd love to.'

'Why don't you take him instead?'

For a moment, Jack felt nauseous. Maybe she'd eaten too fast and the overexcitement had churned her stomach. 'No. If it's not you, then I'll ask Teddy.'

'Teddy?' Danny scowled at her. Had she given up on him too quickly?

'You know, Teddy Garson.'

'Yeah. He's hardly in your league.'

'He's tough and an intelligent climber. Okay, he's a bit on the heavy side and will be difficult to lead for, but he's passionate about the mountains and that's what I'm looking for more than anything.'

Danny sat back. 'You don't even know why he left education.'

Jack paused. Was this just jealousy because he wouldn't be allowed to go? 'You know that outdoor education's in decline. Has been for years. What the hell are you implying?'

'Nothing.' Danny ran his hand through his blond curls. 'It's just that you don't know him. He hasn't been in the game for a while and, frankly, there are far more experienced and skilled climbers out there.'

'Is there something you know about Teddy that I don't?'

Danny shrugged. 'Just rumours. You know what he's like.'

She knew him as a kind and supportive friend. Danny clearly thought differently. And yet, he always had been a good judge of character. Maybe it was her judgement that was failing.

'It needs to be someone I already know and trust.' Someone like Hannah. But, of course, there was no one like her.

Tears pricked her eyes. *Why was this so hard?* On the drive here, she'd been so excited and felt alive for the first time in months. And now Danny was bringing her back down to earth without a crash mat.

It was his turn to lean forward and grab her hands. 'Listen, if you're really sure about this, then I'll help you with everything – deciding on the climb, practising routes, finding sponsors and, above all, finding the right partner.'

There was so much to do and less than a year to do it. He was right, as usual. And then, of course, there was work and she hadn't given up on that. Or had she?

TWENTY-EIGHT

Where's Jack? I haven't seen her for days and this new plan is all for her. She'll be so pleased... but she's not at home and not at work. In fact, there's some older guy now working with the Muslim sergeant. This can't be happening. I'm almost ready.

TWENTY-NINE

Jack didn't go home after visiting Danny. She could at least decide on which mountain to plan to climb, even without confirming a partner. Nanga Parbat was Tom's mountain in her eyes. The famous climber Tom Ballard, for whom she had great respect and had met several times, had died there in recent months. Danny argued that this was due to 'choosing the wrong partner'. Jack had never known him to be so judgemental, but maybe he had a point? And maybe he had a point now about Jack needing the right partner.

Kangchenjunga was a more frightening prospect, in some respects – more of a killer and, like Annapurna, it was prone to avalanches. But more than conquering a mountain, Jack needed to conquer her personal fears. This would be the ultimate challenge.

Jack headed to Blencathra, where the Mountain Heritage Trust housed some of the best collections of mountaineering history in the UK. She needed the time and some headspace to make decisions. She also wanted to get as far away as possible from Birmingham and the Urban Climber case to do it... for now. The drive would give her the time to consider and contemplate. While some might find a five-and-a-half-hour drive daunt-ing, Jack relished it.

She booked a B&B on the edge of Keswick with the most spectacular view of the Lakes. This would be her bolthole for a few days, maybe longer if her suspension dragged on. As soon as she arrived, she quickly unpacked her luggage and her climbing gear. There was a large desk and chair directly under the only window in the room. It would be perfect for spreading out maps and making plans. The bed was king-sized and looked comfort-able enough, and there was even an en-suite shower room. The only issue was the oppressive heat. Jack opened the window as far as it would go and thought about asking for a fan from reception.

Only then did she consider picking up her phone. She'd never seen so many missed calls. There was even one from her mum. So the gossip in Birmingham had reached even her. She might as well get a call to her mum out of the way first as it was likely to be the most difficult. She made herself a coffee and rang her mother, who answered straight away.

'Jack, I've been worried sick. Suspended? Whatever for?'

'It's all bollocks, Mum. And I'm fine.'

'Are you sure? I mean – suspension, that means you might lose your job, doesn't it?'

Jack chewed her lip. 'It won't come to that. I need a break, so maybe it's done me some good.'

There was a pause in the conversation until her mum said, 'I suppose.'

'Don't worry, I've decided to take a holiday in the Lakes.'

'A holiday? What a lovely idea. You should have said. I'd have joined you.'

Jack couldn't imagine anything worse. After a few minutes of small talk about what she was likely to do on her break, she extricated herself from the call.

Next came Shauna. 'You okay?' Jack asked.

'Fine. Just wondered if you fancied a drink, and I'll fill you in on what's happening.'

Jack felt the guilty pull back to the Urban Climber. It wasn't right that she'd been suspended. It was her case, and she did plan to fight to get it back, but she needed time and, maybe, in the short term, this had given her the opportunity to breathe and reassess what was important. 'I'm sure what's-his-name is doing a grand job. Has he caught the UC yet?'

Shauna sniffed. 'You taking the piss? He's borderline useless from what I've heard.'

'Good to know I'm missed. I'm staying in the Lakes for a few days, so I'll give that drink a rain check until I get back.'

'You sure *you're* okay?'

'I'm planning a climb for next year. Since I've got some time now, I might as well put it to good use.'

Shauna didn't answer straight away. 'A climb... that's good. Where?'

'A mountain in the Himalayas. You won't have heard of it.'

'Not Everest then.' Shauna laughed.

'No. Not Everest.'

Jack wanted to leave the stuffy room so brought the call to an end. She knew Shauna would spend the year until the climb worrying about it, then be an emotional mess while she was summiting and only calm down when she was home again.

The curator at the Mountain Heritage Trust had prepared for her visit that afternoon. A climber himself, he knew when to make himself scarce and when to chat about mutual acquaintances and tricky routes. On a large table in the document library, he'd placed maps and documents related to the two mountains. Jack took out a fresh, leather-bound notebook, pencils and pens from her backpack. She laid them down and unrolled one of the larger maps of Kangchenjunga. If she was going to climb it, then she was going to do it differently. She studied the major routes, noting down the positives and negatives of each. There were more commercial climbs on the mountain now than there had been five to ten years ago. You could never completely escape them in the Himalayas unless you went 'off season' and added even more danger to your expedition.

Annapurna was the women's mountain in Hannah and Jack's eyes – a goddess on the grandest scale. Neither Nanga Parbat nor Kangchenjunga had that same pull. As her stomach began to rumble and her eyes became strained and sore, Jack decided that she'd come back the next day when her mind was fresher. What she needed now was a pie and a pint, and possibly some conversation. The landlady at the B&B had mentioned a good place to get all three, so Jack closed her notebook, placed it back in her backpack and headed for the pub.

A few hours later, Jack dragged herself up the stairs to bed. At the Traveller's Rest, a group of young ramblers had taken pity on her and dragged her into their pub quiz team. They may well have decided this was a mistake after the first round, which was primarily on popular culture. Jack didn't even own a television. In the next couple of rounds, her general knowledge came to the fore, but so did theirs, and they were quicker with the answers. Then came the music section and the quizmaster asked two questions related to jazz. Her adopted teammates looked completely flummoxed, so she surprised them with her quick, correct answers. The team finished a credible third and Jack bought a round of real ale to celebrate. She regretted that now as she lay on her back as it didn't sit well with the other pints and her meal.

Sleep didn't come easily either, and when it did, it was cursed with nightmares.

. . .

*The weather had suddenly turned on Annapurna. A whiteout.
Thick, white flakes billowed in front of her. Breathing was hard
enough at this altitude, but even with a buff and goggles, she still
sucked in the freezing air.*

*Hannah had disappeared from view. She should be on the
rope line in front of her. Where had she gone? Heavy step
followed heavy step. There were no footprints in the snow. And
then no line of rope keeping her safe. Another step and she fell
into darkness.*

Jack lurched out of sleep more violently than a hypnic jerk. She
lay awake, staring at the unfamiliar plaster on the ceiling. It took
her a moment before she realised where she was.

* * *

The days that followed were far more fruitful. By Friday, she'd
made some decisions and felt able to return to Birmingham with
plans in place and in a far better place mentally to face her
future.

Her first port of call was home. Jack wanted to put her dirty
clothes on a cold wash and calm herself before visiting the
station. Almost as soon as she entered the flat, she sensed that
something wasn't quite right. There was no sign that anyone
had been in her apartment and certainly no sign of a break-in,
yet it almost felt as though she had entered a new, unfamiliar
space. It didn't feel like her home. The only other person who
spent time in her flat was her cleaner. Jack knew when she'd
been in. The mild smell of bleach gave it away.

Jack checked each room for changes – any object that might
not be exactly where she expected it to be – but didn't spot

anything out of place. Perhaps she was imagining it? She entered the kitchen and shoved her dirty clothes into the washing machine. As she stood, she sensed it again. An almost primal stench of stale sweat. It wasn't her clothes. She'd already shut the door on the washing machine. She sucked in a breath. The Urban Climber had been here in her flat. She shivered. There was no proof. She just knew it.

An hour later, Jack drove to the station. With a letter in hand, she took the stairs up to the DSI's office. She hadn't expected her entrance to be so easy. They'd clearly forgotten to cancel her pass.

A young Muslim woman passed her on the stairs. Their eyes locked in recognition. Jack turned and watched her take another step down before saying, 'Wait.'

The woman turned, re-covering her hairline with her veil.

'You're Basheer's wife, aren't you?'

'DI Kent... I...' The woman looked down at the stairs between them.

'What are you doing here?'

'Is there somewhere we can talk?'

Jack had planned to confront DSI Campbell and demand to be reinstated. She had a letter from Nadia in her hand, ready. They'd talked the night before and decided that it was the only way. Nadia would share her secret and thus expose the corruption in the council, so they'd have nothing on Jack other than the word of this woman's husband. Hopefully, it would be enough proof that the imam was lying.

Yet here was his wife, wanting to talk. Jack could hardly refuse. A few minutes later, Jack and Samira Fawaz sat opposite each other in a booth in a corner coffee shop. Samira appeared to be struggling to find the right words to explain why she was at the station. Jack stirred her coffee and waited.

Eventually, Samira said, 'I can't carry on watching my husband tearing himself apart.'

Jack folded her arms, resting them on the table in front of her. 'He lied. I've been suspended. He could still cost me my job.'

'I know. And I've told him he's wrong and he may never be forgiven.' Samira waved her arms around as though chasing away a wasp. 'A man came to see him not long after you did the other day. I didn't recognise him, but there was something about him. Something nasty. I listened at the door, and he called you all sorts of words I couldn't repeat. He implied you sleep with women and deserved all you get.'

Jack raised her coffee cup and sighed. 'I do sleep with women, but what I'm not is threatening, racist or disrespectful. Or at least I try as hard as I can to *not* be those things.'

Samira sat on her hands. 'I'm not homophobic.'

'I'm glad to hear it. Are you saying Basheer is?'

'No...' It came out more as a question than an answer, her uncertainty chewing at its edges.

'But he hasn't come to the station, has he? So, why were you there?'

Her lips pursed, Samira said, 'To tell the truth. If he won't tell the truth, then I will.'

'Then I guess I should thank you.'

Samira sighed. 'I don't expect your gratitude. You've every right to be angry. They'll let you go back to work now... won't they?'

'Maybe,' Jack mumbled.

There was nothing else to say. Jack finished her coffee in one last gulp and left without looking back at Samira. Let her drown in her guilt.

Of course, she could just go straight from the coffee shop to Campbell's office and demand her job back, but she wanted to speak to Nadia again first. Jack knew that, even if they lifted her suspension, she'd still need to convince Campbell that she deserved to resume running the case and, for that, she needed some insight as to what had happened since she'd left. When she spoke to Nadia last night, they'd concentrated on the blackmail and conspiracy in the depths of the council and what parts of Nadia's story she'd be happy for Jack to share. None of that was necessary now. The best way to expose the corruption would be through the press, and Catherine was still working on that. To be honest, Jack didn't trust the upper echelons of the police to act on it.

Nadia joined her ten minutes later in her car, which was parked near the back entrance of the station. So that Nadia wouldn't assume that she'd delivered the letter to Campbell, Jack filled her in about Basheer's wife.

Nadia rubbed her hands together. 'That's great, boss. So now you can come back to work, surely?'

'You'd hope so,' Jack nodded, 'but they might not let me back on this case.'

'We're getting nowhere with it under O'Donohue. He's convinced Moore's murder is gang-related, so he's concentrating on that. I've even shared the file on Philip Dyson with him and he just told me to shelve it.'

'So, basically, he doesn't think there's a climber involved?'

'He reckons the burglaries and Moore's death are unrelated.'

'But the carabiner on the balcony—'

'He reckons that's been there a while. Maybe our climber had robbed another flat in the block.'

Nadia smiled. 'Anyway, a few of us have been undertaking surveillance of Dyson's flat on the quiet.'

'And?'

'Let's just say... he keeps strange hours. And likes to do walking tours of the city centre late at night.'

'For what reason?'

Nadia shrugged. 'No idea?'

Philip Dyson was still a major person of interest. That was clear.

Jack decided to give DSI Campbell the rest of the day to call her and apologise. If she didn't hear from him by the morning, then she'd go to him and tell him she'd spoken with Basheer's wife.

Over the last few days, she'd considered jacking it all in and concentrating on her climbing for a year. With sponsorship deals, and if she sold her flat, she'd have enough money to get by. She wouldn't be the first climber to live in a van travelling from place to place depending on where she needed to train. But this case was personal, so she may as well try to solve it before disappearing.

An email from Police Complaints pinged into her personal mailbox just over an hour later. It informed her that her suspension had been withdrawn and she was free to return to work the next day. No explanation was given, nor any sign that they'd rescinded the allegation. Typical. She sat on her sofa at home and continued to write an email to one of her Sherpa friends. If she was going to climb Kangchenjunga in the way she hoped, then she'd need the perfect team of support climbers.

The next morning, Jack walked straight into her office and emailed the UC team, asking them to attend a briefing at 2 p.m. that afternoon. No one else was at their desk. In a way, she hoped that O'Donohue was an early riser, too, so she could sound him out before the others arrived. But as far as she was concerned, she'd been given the green light to continue as lead officer.

A couple of PCs arrived first and grinned at her as they entered the office. It was good to see that some people were happy to see her back. Then Nadia and Harry arrived, nodding at her with a brief, 'Boss.'

It was 9.30 a.m. when DI O'Donohue showed up. By this time, Jack had liaised with several members of the team about their recent tasks and possible next steps. O'Donohue approached her and said in a voice hardly above a whisper, 'Can I have a word?'

Jack didn't move, just motioned to the seat next to her.

'No, outside.'

There was no way a same-grade officer was ordering her about. Jack stood her ground. Of course, anyone in the vicinity would have noticed this. Harry was clearly having a hard time stifling a snigger.

Eventually, O'Donohue got the message and sat on the vacant stool next to Jack, who made a show of shutting the lid on her laptop.

'What do you think you're doing?' he said.

'Haven't you heard? They've lifted my suspension.'

'Yes, but—'

'So, I'm here doing my job, leading my team. I guess I could ask you the same question.'

O'Donohue didn't answer. He stood with enough force to almost send his chair over backwards and left the office, heading in the superintendent's direction.

A smattering of applause followed.

O'Donohue hadn't returned by the afternoon, so Jack started the briefing without him. She made it clear to all that, in her view, Philip Dyson was a lead suspect. She also set out a rota for night-time surveillance. Let the DSI complain later.

Harry was given the job of finding out all he could about Philip's history. Nadia was to apply for a warrant to search his address. Then Jack spoke to the room. 'We have a suspect who regularly drives at night and walks around the city centre in the area where burglaries have taken place. He has no alibi and is a reasonably competent climber. Look, it's clearly not enough to charge him or formally bring him in for questioning. We need more and I'm looking to you to provide that.'

PC Brown put up his hand. 'I'm happy to trawl CCTV again for the night of the burglaries. Maybe we can match him to IC1 males. We haven't had a suspect before, so it's worth going back over what footage we have.'

'Great idea.'

Then Nadia said, 'Could we go back to Freddie with a photo of Dyson to see if he recognises him?' She looked down at her pad. 'Also, should we go door-to-door in some of the apartment blocks again with his photo? You never know, someone might have seen him.'

Jack nodded. 'I know we're thin on the ground as we're only a small team. I'll push for more officers and, of course, overtime.' A couple groaned at this. They knew how likely that would be. However, Jack had never felt more confident that her team supported her as a boss. Besides, there was still no sign of O'Donohue. Or DSI Campbell, for that matter.

THIRTY

It's time. Everything's in place. Those familiar feelings of anxiety and excitement bubble up in me. I take deep breaths. Counting 1... 2... 3... breathe. My heart rate slows. I gather my gear and pack it into my daypack. I've stashed ropes and my harness in the building. *Just two more hours.*

1999

On the day I left care, I had a plan. I may have only been sixteen, but I had the basics to get by: a room in a hostel, a small allowance, and my case of possessions. I intended to be someone.

I only ever wanted to do good. I held no malice for those around me who tried to help. This was a system error, and, in my own small way, I vowed to correct it.

At first, I did small things – transferred a few thousand pounds from one account to another. The corrupt local council made a sudden large donation to a hospice, for example. But these didn't impact real people and that didn't seem fair either.

I got a job as a labourer. It paid enough to afford the equipment. For a while, I just concentrated on learning to climb. As the instructor said years earlier, this was something I excelled at.

Every Saturday, I caught a bus to the Peak District and climbed some of the local crags. Occasionally, I spoke to the other climbers and listened fervently to their tips and advice. Every week, I improved a little more. Nothing else seemed important during that time. As I progressed, I made friends with some of the up-and-coming local stars, offering to partner them when they needed help. Many of them shunned me. I didn't wish them well. I'd never get their chances and opportunities. I had no finances, no parent's backing and I was never part of the community of climbers. Always on the edge, an outsider. But that would change. I'd make them sit up and notice.

THIRTY-ONE

Nadia and Jack were heading for Dyson's flat to serve a search warrant that afternoon when a call came across the radio: *'Possible robbery in progress at Trentham Garden Apartments, penthouse suite.'* Jack glanced at Nadia, who nodded. Taking just a moment to do a U-turn, Jack headed in the opposite direction. She spoke into the radio: 'DI Jack Kent, in assistance.'

'It's the middle of the day,' Nadia said. It struck Jack as bizarre too, especially since she had the uneasy feeling that this involved their climber.

Nadia took out her phone and started swiping, making Jack wonder why she was doing that instead of giving directions. Then she missed a right turn that would have provided a good diversion for the midday traffic build-up, making her even more angry about the lack of her colleague's support. Jack sped up again. The Range Rover was fitted with large, blue LEDs that ran across the bumper but gave out no sound. Each time they approached a car slowing at a junction, Jack used her horn to alert them to move to the side. Some didn't comply fast enough, forcing her to brake. Still, Nadia seemed more interested in her phone.

Jack was about to shout at her when she looked up and said, 'Do you know who lives in the penthouse?'

Jack glared back in response, and then immediately turned her attention back to the road. What was this? Twenty questions?

'It's where the mayor lives with his son.' Nadia had clearly accessed the rape case record to check. She let that sink in. 'Though, of course, we know his son currently resides elsewhere.'

Neither of them had time to wonder about this as they turned into Trentham Gardens. Jack began to slow down, planning to block the exit from the underground car park.

It happened so fast – maybe it was the inhuman scream that caused Jack to slam on the brakes. Not far in front of the car, a great mass dropped past the windscreen. It hit the ground with a thud. A moment's silence was followed by Nadia's scream as she covered her face with her hands. Suddenly conscious of her own breathing, Jack unbuckled her seatbelt and flew out of the car.

In front of her was the mangled body of a man, a mass of twisted limbs and a free-flowing river of blood. From his hair colour and height, Jack guessed it was the mayor. She felt for a pulse. Nothing. They were too late. Instinctively, she shielded her eyes and stared up. The top of the building was in direct sunlight and all she could see was the building in silhouette.

Nadia was out of the car by now, leaning on the front in an obvious state of shock, holding her head, staring at the body.

'Call for backup,' Jack said before turning back to the building. There was no way this arrogant bastard had jumped by himself, she thought. Somewhere inside that building was a killer, and she knew in her gut that the UC could be responsible.

It was up to Jack to take up pursuit. She had to trust that her partner would call in what happened as soon as she took stock of the situation. She sprinted to the main entrance to the apartment block. Without thinking, she glanced at the elevators; neither was moving and there was no sign of a concierge or porter. The penthouse was ten floors up. Jack headed for the stairs. Racing up them without thinking about what she'd do if she came face to face with a possible killer, she soon reached the third floor and took a moment to catch her breath. The stairs were concrete, and she couldn't hear anything. Surely, by now, if he was heading this way, she'd hear his feet slapping against the stairs? She opened the stairs door to peer out into the third-floor corridor. The elevators were directly next to the stairs and the lights showed that they were still stationary – one on the ground floor, the other on the third. Pressing the button, she waited for the doors to open and took the elevator to the top floor.

The door to the mayor's flat stood wide open. Jack wasn't armed and couldn't know if the killer was still in the apartment. Swallowing hard, she entered the apartment, careful not to touch the door or any other surface. Listening for the slightest sound, she took one step at a time. Nothing. The apartment was sparsely furnished, making the path to the open sliding doors to the balcony relatively easy. Still no sound. Even the sound of her heart no longer pulsed in her ears. Where could he have gone?

Jack reached the balcony, took hold of the railing and looked down. She could now hear distant sirens. The body was a bloody mess in front of her car. Someone – she assumed Nadia – was keeping people back from the scene. Jack felt suddenly vulnerable. Conscious that she could be next, she stepped back into the flat. Again, she listened for any sound and heard nothing. Where was he?

Jack took her phone from her jacket pocket. She needed to let everyone know she was safe and that she was alone. Still wary in case someone was hiding in the flat, she left and stood at the front door, blocking the exit. It didn't take long for her to describe the situation and only moments passed before a team of officers met her at the door.

The flat was thoroughly searched and found, as she'd expected, to be empty. No one had been seen leaving the building, but Jack knew in her gut that he'd somehow escaped. Just in case, she sent a couple of officers to check that there wasn't anyone above them on the small strip of roof that covered the top of the penthouse but that, too, was clear. He'd got away.

CCTV would be monitored, and any sign of the fleeing suspect would be relayed to cars on the ground. Jack made the snap decision that she needed transport to be ready to give chase. Her car wasn't damaged by the impact of the falling body, which had landed on the tarmac a few feet from the front. She couldn't see any visible signs of transfer of evidence from the body. Before anyone could stop her, Jack got into her car and hit reverse. The road cleared behind her and a quick-thinking officer stepped out of the way just as he was about to place police tape across the road.

The radio blared out a possible sighting. '*IC1 male running on foot towards the Convention Centre on Brindley Place.*' Good job she'd got the car; it would save her a good few minutes. If she put her foot down, she could meet him coming out of the entrance onto Centenary Square.

Jack screeched the Range Rover to a halt at the side of the Repertory Theatre and leapt out. A white male streaked past in front of her, and she gave chase. He'd clearly been running for a while as she could hear his panting from strides away. She shouted, 'Police!' but he failed to stop. She soon caught up with him, lunged at him and sent him flying to the ground. Only then did she spot the woman's red handbag as it slid across the pavement. He was nothing but a bag snatcher. She was tempted to leave him grovelling on the floor, but she grabbed his arm and pulled him to his feet, reading him his rights. Picking up the handbag, she led him to her car. In the boot was a holdall containing her torch, handcuffs and other tools of the trade. He remained compliant as she cuffed him and called for backup.

Within an hour, Jack was back at the mayor's apartment explaining to her boss why she'd left the scene. The fact that he'd left the comfort of his office only showed the significance of the victim.

There had been no other sightings of anyone suspicious in the area and CCTV recordings didn't show anyone leaving the flats. There were plenty of officers scurrying about going door-to-door and removing evidence bags under the watchful eye of the local press. The mayor's body lay undisturbed under the white shroud of a murder tent.

Campbell glared at Jack. 'I really don't care that you accosted a petty thief. You should have been here, protecting the scene.'

'To be fair, when I left, there were plenty of other officers around to do that.' She didn't meet his gaze.

'Moving your car could mean we've lost evidence.'

That much was true – she'd give him that. If he wished to throw the book at her, she'd have no defence. Of course, it would have been a different story if she'd caught the fleeing killer.

Nadia saved her any further embarrassment. 'The car park's been checked. No one's hiding in there. No vehicles have left since the attack and there were no arrivals in the past five hours. I think we can be reasonably sure our perp didn't enter the building that way. Oh, and the pathologist's arrived.'

Jack followed her colleague to meet Shauna, who was

already suited up and about to enter the tent. 'You're not coming in here without the correct gear.'

Jack grimaced. 'I wasn't planning to.' She wondered what her friend would make of the fact that she'd moved the car. No doubt she was due another dressing down. It was unlikely that anything of significance had hit her car as he fell, and she'd briefly checked that there weren't any body parts tangled in her mudguard, radiator or bumper. It had been far enough back from the impact to make that unlikely.

By the time Jack returned to the tent in the correct gear, Shauna had started her preliminary examination of the body. The position of his legs and arms showed multiple breaks in all his limbs.

'Help me roll him.'

Jack stepped forward and between them, they rolled the corpse onto its back. The photographer took several snaps before Shauna continued to probe the body. The face was unrecognisable. Even if Jack had been a relative of the mayor, she didn't think she could say for definite that this was the same person. There were no discernible features present; they'd all been turned to a pulp when he hit the concrete.

She'd been so sure it was him – the expensive suit, the neatly trimmed hair – but maybe she'd been wrong? Either way, DNA would need to be sought to confirm identity.

It was late that night when Jack arrived home. She stripped and showered before raiding the fridge for food and a small glass of Pinot. There was something niggling her like an object on the periphery of her vision that she couldn't quite make out. As she waited for the familiar ping of her microwave, she opened her laptop and began to check the reports from her colleagues. The entire building had been searched and they'd found nothing.

She was beginning to wonder whether their victim had jumped to his death.

Shovelling in forkfuls of bland lasagne, she considered how possible it was to escape the flats without being picked up by even one camera. You'd need to know the blind spots really well. And how had he got out of the building unseen? She'd entered the lobby within minutes of the fall. Jack wondered if the call reporting the robbery held any clues. Fortunately, the radio operator had the foresight to upload it and send it to her department. Putting her plate to one side, Jack pressed play.

A woman's anxious voice said, 'I can hear banging and shouting from the balcony above me. I think someone is breaking in.'

The operator asked her to confirm the address and her details. Then the woman said, 'It's all gone quiet. They must be inside the flat.'

The operator then asked if the flat's occupants could be arguing. 'It's the mayor's flat. He lives alone now. It's usually so quiet I even wondered if he might have moved out.'

'And have you heard the mayor there today?' asked the operator.

'Yes, actually, this morning.'

'Don't worry. Help is on its way.'

A few seconds later, she said, 'I can hear yelling outside again... oh my god, oh my god! Something's fallen past my window.'

It was then Jack remembered that they still needed to search Philip Dyson's flat. Could this have been him? Had he pushed the mayor off the balcony and disappeared into the shadows? If it was him, then he could be getting rid of the evidence as she sat there. Picking up her coat, she made a snap decision.

THIRTY-TWO

It didn't matter to Jack that she was one of the few detectives in the building. The search warrant and associated risk assessments for Dyson needed to be updated. The plan was to serve them at first light, but something nagged at her. It just didn't feel right. Philip Dyson was nervous and slight, whereas Mayor Jacobs had been tall and muscular. The balcony railing was at least forty-two inches high, and the mayor wasn't going to throw himself over. It would take a huge amount of force to both topple him and push his whole body over.

Over the next few hours, she sifted through the evidence on Dyson. It was flimsy at best. In some ways, she was surprised that they'd convinced a judge to grant the property search. An arrest warrant would be a bigger deal, dependent on what they found at the flat. Clothing would be a major find. It was possible that Shauna would find shredded fibres on Jacobs' body, clothes or under his fingernails from where he struggled. Dyson may have had time to wash the clothes that he'd worn, but that was a risk they took. Maybe they should have gone straight from the crime scene to his home? That could turn out to be a fatal error if she was wrong, but in her gut, Jack didn't believe the Urban Climber was Philip Dyson.

The cars pulled up on one of the side roads off the main shopping arcade. DS Begum had the warrant in hand. It didn't take more than a minute for the team to reach Dyson's flat. Jack knocked on the door. This wasn't a raid needing the enforcer. She knocked again and shouted out, 'Police, Mr Dyson. Open up.'

Dyson opened the door wearing pyjama bottoms and rubbing his eyes. The sight of his naked upper body only reaffirmed Jack's growing unease that this wasn't their man. But they were here now, so they might at least conduct a search. He could know the UC, or they could even be working together. She couldn't rule that out.

Nadia told Dyson to sit on a chair in the living room while they searched each room. On the table were more laptops with their innards hanging out of their cases. Forensics placed these in evidence bags.

'They're not mine. They belong to clients—' Dyson stood and was gently told to sit back down by Nadia.

'Do you have any proof of that?' Jack asked.

Philip shook his head before folding his arms across his bare chest.

'If you can get us some proof from the client, then we might be able to return it to you sooner.' Jack didn't know whether the tech team would bother with the shells. They'd probably be able to read the hard drive and any saved files, but it wasn't her field.

Dyson began to shiver.

'What clothes were you wearing yesterday?' DS Begum asked.

Dyson stared from Nadia to Jack. 'Look, what's this about?'

'What were you wearing yesterday?' Nadia repeated.

'The clothes on the floor in my bedroom.' He held his crossed arms closer to his chest. 'Can I get a jacket?'

It was a warm June day. Jack was sweating in her short-sleeved shirt. 'Help us find your clothes and you can get something to cover yourself with.'

Dyson muttered, 'Thank you.'

There were only three rooms in the flat: a living room/kitchen, a bedroom and a bathroom. It didn't take long to complete the search. Nadia pulled Jack to one side. 'Shall we take him in for questioning now?'

Jack paused before answering, unsure for a moment. 'We can ask him to accompany us, but we've got no reason, as yet, to arrest him.'

Nadia screwed up her face into a frown. 'I'm not sure whether we should do this formally. I mean, he fits some of the profile.'

'Does he?' Jack let her doubt temper her voice.

'Okay, informally. I'll ask him to come with us.'

He didn't protest other than to ask if he could get dressed first. It only took him seconds to change into a pair of black jogging bottoms, socks and trainers. He kept on the hoodie that he'd picked up earlier to cover his naked chest.

Back at the station, DS Begum and DC Harry Martin conducted the interview. Jack watched the recording, noting Dyson's general demeanour and body language. It was easy to see that he was scared stiff, the line of questioning making it clear in the first few minutes that they were linking him to the murder of Christopher Jacobs, the mayor. By the time they reached the question about where he was at midday, he was shaking from head to foot rather than shivering. His hand shook as he reached for the can of Coke that had been provided.

Jack stopped tapping her pencil and wrote her concerns on her notepad. She hoped her colleagues shared them. The alibi he provided was weak but verifiable. He'd been to the rag market to get some wiring supplies. He'd visited a couple of stalls and they should recognise him as a regular customer.

As Nadia completed the interview, Jack's mind wandered. She felt like she'd spent the day pulling at a jumper thread. The case was unravelling in front of them, but there was something she was missing, something she should have taken notice of or attached more importance to. Now, though, the stakes had been raised. The deaths of a wealthy Russian and a drug dealer were newsworthy, but not in the same league as Jacobs. If she didn't get a quick result, then they'd soon ship someone in to take over. And it probably wouldn't be bumbling O'Donohue either. She'd seen nothing of him.

The interview now over, Nadia entered the incident room. Jack called her over. 'How do you think it went?'

Nadia shrugged. 'We've got to check his alibi, but to be honest—'

'It's not him.'

'Unless we get forensics and he's been lying to us.'

Jack sucked at her teeth and then realised what was bothering her. 'He never left the flats.'

Nadia looked confused. 'Who didn't?'

'The killer. The UC. He never left. Whoever has been doing this knows the flats well, and he knows the residents. I know we've checked employees and there's little crossover with management companies.' It couldn't be, surely... 'No. I'm *sure* he works there or lives there. Check again.'

Nadia nodded and spoke to the rest of the team. 'Listen up. I want a list of everyone who works and lives in all the flats involved in this case. Any similarities between the workers, whether it's their age or appearance, anything that stands out, then bring it to me.'

Jack entered Teddy Garson's name into the force database. It came up with his birth name, current job at the management company and his address, a flat in Selly Oak. She then looked up the details of his DBS history from when he worked in education. It was all clean. No record of any safeguarding issues. Nothing. The management company that he worked for did, however, cover three of the blocks of flats that had been targeted.

Teddy was strong enough to throw a man over a balcony. Jack didn't doubt that. But what reason would he have?

Jack reached for her phone and car keys. When she reached her car, she rang Ted. He was at home, so she arranged to meet him there.

When she reached his flat after a difficult drive through rush hour, Jack must have looked tense. Ted was clearly pleased to see her and pulled her into a hug on the doorstep. As soon as she took a seat at the kitchen table, he flicked the switch on the kettle.

'Tea?' he asked.

'No, it's fine. Sit down, Ted. I've got to ask you something.'

Ted plonked himself down on the chair opposite her. Maybe he now sensed the tension in the air. 'What's up?'

Jack took a breath. 'Where were you yesterday from 1 p.m. until, say, 3 p.m.?'

She could almost see the cogs turning and the alarm sounding in Ted's head. 'Wait. Jack... you're not suggesting...?'

'Where were you, Ted?'

He stood, running his large hands through his curly hair. 'What the hell do you...?'

For just a moment, Jack felt afraid.

He slammed his hand down on the table, causing a vase that sat in the centre to rock. A black storm cloud settled between them. Jack knew there was no going back from this, but she persisted. 'Just tell me. You're a climber. You have connections to some of the flats. Just tell me.'

'And if I don't have an alibi? What then, Jack? You going to arrest me?' Teddy grabbed the edge of the table.

Was she?

'You really think—'

'I don't think anything.'

'I'm a damn teacher, not a murderer!' He sat back down then. Jack noticed the tears fall before she heard his sobs.

She stayed where she was, despite her whole being wanting to comfort this broken man. 'I'm sorry.'

He stopped, looked up and stared at her before wiping his face with his sleeve. 'I lost everything.'

A tightness grabbed her chest.

'They cut the funding from the centre for the second year running. And they started to question my fitness.' He paused and took a deep breath. 'You know I'm a good climber. None of the younger, cheaper climbers they employed was half as skilled as me. But they questioned my competence. And then I started to believe them and... I started drinking, to my shame.'

'I'm sorry, Ted. I didn't know.' She should have kept track of what he was doing. She should have cared enough.

'So, they let me go. I lost my job, my home at the centre... I lost everything. The centre closed two years later, but I'd already gone. Didn't even get a leaving party. They sacked me. Claimed I was drunk on the job – which I never was.'

The kitchen walls seemed to close in further, squeezing the air out of the room. Neither spoke until Ted said, his voice breaking, 'And now you accuse me of *this*.'

Jack held out her hands across the table, laying herself bare. 'I haven't accused you of anything. I—'

'I was visiting my mum yesterday. She's in the sheltered housing on the corner of Hayfield Lane. Her carer was there, too, so even if my mum doesn't remember, then she will. And I think it's time you left, Jack.'

Jack sat in her car outside Ted's place for what felt like an age. The vibration of her phone broke her out of her melancholy.

It was Nadia. 'Boss. We think we might have something.'

If only she'd waited and not jumped to ridiculous conclusions, she wouldn't have just lost a friend.

Ten minutes later, the address entered into her sat nav, Jack started her car.

As soon as she pulled up outside the apartment block in the centre of town that Nadia had directed her to, an SUV shot out of the underground car park. Jack recognised the occupant as he raced by. She quickly made a three-point turn and followed him, alerting the control centre and all the other cars that she was in pursuit.

For once, the usual congestion in central Birmingham had dissipated. He was at least a couple of cars ahead of her and heading out of town. Jack knew you couldn't floor it when navigating the inner ring road unless you wanted to be involved in an accident. But the driver of the other car didn't seem to share her concern as he sped into an underground section. Jack tried to pull across into the outer lane, but a BMW driver seemed to have other ideas, not even noticing the flashing blue light in her back window. Jack swerved back into her lane and tried again. This time, she was successful.

Cars pulled out of her way, but the delay had cost her. She couldn't see the SUV. Maybe it had pulled off onto one of the side roads. She slammed the steering wheel with her palm. 'Damn! Control: suspect has exited the ring road at Smallbrook Queensway. Be advised he's travelling at speed and may pose a danger.'

Jack pulled off at the next roundabout waiting for someone – anyone – to pick up the chase but no one did. After five minutes, she returned to the office. At least they now knew who they were chasing. She'd only got a brief glimpse of the driver as he pulled out in front of her. But she recognised him. Now all they had to do was find him.

THIRTY-THREE

An hour later, there were still no sightings of the SUV, but they had discovered more about their suspect: his address, several aliases, and links to at least two-thirds of the robbery sites.

DS Begum vented her frustration. 'Why didn't we see it?'

Jack shook her head. The couple of times she'd met him, he'd practically told her that he was the Urban Climber. 'It's my fault,' she muttered, as her phone vibrated on the table.

She noted it was an unknown number as she answered. 'DI Jack Kent.'

'Hi, Jack. I think we should meet. Have you got a pen handy? What would you prefer – coordinates or What3Words?'

'Who is this?'

'Don't be silly, Jack. You know who it is.' And she did. The voice wasn't familiar. Maybe this was his normal voice, not the one that he used for all other situations.

'Coordinates are fine.'

She wrote them down as he reeled them off but didn't need to check where he was. She knew this particular location off by heart.

'Come alone. There are things I need to tell you. Just you,

Jack. If anyone else is there, you won't get anything out of me.'
Then he cut the call.

Jack grabbed her coat. 'He's at Raven Tor and he wants to talk.'

'Boss—'

She could hear Nadia running behind her, so she called over her shoulder, 'Follow me. I'll brief you on the way.'

He'd set up two sets of ropes, one for himself and the other for her. The light was fading as the sun descended behind the natural curves of the Derbyshire peaks, but the brightly coloured rope made enough of a contrast to the grey limestone rock to stand out. Jack had clipped a torch to her harness and wasn't concerned. Like a scout, she was always prepared, particularly for a climb.

Peter Jennings was already halfway up the Tor. He hung there, no doubt waiting for Jack to join him. She concentrated on her part of the climb, grazing her fingers, trying to find suitable holds. Hugging the wall, she ignored the purpose of the climb, feeling more at risk of losing her footing than from the man above her. He'd chosen a tricky but assailable route.

After half an hour, she was in line with him. He looked different. This was the real Peter with no wigs or make-up or fake broken arm casts. She remembered he'd introduced himself as Pete at the first flat that she'd visited.

Then he disappeared into the background of each subsequent block of flats, fixing the plumbing, making sure the entrances were clean, checking that the heating worked. He was the caretaker hired by different management companies under different names. No wonder they hadn't tracked him from one location to another.

'Glad you could make it,' he said in a soft, local accent.

'You wanted to speak to me. We could have done that anywhere.'

'I wasn't sure you'd come, seeing as it's here, and this particular crag.' He stroked the rock face with his hand.

She didn't tell him that she'd climbed it recently. She still didn't quite believe it herself. 'What did you want to tell me?'

He stared across at her. She could see the sorrow in his eyes. 'The reasons... the truth... why I did it.'

'Go on.'

'I know you'll understand. You've lost a parent... but my mum was everything to me.' He leant back on the rope. 'She became ill. Cancer. They kept saying to me, Jack, "There's nothing we can do". But there was.'

Jack listened. This was his time.

'There was a treatment that could have saved her, but it was too expensive. The hospital wouldn't fund it. So they made me watch her die. At least you didn't have to do that... with your dad, I mean.'

Would that have helped her, though? Maybe. At least she'd know for certain how he died.

'So I decided to make amends in any way I could.' His face changed. Gone was the softness of grief; now she saw only the harsh frown lines of anger. 'I wanted to redress the balance.'

'So, you stole from the rich and gave to the poor?'

He laughed. 'Is that what you think I am? I guessed as much. Robin Hood, mythical superhero.'

He adjusted his line and continued. 'But then it wasn't enough. They barely noticed their missing cash or jewels. The first death might have been an accident, but actually, why should those bastards live when my mum didn't?'

'Do you admit you killed Ana Marlova, Moore and Jacobs?'

'Yes, and I would again. They were vile people, Jack. Well, except for Ana. She was beautiful, like a tiny bird. She'd been caged by her husband for long enough. I set her free. As for the others, I didn't even need to break into their computers to discover that they deserved to die. It was obvious – the way they carried themselves, the lies they told, the people they hurt. Take the mayor: if I hadn't stopped him, he'd have taken out the jury in his son's case one way or another. You know that.'

'You killed them.' She needed absolute clarity on this.

'Yes, I did.'

'Then I'm arresting you—'

It was all she managed to say. At that point, he removed his knife from his harness. She saw it glint in the last rays of the sun.

For a moment, she thought he was going to cut his own rope. But then he lurched across the gap between them and caught hold of the rope above her. He began to cut, and she gasped, realising he wanted her dead.

'No!' she cried, and she pushed up with her feet in an attempt to bridge the gap between them and reach him. This just made him saw the rope with more intent. There was no way she could stop him in time. She needed to try something else. 'There are ways out of this. If you explain—'

Peter stared across at her but continued to cut. 'This is my way out. You're not going to arrest me.'

Perhaps she could stall him. 'Tell me more about your mother. Is this what she would want?'

He briefly smiled as though a memory had sparked a light. 'To be honest, Jack, she would have wanted me to be happy. But that wasn't going to happen.' He paused for a moment, one final touch of the cold rock face. 'This is my happy. But I was never good enough. Not like you.'

Jack knew he was going to prison whether he killed her or not, there was no getting out of that, so she thought fast. 'There's still time. There are climbers in their sixties climbing the most impossible of routes.'

He'd cut through the sheath of the rope by now. Only the

thick, white strands of the kern remained. Jack dropped a few inches. It wouldn't be long. She scrambled to get a good hand and foothold taking a little weight off the rope. 'I did this for you, you know.'

For a moment, Jack couldn't speak. A huge lump formed in her throat that she found impossible to swallow. Peter continued to saw into the rope.

'What do you mean, for me?' she eventually asked.

'I've read your articles, seen your interviews... you hate it as much as I do.'

There was little left of the core of the rope. It could only be seconds. Surely, he wasn't blaming her. 'Hate what?'

'The inequality, unfairness. You seek justice in your work and—'

Just as she was about to drop, Jack moved. Not thinking this time about whether she would get hurt in the process, she traversed the space between them, one leg after the other at lightning speed. At the last possible second, as her rope failed, she caught up to him, wrapping her legs around his body, holding him close.

He opened his eyes and stared at her. 'Get off me, Jack. I'm stronger than you.'

Her right hand grabbed for the back of his harness, she pulled him upwards, wrenching the muscles in her shoulder as she did. Now she had a firmer grip with both her arms and legs tight around him, she could relax for a moment. 'I'm sorry, but you have to pay for your crimes. I'm not giving up that easily.'

They swung for a moment. Two bodies entwined. Jack hoped that her colleagues had seen them and were working out a way to save her. She couldn't hold on forever. Her heartbeat quickened under the strain and the air around her froze. Thoughts of Hannah filled her head. Thoughts of the day of her death invading. But this wasn't her love that she was holding onto, this was a killer.

'You've forgotten something. I still have this.' She felt the sudden coldness of the knife at her neck and the staleness of his breath on her face. 'Shall we go together?'

And then she would finally pay her debt too. If it wasn't for her, Hannah would be alive. Maybe even her father would be alive. Perhaps he was right, perhaps it was her time. She bit her tongue. The edge of the knife dug deeper into her skin. It stung and she felt something warm and wet trickle down her neck. *Decision time.*

Without any warning, she took out her knife from its sheaf on her belt and sliced through the back of his harness. The cheapness of the fabric was no match for her regularly sharpened blade. With no rope attached and nothing to hold onto, he slid down her body at speed. Too quick to use his knife, which he swung as he fell. Clearly, he didn't expect her to save herself and let him die. But she was a climber and self-preservation was, after all, in her DNA.

Below, officers rushed from their hiding places under the overhanging rock and swooped around like vultures. They knew it would be moments before he hit the ground.

She looked down and watched his body slam against the rock face as he fell. His chances of survival were slim to non-existent.

Is that what happened to her father?

THIRTY-FOUR

Jack pulled up outside the cottage. She'd rung ahead that morning, so she knew Janet and Ian were expecting her. She didn't need to knock on the door as Janet opened it as she walked up the path. 'Jack, it's so good to see you.' Janet wrapped her in a hug.

After the usual pleasantries and the offer of tea, Janet and Ian sat opposite Jack, waiting expectantly. For Jack, this reminded her of the worst of times, those conversations that you have with a set of parents when something unthinkable has happened to their child. She took a deep breath and held her hands together in her lap. 'I loved Hannah.'

Janet smiled. 'We know.' She turned to her husband. 'And she loved you.' Ian didn't move or smile. Maybe he was trying to keep himself together.

Jack continued. This is what she'd come here to say. 'I want to tell you how Hannah died.'

Ian waved an arm. 'We know how she died. She died on that bloody mountain.'

'Ian.' Janet whispered. 'It's okay.'

'The avalanche hit and wrenched her off the mountain beneath me. There was nothing I could do but cling to the ice.'

Janet looked confused; her brow scrunched. 'We know this.'

Jack looked from one to the other and took another deep breath. 'The weight of her body added to mine was tugging me off the cliff. You have to understand... I had no choice.'

'No choice...?' Janet said, in little more than a whisper.

Ian must have realised what she was saying. He leant forward with his hands on his knees. 'Jack. It's not anyone's fault. She was doing what she loved to do. What she lived to do.'

'If I hadn't convinced her to climb with me—'

'She'd have climbed with someone else and might still be dead.' Ian reached for the teapot and poured himself another cup. 'Would you like another?' He glanced first at Jack and then his wife, who was dabbing at her eyes with a hankie.

'I had to cut the rope. She was attached to me, and I cut the rope.' Jack had finally said it.

Tears fell. Jack hadn't come for forgiveness. Hannah's parents knew about climbing. They'd helped their daughter learn to climb, paid for lessons and re-mortgaged their house to pay for expeditions. Jack wasn't the first to save her own life in this way. It was almost expected in the circumstance.

Jack sobbed. Holding her head in her hands, she let Hannah go. Not with guilt this time, but with love. The tears wouldn't stop as she curled up into a ball on the couple's sofa. Janet left her chair, sat beside her and held her like she was her own daughter. They both cried.

Ian finally said, 'She was dead, Jack, before you cut the rope. The fall, being suffocated by snow and ice, the crevasse she fell into... she was dead, and it wasn't your fault.'

Later, Jack sat in her car, unable to drive away. She thought that telling Hannah's parents would be the ending she needed, but nothing was ever fully resolved. The guilt would remain, and she had to learn to deal with it. Guilt for Hannah. If she hadn't persuaded her that they could follow in the footsteps of the all-woman American team that conquered Annapurna, she wouldn't have died on the mountain. If she hadn't cut the rope... maybe she, too, would have died, or Hannah would still have perished. But maybe, just maybe, she wouldn't then need to keep reliving it.

And now, guilt for all the victims of the Urban Climber. It was unfair that he'd placed the blame on her, of course it was. He clearly had his own demons to fight, but, inside, where her frailties lay, it would gnaw away at her. His motives were another unsolvable mystery like her father's death.

THIRTY-FIVE

Jack loved her team. The rest of the police force may see them as a disjointed, strange crew of misfits, but they worked their socks off. Nadia was well on her way to being a competent detective, now she had gained confidence. Without interrupting, Jack listened to her conclude the case against Peter Jennings in the final team briefing. Jack didn't feel it was her place to sum up the death of the man that nearly brought her to her own demise.

It also gave her time to reflect. Why hadn't she seen the caretaker as a threat? When they'd searched his flat, they had found wigs, theatrical make-up, even prosthetics. It became clear that, over a long period of time, Peter Jennings had fooled her and others. Each apartment block employed him in some capacity to service their buildings. Despite Jack standing next to him, she hadn't recognised him as the same person. She would have to live with that.

What bothered her more was how personal the case became. Jennings may have killed for her. She would never really know what motivated him. If it wasn't her that he looked up to, it could well have been someone else, another climber perhaps, but even the thought that it might be personal to her chilled her to the bone.

As the team started to pack away the photographs on the evidence board, Jayden came over to her desk. 'Something odd's come up.'

'Huh?' Jack continued to watch Nadia as she shared a joke with Georgia.

'You know that young lad that was beaten up in town.'

Jack faced Jayden, confused. 'What lad?'

'Few weeks ago. He was in a coma for days. Attacked outside a pub – The Wellington. Harry worked the case.'

Then it hit her. It was the night that she'd met Teddy in the Wellington. 'I remember. It was The Wellington? I was there that night.'

'Oh, well, they found Peter Jennings' DNA on him. He must have been the attacker.' Jayden passed her a file. 'It hardly fits his MO. Do you want me to file this away with the rest of the case?'

Jack shivered. She'd spoken to a lad that night while she waited for a taxi – the one who had tried to buy her a drink. Surely it couldn't be him?

She opened the file and stared at the photo of the victim. Of course, it was raining and she'd had a couple of drinks, but it could have been the same lad. In fact, the more she looked at the photograph, the more sure she was that it was him. Jennings had hurt this lad – nearly killed him – for *her*. Something else she'd need to live with.

DSI Campbell entered the room as she placed the file into the last evidence box. He handed Jack a slip of paper. 'Your leave has been agreed. Thought you'd want to know. Which bloody mountain is it this time?'

Jack smiled and held the piece of paper to her chest. She could put this case to bed. In just ten months, she'd be climbing Kangchenjunga.

A LETTER FROM THE AUTHOR

Dear reader,

Huge thanks for reading *Silent Fall*. I hope you were hooked on Jack's journey. If you want to join other readers in hearing all about my new releases and bonus content, you can sign up here:

www.stormpublishing.co/nicky-downes

If you enjoyed this book and could spare a few moments to leave a review, that would be hugely appreciated. Even a short review can make all the difference in encouraging a reader to discover my books for the first time. Thank you so much!

As a voracious reader of crime since a child, I have always loved diving into novels with strong female characters that I could aspire to. DI Jack Kent is such a joy to write stories about. I've particularly loved learning about the climbing world she inhabits. I hope you love it too!

Thanks again for being part of this amazing journey with me and I hope you'll stay in touch – I have so many more stories and ideas to entertain you with!

Nicky

www.nickydownescrimeauthor.com

 twitter.com/nicky_downes

ACKNOWLEDGMENTS

I know I can't be the only person in awe of those that seek to climb the highest mountains in the world. (I'm afraid as an over-weight asthmatic, I will never join them.) Mountaineers never climb completely alone. They have a team of people behind them. In the Himalayas, these are often Sherpas.

After watching a film about the plight of Sherpas, I wanted to learn about mountaineers and their reasons for climbing. Over months, I devoured stories of achievement and disaster, victorious ascents and death. From this, DI Jack Kent was born.

I wouldn't be able to share her story without the support of my team.

I started this journey with a wonderful, talented band of authors that I met through Jericho Writers. Their comments on my work and help with edits were invaluable. Jackie Kowalczyk, Becky Jones, Harriet Martin, Kate McDermott, James Pierson, Alan Fraser, Anne McMeehan Roberts and Barbara Muszyn-ski-Webb, thank you! I wish you every success with your novels.

Thank you to my mentor at Jericho, Helen Francis, who loved my messy draft manuscript and helped me mould it into something readable.

Thank you to my amazing editor and publisher at Storm, Kathryn Taussig for understanding and loving Jack as much as I do.

To the whole team at Storm, who takes such care of all of their authors, thank you for believing in me.

Finally, my family who have gone above and beyond to support my writing. You all make me proud.